# IT'S RAINING MEN

Also by Naomi Rand

*Stealing for a Living*
*The One That Got Away*

# IT'S
# RAINING
# MEN

## AN EMMA PRICE MYSTERY

## Naomi Rand

HarperCollins*Publishers*

This is a work of fiction. The characters, incidents, and dialogues are products of the author's imagination and are not to be construed as real. Any resemblance to actual persons, living or dead, is entirely co-incidental.

HarperCollins books may be purchased for educational, business, or sales promotional use. For information, please write: Special Markets Department, HarperCollins Publishers, 10 East 53rd Street, New York, NY 10022.

FIRST EDITION

*Designed by Joy O'Meara*

Printed on acid-free paper

Library of Congress Cataloging-in-Publication Data

Rand, Naomi R.
   It's raining men / Naomi Rand.—1st ed.
      p.   cm.
   ISBN 0-06-072371-8
   1. Price, Emma (Fictitious character)—Fiction. 2. Women private investigators—New York (State)—New York—Fiction. 3. New York (N.Y.)—Fiction.   I. Title

   PS3568.A478I87 2005
   813'.54—dc22                                                      2004053940

05  06  07  08  09  ❖/RRD   10 9 8 7 6 5 4 3 2 1

For my father,
Harry Israel Rand

# Acknowledgments

I would like to thank the early readers of this book, Hallie Ephron and Jan Brogan, for taking the time and being honest. Such wonderful friends. Such generous colleagues. And thanks to D. P. Lyle, M.D., for his help in answering a critical question about forensics. Thanks to my gracious and excellent editor, Carolyn Marino, for her insight and for her political smarts. Thanks to Flip Brophy, my agent, who's an ace at her job. And a mensch to boot. Thanks to Jennifer Civiletto and Tim Brazier at HarperCollins for all their hard work. And thanks to the three men in my life who make every day better than the last: my sons, Cody and Travis, and my husband, David.

# IT'S
# RAINING
# MEN

Before they were ever *together, he wanted her so badly it hurt. Not that she knew anything about it. He memorized every little detail there was, down to the way she wiped her bangs off her forehead, then did this absentminded toss of the head. Her name was Julie. She was seventeen.*

*He took her out for breakfast, watched as she used a fork to stir what was left of her eggs, moving them across the plate, then back.*

*The city was full of them, almost-women, the fashion that summer was microminis with tube tops and high-heeled slip-on sandals. Girls wore dark raccoon rings around their eyes. Julie didn't bother; when she had on clothes, they were cutoff jean shorts and a man's undershirt, no bra, ever.*

*Heat in the city whipped off the pavement, curling up to your nostrils. He had the T-bird that summer, and he took her out for a ride, onto the Southern State. Glancing over, he saw she didn't notice him, she had her head tipped back, her eyes narrowed to slits, the radio played hits, Madonna. She sang along.*

*When he thought back, he told himself it was her fault, all of it. Julie next to him, laughing, while the sea-salt smell rose up, the cattails purred.*

*Later, in the hotel room, her hair was a mess, witches' knots. Stepping out of the shower, he caught her, pushed her back against*

*the wall, thought this was perfect, holding her up, tight, white tile be-
hind her, her eyes shut, like she was inventing something. Someone.*

*In the mirror he saw the two of them, saw what he had, what he
held, saw her spirit sliding away.*

*Grabbing her face, he forced her to watch.*

*The rain came in spurts, gathering power. He pulled the blanket up,
turning on his side. It had been raining that other night too. He'd
walked up the road, and all that long walk, he turned over the things
he was going to say that would convince her.*

*He was good at that, wasn't he?*

*But when she opened the door to him, he knew it was all bullshit.
She was never going to listen to one word he had to tell her.*

*Julie stretched like a cat.*

*"You're late," she told him, walking to the fridge, taking out a beer,
and unscrewing the cap, tanking it down; then giving him that wicked,
knowing smile.*

*Later on, when he turned it over in his mind, he realized there was
nothing he could have done. It was inevitable, and if she'd been less
willful and more intelligent, she would have known. After all, he was a
reasonable man, but even a reasonable man has limits. As the years
passed, his conviction hardened. At first, he changed little things, the
way she'd looked at him, the tone of her voice, so that, eventually,
he rewrote the script, diagrammed out the entire scene differently,
Julie taunting him, laughing meanly, so that really, there was nothing
else he could have been expected to do.*

*Was there?*

*It was her fault, everything that happened.*

# Chapter One

Shake, rattle, then roll. Emma Price awoke to the sound of a wailing siren too near. Adjusting her vision, she realized she was staring at a blue pants leg, and moving up, past the waist and upper body, she found a man's face. He boasted a handlebar mustache and an arresting shock of black hair. "Hey," he said, catching her eye. "Don't worry, sweetheart, you're doing fine."

There was a flutter just out of her field of vision. Turning was painful, but she did, and found the source: a female companion, who was also dressed in blue. She was plumping an IV bag. Emma's eyes followed the trail of clear liquid, dripping down, down, down, and realized that the shunt was taped to her arm.

She was in an ambulance then, on her way to a hospital. "Thank you," she said softly.

"She say something?" the woman asked.

Emma didn't have the strength to repeat herself.

"I guess not. So you want to hear what happened next?"

"All ears," the male voice replied.

"It was like in a fairy tale, you know, he got right down onto his knees, people were giving us looks. He says, 'Will you marry me?' I tell you what, I got all light-headed and I guess I must have nodded, because that's when he slid the ring on."

"Let's see that again."

Air shifted overhead. Emma opened her eyes and watched their fingertips touching, a Sistine Chapel moment. Then the man's face loomed close, his jaws opening.

Emma didn't even have the strength to flinch.

"What the hell you think you're doing!" the woman screeched as she jerked her hand away.

"That's how you test it." And the smirk was there, in his voice. "You know, making sure the guy's not playing you, giving you some good-looking fake."

"You know what? You're out of your fucking mind."

"Just doing you a favor."

"How the hell you figure that?"

"Please. The financial aspect is all any of you ladies cares about."

"Is not."

"Is so. Baby doll, you can sweet-talk that Joe you got trailing along behind you all you want, but don't try that shit with me. I know you a whole hell of a lot better." His laugh insinuated how.

A pause, the woman apparently considering what to do with this, then she said, "Samuel, you are so damn nasty."

"Baby," he replied. "Nasty is as nasty does."

Emma was in a room stuffed with gray cotton. Closing her eyes, she counted to a hundred, then opened them again. This time, the walls came into focus. A television hung on the wall just inside her line of sight. By her right arm, bars to prevent an escape. And on that arm, a hospital bracelet. She lifted it, bringing her wrist up to her face. Scratches in black on the white band slowly morphed into words: Jane Doe; 3:17 A.M.

Dropping her arm, she lay there for a while, then turned her head, incrementally, to take in a window with a slatted Venetian blind. From behind it, a tap-tap-tapping. Rain, Emma decided.

"Okay, sleeping beauty, up you get."

Emma blinked. The woman had on a white nurse's uniform. "I'm tired," Emma protested.

"Tired or not, you're going to do this for me. No more messes to clean up. You're too big a girl, honey. You don't help me here, I got to catheterize you, and believe you me, you don't want to go there. Now, be good, all you got to do is help me slide this underneath and try for Freddy."

Her sheet was pulled up, something cold, and Emma realized what—a bedpan. She felt a rush of embarrassment. "Here's what you got to do, think about a water-main break, okay, there's the water pumping up and up and up, it's a regular flood like what happened up in the Bronx the other day, you got water coming out of nowhere, okay, everything's soaking and there's more coming, a great big river of water. See, there you go."

Sunlight, too bright to bear. Emma tried to cover her face with her hands, but someone had her arms. "You're a wild one," the nurse said. Adjusting her gaze, Emma took in the woman's neck; there were folds of soft flesh, a slightly doubled chin, the pink flush of lipstick, and liquid brown eyes. "There now, you're awake for good this time, right? And you're not gonna give me no more trouble, right? Tell Loreen you're going to be a good girl."

Did she have a choice?

"Good girl," Emma mumbled.

Her arms were released, the hands hanging there a minute more, just in case, then dropping to her sides. "There you go," Loreen said, although she didn't sound completely convinced. "You got to give up waiting on that damn prince," she added. Emma read her name, "Loreen Smith, RN."

The television set was still hanging midway up the far wall; other than that, the room held a chair and a small bedside table. She remembered collapsing in front of the boarded-up door to the Tiki Bar, which, despite the claims in the song, was most definitely not open. She'd sunk onto a mat of broken glass and burned-up boards and then, somehow, there had been that ambulance ride. "How's it feel?" Nurse Smith asked.

There was only one answer that wouldn't disappoint. "Fine," Emma offered weakly.

"Really, you don't say?" Lifting an eyebrow to inflect some additional humor. "So how about we start with a name—you've got a name, right?"

"Emma. Emma Price."

"Well, Emma, looks like you had yourself a real party."

That was one way of looking at it, Emma supposed. Trying to take stock, she realized there was not one inch of her body that didn't express outrage. And with good reason. Her arms resting on top of the sheet sported several mottled bruises, the palms of both hands were scraped raw—a preview of what was hidden from sight.

"So how about a little something to eat?" the nurse said.

"I'm not hungry."

"Sure you are," the nurse said, clucking her tongue as she pushed the food tray closer to the bed.

There was a telephone on the side table. Emma stretched her hand to it and got a cluck of disapproval for her trouble.

"I say eat, you reach for the phone."

"But I need to tell someone—"

The nurse finishing up for her, "—about all this. I don't blame you, but there's no service. Got to fill out the paperwork before they turn it on. That and the TV. Tell you what, you eat something, I'll see what I can do to hurry things up." She pressed down on the remote button, and Emma was lifted to a sitting position. "There you go." The tray swinging over her prone body; trapped by mystery meat.

"Don't you have a cell phone?"

Another cluck of the tongue.

"I have kids," Emma said. "They need to know I'm okay. Please, just one call."

This time, she got a little more sympathy. "Can't use them on this floor," the nurse said. "You want me to make the call for you? I can do that."

"No," Emma said, a little too quickly. "Better if I do it."

If there was doubt, Nurse Smith didn't show it. "I understand, don't want anyone throwing a fit." She shot Emma a motherly smile, warm but no-nonsense, then lifted the plastic cover off the tray with a flourish. "Eat," she said.

And off she went, to do what she could.

Emma began with the mystery meat and moved on to the freeze-dried potatoes, the rock-hard roll, the limp green beans. Plus, green Jell-O for dessert and a cup of soup that looked more like mud-colored water. Gourmet fare it was not, but Emma cleaned her plate. Indeed, she was upending the Styrofoam cup to get the last drop of the purported soup when she heard the sound of someone clearing his or her throat. His. The man had appeared from behind the curtain that hid her from her roommate. "That good?" he asked. Moving close, he flashed his ID, a police badge in embossed metal, then took a seat.

Out of uniform. He wore a leather jacket over a white T-shirt, and a pair of manufacturer-stressed blue jeans. He looked to be in his twenties, but lines on his face gave the lie to that.

"Bobby Fitzsimmons," he said. "I didn't mean to interrupt your meal."

His presence prompted her to lift the phone still no dial tone.

"Calling your lawyer already?"

The expression on her face was a warning against further levity. "Look," he said, leaning forward to show his earnest intent. "I only want to find out what happened with you. No need to stress. Nurse says your name is Emma?"

"Emma Price. And I really need to make a phone call." The food had given her enough strength to think she could make trouble. Yet, as she reached for the guardrail and pulled herself vertical, the light-headedness returned. She must have gone white, because he was out of the chair like a shot.

"Breathe," he told her. She realized she hadn't been, not exactly. His hands were on her shoulders, and he was helping her sink back onto the pillow. "Sure. I understand. You want to let your loved ones know you're in the here and now. I'll take care of all that for you, just let's get a few things squared away first."

He had found pad and pencil. "You spell that last name Price, like the price is right?"

"718-222-5555."

He waited.

"Please. Let me talk to whoever answers. It won't take any time at all."

He did have a cell phone and was apparently willing to break the ban. Flourishing it, he asked, "Who am I calling?"

"A friend," Emma said.

Cupping it in his hand, to indicate that all she really had to do was work with him on this: "Friend's got a name?"

"Dawn," Emma said.

"Last name too, I'm assuming?"

Emma was getting exasperated. Why was this so hard to accomplish? Even an arrested suspect got to make one phone call. Then she had a brainstorm, or so it seemed to her at the time. "Do you know Detective Solomon?" she asked. There was a flicker of recognition, which he quieted almost immediately. Instead of responding with a simple yes or no, he tried the time-tested interviewing approach. "Why would I know him?"

"He worked at Brooklyn South for a while."

"Might have heard the name."

"He's a good friend. He can vouch for me."

"Can he? Vouch for you how exactly?" His eyes crinkled at the corners, accordion-like. The smile made her exceedingly uncomfortable. "So which one am I supposed to call, this Dawn woman, or Detective Solomon?"

Calling Laurence Solomon would not advance her cause overmuch. He was in Florida, attending his son's wedding. If he hadn't been away, she knew that things would have gone differently, because more than likely she wouldn't have been alone on Friday night, she would have been with him, and Dawn would have known better than to place that call to her, to ask her for that particular favor.

Meanwhile, Fitzsimmons was waiting. She made an assessment of him, a head of reddish-brown hair, an incipient mustache, that impish look on his face like he knew everything she would ever say, like he was always one step ahead of her kind. Her kind being what, she wondered, what did this guy think? And then she realized, even as he opened his mouth, to try to tug the rest of her statement out.

"Look, they found you passed out in a lot over by the bay. There are bruises on your arms and legs. Now, I'm just taking a wild guess, but I'm thinking somebody beat the shit out of you. So who you know in the department, or even outside of it, doesn't exactly matter to me. What does matter is finding out who did this to you, and making sure it doesn't happen again."

"I didn't know them," Emma said. He probably didn't believe her, of course. Ninety-nine point nine percent of victims knew their attackers, whether casually or intimately.

"Them. Okay, so there's more than one."

"Two men. This is the thing." Emma paused; how to convince him? "It was Dawn they were after."

"So they got confused. You two look alike."

Not at all, but she knew better than to tell him that.

"This Dawn, what did they want with her?"

"Use your imagination," Emma said.

He sighed. Been there, done that, a million times before.

"These two guys, they have names?"

"They neglected to make formal introductions," Emma said, losing patience. "I'm not making this up."

"Look, this guy—" He corrected himself—"These guys, someone who's prone to violence, they don't just find the cure overnight."

Emma's hand reached for the phone, he set his on top.

"Are you listening?" he asked. "I'm here to help you. But I can't, unless you start helping yourself. The nurse says you have kids."

Now he was trying to pull her children into it.

She retrieved her hand, tucked it under the sheet. She'd spent enough time with the two men to physically distinguish them. TBH, Emma thought, shorthand for assailant number one, whom she'd tagged, in a flash, as tall, blond, handsome. His companion was dark, swarthy, and muscular. "One was tall, probably close to six feet. He had dirty-blond hair and one of those 'I forgot to shave today' beards. You know, the kind where you think to yourself, Why even bother?" Emma had a moment of true clarity, as if he was standing there, in front of her; her breathing quickened, she felt the fear embrace her. Stop, she told herself, but it was impossible. Animals had the same response to danger, the surge of adrenaline, the sharpening of every sense.

It took a while for her to recover, and when she did, she realized Fitzsimmons was watching her intently.

"You all right?" he asked.

*Terrific.* Another smart response she knew better than to make. Defensiveness? Perhaps, but Emma preferred that to recalling the rest, how those men's dishonorable intentions had not called forth either pluck or even street smarts; when the stranger had approached, she hadn't even thought to suspect anything. Then he'd grabbed her, pulled her arm behind her back, shoved the gun into the small of it, pushed her facedown onto the floor of the car. She hadn't even had a moment to do anything—to scream, to kick at him, to bolt.

"Anything else?" Perhaps he could read her mind. Emma was grateful that he'd stopped the self-flagellating free fall.

"The taller one wore expensive clothing, black pants, a light blue silk shirt. His watch was nice too, not ostentatious, but thin with a . . ." She squinted, trying to visualize. "A black leather band. He seemed a lot more nervous than the guy who was driving the car."

"And this driver?"

"Short for a guy. No taller than I am, five-six, possibly five-seven. He obviously liked to work out, his biceps were huge, and he had this oddly high-pitched voice, like a eunuch." Emma laughed harshly. "You can always hope," she added.

Fitzsimmons was jotting everything down, but without the requisite fervor.

Tapping the pen as he finished, he raised his eyes. "Quite a description."

"You don't believe me, I get that."

"Look, in my experience victims don't tend to have such good memories for what a guy's wearing when they're getting the shit kicked out of them."

"I only got hit once, here." She lifted her hand to her cheek, to offer visual corroboration.

He raised an eyebrow. "Really. So how'd you end up like this?"

"The swim," Emma said.

"Ah yes, the swim."

"Remembering details is part of my job."

"Okay." Put acerbically.

She let out an exasperated sigh. "I work for New York Capital Crimes. My boss's name is Dawn Prescott, call her up, she'll vouch for me."

"Capital Crimes?" Like a dog, pricking up its ears. "What is it you do?"

"Lead investigator."

But she saw something working in his face, some question.

"What?" she asked. And wanted to add "What's wrong?" but Fitzsimmons was already standing, putting away pad and pencil.

"Back in a sec," he told her. "Just want to check up on your story."

No sec. No minute, either. Five turned into ten, ten into fifteen, and the phone was still dead, likewise the TV. Emma buzzed for the nurse. But no one showed. She could have been gasping her last breath, for all they knew. Or cared.

I'm not lying here waiting forever, she thought. Plus, it felt like worse than forever, the minutes spinning away. Trying yet again, she held down the buzzer and simply waited. This time an aide showed up.

"Can I help you?" His tone belying the content of the question.

"I was supposed to get phone service. Could you please see what's holding things up?"

"Sweet Jesus in heaven." He stomped away.

So much for that. Emma knew from long experience, as in her recently extinguished marriage, if you wanted something done, you basically had to do it yourself. She pulled herself up to a sitting position and waited for the haze to abate. That done, it took her another few minutes to figure out how to get the guardrail down; pulling on it and pounding had no apparent effect. She felt tears of frustration come, and had all but given up, wondering if she could actually manage to fling her unreliable body over, when she discovered the easy-to-read directions. They were literally under her nose, written on the metal strip underneath the railing.

It lifted. Her legs slid out. Her feet touched the floor and, as they did, a tremor ran through her body.

Looking down, she found her almost-naked self, clothed only in a hospital gown, and couldn't help wincing. Her knees had been scraped raw, the product of that seemingly endless crawl across a rock jetty; there were bruises up and down the length of her legs; and her arms were similarly mangled. It was hardly surprising Fitzsimmons had assumed she was a beating victim. Holding onto the bed, she managed to avoid crumpling onto the floor, then slowly, ever so slowly, raised her head. There. She was more or less erect; she took a crablike step and immediately listed to one side. Emma would have laughed at her plight, but that would have required too much energy. Instead, she focused on finding her sea legs. Pinpricks of light danced in front of her eyes. Then nausea broke in chilly waves. She tried counting to a hundred, in an effort to counteract the misery. Halfway through, she forgot the sequence and had to begin again. And again.

Finally, the fog abated, her stomach settled, and she focused. To the wall, she told herself, and then wryly added an internal jibe. *One small step for womankind.* Once there, she set course for her roommate behind the curtain, finding an elderly woman who was either fast asleep or dead. Monitors were piled on top of a cart next to the bed, emitting a chorus of unsynchronized beeps. Emma grabbed onto the metal safety bar and guided herself, hand over hand, right to the bedside chair. Sitting with an oomph of exhaled air, she dialed Dawn's number. It rang twice before she got the recording: "I'm sorry, you are not authorized to make outgoing calls from this number."

"Christ!" she exclaimed.

The remote was next to the phone. Lifting it, she tried the TV. This time, at least, there was ignition. Finding CNN, Emma read the tickertape underneath the talking head. The world was still a mess. Civil war was raging in the Congo. A train wreck in India had killed over six hundred people. Flash floods were, at this very moment, destroying priceless artworks in Berlin. There was a famine in Timor. And Al Qaeda was claiming responsibility for an attack on an army base in Qatar. Meanwhile, back in America, the Academy Awards were being televised live, tomorrow, from the Shrine Auditorium.

She hadn't forgotten. After all, her ex-husband, Will, was out there with his new wife and baby girl. He'd also taken along his two kids by Emma for the joyride. She'd personally heard his acceptance speech four times. Followed by the obligatory caveat, "But I'll probably never win." He was up for Best Editing in a Major Motion Picture.

Just then, the breaking news banner flashed across the screen: "Connecticut Senator Hamilton Prescott's Daughter Missing."

Dawn!

It was Dawn they were talking about.

Emma held her breath as the female talking head recounted the latest developments. "Apparently, the disappearance of Dawn Prescott, head of New York Capital Crimes Division, was noted only this morning. Her child's nanny, Celeste Virgin, discovered Prescott's baby daughter, alone in her Brooklyn brownstone. Police and the FBI are declining comment, but are asking anyone who might have information on Prescott's whereabouts to contact the authorities." Then an 800 number scrolled across the bottom of the screen.

Emma scrambled to find writing utensils. The bedside table was completely bare. Opening the drawer, she discovered it was empty except for a plain gold wedding band. The elderly woman's naked fingers clutched the sheet. Her crumpled face looked anything but peaceful, and Emma felt a stab of pity.

Pushing herself up, she listened. Was this Fitzsimmons ever going to return? No sound came from the hall, and although her head was pounding, she toughed her way to the door. Pushing it open, she stepped out. The lighting was dim, or perhaps her eyes were going. She blinked hard, but there was no improvement. Veering out, she made the opposite wall, and tried to evaluate direction. Somewhere, there was a desk with the hospital staff undoubtedly gathered around it, bent on ignoring the patients' needs. So much for managed care, or the lack thereof. Now, was it up or down this seemingly endless tunnel of mustard-yellow walls and numbered doors? She turned her head one way, then the other. The sound of laughter filtered toward her. It was coming from the left, wasn't it?

She lurched in that direction, stopped, then started again, shambling on and feeling centuries old. As she made her way, she tried to plot out strategies; the 800 tip number was gone, long gone from the catacombs of her mind. She'd call Brian, Emma thought, he'd know what to do. He'd believe her. He'd get the word out to the people who matter in time.

She cringed, flashing on the alternate possibilities, then told herself not to go there.

It had been Friday night, a little after nine P.M.

Emma had been comfortable, ensconced in her queen-size bed, rereading page 97 of *Jude the Obscure*, her book group's choice for the month, wondering why she was bothering, since nothing good could ever come to a Hardy hero or heroine; the novels were as she remembered them from college, unrelentingly bleak and depressing. She got enough of that at work, not to mention from the news. Her attention wandered peacefully into greener pastures. She would suggest the next book, something trashy or at least humorous. Her eyes had shut, and she had drifted off with the book collapsed on her chest, when the phone rang.

It had been Dawn. "I need you to meet me," she'd insisted. "Look, I know it's short notice, but I wouldn't ask unless it was important. I want you to get over to the corner of Carroll and Third Avenue. I'll explain everything when I see you."

"Now?" Emma had asked, stalling. The bed had been so comfortable, the nap so delicious.

"Yes, now. Emma, come on. I wouldn't ask unless it was really important."

Except that everything was equally important to Dawn. There was the rub. Still, Emma had known there was no way to squirm out without getting into a fight about it. Her usual excuses, the kids, were out of town, so was her boyfriend, Laurence. And, as if that wasn't enough, she'd sounded asleep. It was only a little before nine at night; she wasn't sick, after all.

"See you there," Dawn had said, firmly.

So Emma had gotten up, gotten dressed, bitching and moaning as she did, called a car service, took it to the corner of Carroll and Third, and saw there was a warehouse, shut up for the night. She waited under the sign—the Acme sign, of all things. This Acme sold surgical supplies, not exploding contraptions.

Emma came to a room with a half-open door. Inside, a patient was propped up in bed, amiably chatting with his visitors. Emma leaned hard against the wall and took a deep, cleansing breath. As she did, a little girl peeked from behind the door.

"Who are you?" the girl asked. Apparently, she didn't suffer from shyness.

"Emma."

"You have a really big boo-boo." Her index finger indicated Emma's forehead.

"No kidding."

It was time to soldier on.

Which was, Emma thought, the story of her life. The self-pity shamed her; what was she complaining about? She was alive, wasn't she?

Whereas Dawn?

"Shit," she said, under her breath, but the little girl had heard her.

"That's a bad word."

"Sorry."

A reflexive apology.

Past door number 703.

It had been Dawn she was waiting for when the man came up,

holding a cigarette in one hand and saying, "Excuse me, do you know where Smith Street is?" She had assumed he was another tourist looking for Restaurant Row.

Minutes later she was facedown on the floor of that car, scared out of her wits. As they made that drive to God knows where, she was working furiously on trying to assess the odds, although there was a part of her that was already defeated by the easy way it had happened.

"You're making a mistake," Emma had insisted. How original was that?

They had been stopped at the time; she figured it was a red light and had a fleeting image of herself making good her escape, launching out the door and onto the pavement, somehow managing to end up on her feet when she did.

Not likely. Not with this man putting his own right on top of her bent body; how would she get up fast enough, get the locked doors open? Invisible Girl, from one of Liam's comics, was the only one who could have done it. She learned in the next second just how different she was, only flesh and blood, as the gun slammed into her cheek.

"Shut up, bitch!"

The pain was unbelievable, the bone was definitely broken, her eyes teared, she sobbed, then shut it off, hating him, hating both of them.

"Jesus fucking Christ. Why'd you do that?" From the man in the back.

"Now she knows," the driver said. "A woman can talk you to death, you let them."

The pain was vicious, but she had managed worse; childbirth, after all, was unendurable, but she'd gotten through. Emma wasn't going to lose it, wasn't going to let her emotions overwhelm her. She had her children to think of.

Emma's face was pressed into the mat. She saw it was littered with cigarette butts and old candy wrappers, Dubble Bubble, Mary Janes. Someone had a very sweet tooth.

They drove. It couldn't have been more than thirty minutes, but it seemed to go on for hours. "Get up," the man who was using her as a footrest said. She did, slowly, searching for her opportunity, but his partner knew better than to give her an opening. He grabbed her arm, pulled her off the floor backwards, and as she tried to swing at him, he sidestepped.

"You want I should hit you again?" he offered, like it would make him more than glad.

That was when she named him Squeaky. Fuck you, Squeaky. She turned to find his companion, and was surprised to see the fear in his eyes.

And the apology.

He's the one I can go to, she told herself. And raised her eyes to his, pleading, but he looked away, at the ground; there was garbage on it, old rusty beer cans, scraps of paper. They were standing in an empty lot, a streetlight nearby illuminated weeds popping up through the cracked cement. Squeaky shoved her toward a chain-link fence. She heard the sound of waves lapping, and then she could see the water, white crests popping up, lights suddenly visible from across—Staten Island? Jersey? How far had they driven?

She couldn't say.

He had a flashlight, he tossed it to the other man. "Make yourself useful," he said derisively.

His partner, his accomplice, his dupe, shone it on the lock. The key worked. The three of them walked through and they were on a dock. Emma tried to orient herself. To her right, about a hundred yards away, she made out a spit of rock, a jetty, thrust into the water. The dock was old, in bad shape, there were holes here and there, almost big enough to drop through. As they moved, the planking creaked.

"You, keep quiet," Squeaky ordered Emma. "Hold onto her," he said. "Try to do that right at least."

Then he flipped open a cell phone. The hands-free headset made it possible to hold the gun and talk at the same time. He was adept, she'd give him that much. "It's me, we're set. Yeah, Prescott was standing right there, didn't give us any trouble. Yeah, that's what I said, alone, yeah. So what now?"

Prescott.

"I'm not Prescott," Emma said, aware that the way she rushed to say it made it seem like a lie.

Squeaky gave her a mean look. "Of course not," he said.

"My name is Emma Price. Please, look in my purse. You'll see."

"How can it hurt?" The other man said it, and just for that, Emma decided she would let him live; she'd shoot him in the kneecaps, of course, but then she'd call the proper authorities.

His hand grasped her collar, she could feel his fingers sliding along the back of her neck. She could hear the hope in his voice. He's never done anything like this before, she decided.

"Fucking amateur," Squeaky muttered, confirming her suspicions. "All right. Go get the purse."

He took over watching Emma.

So near she could smell his sour breath, smell his sweat.

The waiting took longer than the drive. Sixty seconds stretching out to an eternity. When his companion returned, he had her wallet out.

"It's true," he said. "Her name's Price."

"Let me see that."

The ID held under the light. "Fuck," he said. Then into the head-set: "We've got a little hitch."

Then he moved away, as if that would somehow make the conversation inaudible. "Okay, don't go blaming me, it was short notice. What was I supposed to do, go up and introduce myself first? She was where you said she'd be, she had blond hair, she looked like she was waiting on someone, what else was I supposed to think? Okay, all right, don't get crazy on me. Yeah, I know. I'll take care of it."

"Fucking moron," he added as he took the headset off, stuck it in his pocket, moved the gun to his right hand from his left. "Sorry, lady," he added. "Sometimes shit happens."

"Over there." He pushed, then gestured with the gun and encouraged her by putting his knee into her back. Emma fell forward, and he righted her, grabbing onto the collar of her shirt.

"Please, I have kids."

"What can I do?" he asked.

The shirt lifted, the top button choking her, closing in on her windpipe. Liam. Katherine Rose. Emma resisted, pulling away from him, trying to reverse the flow and turn back time. As she did, the button popped, the shirt bunching up at her neck, and then that second button went too and the next, until suddenly he was left holding her shirt in his hand.

She caught him looking down at it, in amazement.

Squeaky's reluctant accomplice was the only thing standing between Emma and the water. He stepped aside, and she dove off the pier. When she hit, her entire body went numb. Clawing up, she caught a breath and wrapped her arms around one of the pilings.

"Excuse me," Emma said. The desk was painted an olive green, a lovely complement to the mustard yellow. Two nurses and an attendant were there, pointedly ignoring her presence. One of the nurses held up a finger, without even looking her way. "So you know what I say, I tell her, what? You think I'm born yesterday, I'm going to let some boy sleep over at my house? Little sassy miss, you got another think coming."

Laughter all round.

Emma was down, sprawling on the floor. She noted that the tile was dingy, apparently the custodial staff was less than efficient. What a surprise that was.

"Miss," the nurse's voice said. "Now, where did she go?" Louder. "Miss? Gets all up in my face and can't even wait a minute, that's the trouble with people these days, they got no damn patience at all."

# Chapter Two

"We can fly back tonight," Will insisted.

"I said no, and I meant it," Emma said.

"Don't be a martyr."

"Right. Me."

That brought him up short. "If you really think it's better this way." She knew he had hoped to milk the selflessness angle for all it was worth.

"It's better," she told him.

"Okay." His voice diminishing, as if he was moving farther and farther away as he spoke. "I guess you know what's best."

Once again, her ex had managed to get exactly what he wanted. Now Will could advertise his generosity, slipping his willingness to forgo the Oscar ceremony into polite conversation, how, even though it was the most important moment of his life, he had offered to fly to his ex-wife's side. What a good guy! What a saint in Armani couture he was, shoes by Bruno Magli, while his wife, Jolene Pruitt Hayes, had chosen vintage Gucci. Her diamond necklace and drop earrings were on loan from Cartier's, and she also had Manolo Blahniks, albeit with Eiffel Tower heels.

"You think Dawn's okay?"

"I hope so," Emma said.

"Me too," Will agreed somberly. He and Dawn had never been

close. Indeed, when Will showed up and whisked Emma off to his castle of married, then pregnant, bliss, Dawn had shown signs of incipient jealousy. But that was years ago. "Her parents must be going nuts," Will added. The pause that followed definitely did not refresh, it just created new anxiety. "Let me get Liam. He's been worried sick. I told him what we agreed on, that you'd fallen down the steps in front of the house, but I don't know how long that's going to fly. There was a story about Dawn in the *Los Angeles Times*. Lucky I was up before him. Then again, who isn't."

He set the phone down. In the background, she could hear Jolene's voice, "I can't believe you . . ." The rest of the complaint was thankfully muffled. Then, "Mom?"

Hearing Liam's voice was all it took. Emma burst into tears.

"Mom, are you there?"

Emma cleared her throat, then croaked out, "Yeah, it's me."

"Why are you in the hospital?"

"Dad told you, I fell down the stairs. I hit my head, and they kept me overnight, they wanted to make sure I didn't have a concussion. I'm going home later today, Suzanne's coming to drive me."

"Are you sure you're okay?"

"I'm fine," Emma insisted.

"You're all by yourself."

"It's not a problem."

"I can come home."

And he meant it, this from her fourteen-year-old.

"Suzanne's spending the night." Another lie, although God knows Suzanne had offered. And Emma had resisted it obstinately. "I'm just going to lie there in bed and watch the awards. Don't forget to wave to me."

"Mom!" Moving directly from worry to embarrassment. Better, Emma thought; a much more appropriate feeling for a boy of such tender years.

"So what stars have you spotted?" The gaiety she injected was false, not to mention uncharacteristic.

"You sound weird," he countered.

"It's just . . ." she began and heard the hitch in her voice, "I'm sharing a room here. No privacy."

"Oh." Smart kid, didn't buy it for a millisecond.

Desperate times call for desperate measures. "Plus, they gave me a painkiller, it makes me a little dopey."

"I thought you said you were fine."

"I am."

"So what did they give you?"

Nothing actually, except plain old Tylenol, which wasn't even good for the headache she most definitely had.

"Vicodin," she said.

"That's a downer, right? Cool."

Now it was her turn to worry.

"Where did you learn about Vicodin?"

"God, Mom, that was FLE, sixth grade."

She was, without question, a dope.

"I really want to come home. I told Dad too. Awards are just superficial bullshit."

"You said that to him?" She couldn't help hoping.

A giggle. "Not exactly." And then she heard a scraping, someone picking up the receiver, then "'Lo?" Katherine Rose.

"Katie, get off the phone," Liam said.

*No, let her stay on.* Only Emma couldn't manage to talk. It was a sweet second, listening to her two-and-a-half-year-old panting.

"Katie," Emma said.

"Who?"

"It's Mom."

"Mamamamamama. Mamamamama." Then she could hear Jolene in the background, saying, "Didn't I tell you not to play with the phone? Put it down. Put it down now! Don't you run away from me, you little witch . . . I swear, I'm going to give you a spanking." The phone was slammed down. Good to know her children were in the very best hands.

"I better go," Liam said. Meaning, *I'd better save Katie.*

"Love you too." Into the phone. After the fact. Guilt muscling in from every side. She couldn't help visualizing the scene that was taking place three thousand miles west, but there was nothing for it. Better, much better, they were in La-La Land than back here, with her at half strength, with Dawn missing.

"Breakfast, ladies." A timely diversion. Lifting the lid, Emma admired the rubberized eggs and blackened toast. She sipped on the cup of lukewarm coffee and ate to the accompaniment of CNN. No news on Dawn. Fortified, she turned off the TV and decided she had the energy to shower. Inside the bathroom, she took a deep breath before lifting her eyes to the mirror. The bruise on her cheek had yellowed at the edges, and the left side of her face was triple the size of the right. She could already imagine how many looks would come with it, but at least New Yorkers were cagey, their eyes skirting tragedy as quickly as possible.

The shower was warm, stinging her body. She gritted her teeth and bore it as the spray scraped knees and palms alike. Eventually, her shoulders began to unknot, and she turned the hot to scalding, using the pine-scented industrial-strength soap to wash her hair till it was squeaky clean and undoubtedly impossible to comb. Patting her body dry, tentatively, she opened the door and slipped past her still-dreaming roommate. A violent snore erupted on schedule. It amazed her that such a tiny, seemingly frail body could emit such an outsized noise; it had kept Emma awake most of the night. She longed for her own bed. For peace and relative quiet.

The clothes her best friend, Suzanne, had brought were on the chair. Emma started with the jeans, wincing as she pulled them up over her legs. It felt as if she was rubbing sandpaper along baby-tender skin. The cotton T-shirt worked better, and with those on, she felt moderately presentable. Sitting on the bed, she beat an impatient tattoo on her thighs, with both hands. Suzanne had said she'd be back after lunch to take her home. Suzanne had also made clear, twelve times over, how much she thought this was a mistake.

"Stay with us," she'd offered yet again. When Emma had predictably resisted, she'd said, "Then I'm sleeping there with you, don't tell me no again."

"No, again," Emma had said firmly.

"You're out of your mind," Suzanne had told her.

True. Looking out the window, she saw a raccoon opening a black garbage bag and picking at the remains of the day. Emma crumpled into the chair and lifted the remote. The channel still was turned to CNN. The tickertape threaded across the bottom of the screen—then, suddenly, the flash for breaking news.

"Shit," Emma said aloud, raising the volume button a notch, in time for the correspondent to announce, "We're going live to Senator Prescott's home." There was the copter's-eye view from above, the senator's private bay beach, his yacht, tethered to the dock, his lap-length swimming pool in crystalline blue, the guest and gatehouses, and the pièce de résistance, that modest, nine-bedroom Tudor.

The camera angle changed, zooming in on the first-term Republican senator from Connecticut, Hamilton Prescott, and his wife, Ruth Darlington Prescott. The couple stood on the front steps, flanked by men in uniform and FBI agents. There was the audible sound of shutters clicking, as the photographers pressed forward. A gust of wind lifted the cap off one of the policemen's heads. He furtively glanced around, then ducked to retrieve it.

Hamilton cleared his throat, which resulted in a quieting of the insistent voices. He stood ramrod-straight. "This has been an extremely difficult time for us as a family, but we wanted to come forward to thank all of you. We're grateful for your expressions of concern. It has been a comfort to know that so many strangers are thinking of us, and of our daughter." Hamilton's expression was grim, his words deliberate; he was the sort who gave no quarter, Emma decided, even when tragedy struck. It was Ruth who appeared to have taken the direct hit; her lips quivered, her skin was ashen and her eyes glassy.

Emma had met Dawn's parents once in their home, three other times at awkward dinners in restaurants, and then said hello in passing, at holiday and birthday parties. Dawn had a set way of dealing with her mother. She'd attempt to involve Ruth in a dispute. Ruth would always refuse, clucking her tongue, muttering a "Now, dear," or changing the subject. Which of course inflamed Dawn more. "The

Mistress of Denial," Dawn called her. "I swear, if I set myself on fire in front of her, she'd douse me with a glass of ice water and then make some insipid comment about the weather."

Over the years, Emma had wondered why Dawn couldn't just give up. Ruth was clearly never going to change. But Dawn kept banging her head hard against the impervious wall. When Ruth offered her a birdlike peck on the cheek, Dawn made sure to grab onto her mother and force her into a hug. Ruth's response to this had been classic: she'd stand completely still, as if it was her nature to endure without complaint.

If Dawn could have seen her now, all would have been forgiven, Emma thought, especially now that Dawn had her own daughter. It looked to Emma as if someone had plucked Ruth's heart from her body and trampled it.

Senator Hamilton Prescott was blue blood, old blood, at least as far back as America went. Unlike many of his brethren, who had inherited old money, he'd worked hard to go from prosperous to filthy rich, investing wisely in diverse areas: timber, mining, computer chips, and overseas sweatshops that produced an array of designer clothing. Before deciding to run for public office, he had contributed heavily to the party that made the most sense: he was a staunch Republican. During those dinners, Dawn had never had any trouble getting a rise out of her father. Their arguments would escalate in volume and intensity. Once, Ruth and Emma had left the table together, reconnoitering in the bathroom. There, they'd passed a civil few minutes washing their hands and talking about the weather. Dawn would have laughed, had she known.

Families were crazy, the world over. Which didn't mean Hamilton Prescott didn't love his daughter, Emma noted. Of course, Dawn had been appalled when he'd decided to run on a "throw out the scoundrels" platform. "Too Rich to Be Corrupt" was one of his slogans. He had won by a landslide.

"We wish to extend our gratitude to all of you who have called in tips to the authorities. I know they are working diligently to find our daughter Dawn and bring her back to us. In order to facilitate this, our family is offering a reward of one hundred thousand dollars for any information that leads to her safe return." He cleared his throat again, then added, "That's all. Thank you." He attempted a graceful retreat, but that was not to be. The fourth estate was peppering him with questions.

"Senator, most missing-persons cases aren't even announced for twenty-four hours. Why did you go public so quickly?"

"Senator, if your daughter's been kidnapped, wouldn't offering this sort of reward conflict with their possible demands?"

"Senator, how are you and your wife coping?"

"Senator, do you think terrorists may have something to do with this?"

"Senator, could this be related to your daughter's role as head of the New York Capital Crimes division?"

And finally, "What aren't you saying, Senator? Don't you think the public has a right to know?"

"Right to know?" he exclaimed. Then he gave his tormentors an imperious look. "Shame on you. Shame on you all," he pronounced before turning his back.

Once more, the camera retreated, displaying Dawn's ancestral home. There was no avoiding the implication, the Prescotts had been cushioned from trouble by their money, their privileged perch; now, finally, they were getting their comeuppance.

"How's it going?" The voice belonged to Fitzsimmons. He breezed in from around the curtain. "You look a hell of a lot better."

"Thanks," Emma said.

Behind him, the screen was displaying an advertisement, a crowd of middle-aged men wearing demented, ivory-white smiles. They loped through a field of bright orange poppies. Underneath, the words advised: "Choose wisely, choose Fracanox. And learn to live again."

Fitzsimmons reached up and clicked off the tube. He turned to her, and she saw his somber expression.

No, she thought. Her hands went up, as if to ward off a physical blow. She flashed on Laurence, her lover, detailing the first time he'd had to give bad news. Only a rookie cop, he'd knocked on a door over on Bedford. "That mother knew before I said anything. Shut the door right in my face, before I could even get the words out." The woman's son had been lying only a block away, a fourteen-year-old boy—the collateral damage of a drug deal gone sour.

Fitzsimmons was saying, "There's no good way to do this." The shrug in his shoulders, the commiseration on his face. She turned to stare out the window. Across the way, in the next wing, a woman pulled down the blind.

At the Nassau County Medical Center, perennial plantings had been used to offset the mediocrity of the architecture, trimmed hedges roping off the sandstone edifice. As Emma stepped onto the rubber welcome mat, the doors swooshed open.

"You can still rethink this," Fitzsimmons said.

Not a chance. She was going to bear witness, she'd known before the words were out of his mouth. He'd argued against it, first in the hospital room, then as they rode out together, saying they could send her morgue photos via computer, saying often it was easier, better, less emotional, more cut-and-dried.

The bodies of Dawn Prescott and an unknown male companion had been discovered only an hour earlier, by a cleaning woman turning down the beds at the Sunrise Motel in Merrick. Dawn had been easy to place, what with her face plastered all over the news.

Fitzsimmons flashed his badge at the guard; they walked to elevator C and rode down to the sub-basement. He rapped on the door to room 2. As the handle turned, she felt his hand settle on her shoulder, giving it a quick, comforting squeeze.

"I guess I'd do the same," he told her just as the door pulled back, revealing Lieutenant Shane Lowry.

"You're Fitzsimmons." Put as a statement. "Go on in, help yourself to some coffee. We won't be long."

Lowry led the way down the hall, without acknowledging that she was meant to follow. She did. What choice did she have? He hadn't even bothered to offer a cursory hello, but then he'd already made it clear, in the few encounters they'd had, just how much he disliked her.

Lowry was the sort of man who people liked to say "looked good for his age," this despite the thickness in his girth and the thinning brown hair up top. He'd spent too much quality time in the sun; now his skin was leathery, the lines dug into it. They'd last met barely three weeks ago. She and Dawn had arrived to vet him, once again, as they laid the groundwork for the appeal in the Arthur Nevins case. Lowry had kept them waiting for a good hour, then he'd taken them back to his office and announced that he had a meeting and he was running late, they'd have to make it "snappy."

To every question, he had a textbook answer. As in, look at the text. "It's all in the report," he'd said. Or, "I testified on this at the trial."

Stonewalling was a very old and trusted tactic. One he'd apparently perfected. Emma had never been in his office before, her encounters taking place on the phone or at the county courthouse. During their all-too-brief visit, she had had time to do a survey of the place, noting the photographs of Lowry glad-handing various members of the local elite, stars of stage, screen, and business, as well as the governor and one retired Republican president.

That day he'd worn his uniform, complete with cap; today he was dressed way down, sporting a madras shirt atop khaki shorts. His feet were noticeably bare inside his over-wide Docksiders.

The elevators were marked FOR HOSPITAL PERSONNEL ONLY. Lowry tagged the down button, without checking to see if she was close.

To Hades, Emma thought. When they emerged, would Cerberus be guarding the door to the mortuary? She imagined a dog of prehistoric size, adorned with a spiked collar. Drool foamed off its tongue.

Of course, when the doors opened to the sub-sub-sub-basement, there was no dog, just an orderly reading a romance novel; on the cover, a long-haired Greek god–like male ripping off a woman's bodice. The chill in the air made the goose bumps rise on her bare arms. The orderly barely looked up as Lowry passed.

Inside, the temperature descended another ten degrees, and the harsh smell of antiseptic coated her nostrils. Lowry signed the visitor's ledger, then tapped on the medical examiner's half-shut door. Simpson

Hobart, M.D., led them into the morgue, he and Lowry exchanging golf tips as they went. Emma found she couldn't really understand the words; there was this buzzing noise in her head. Drawer 17 was unlocked, the wheels so greased they didn't make a sound.

The man's eyes were no longer blue. How had that happened? They were hazel, but in every other respect he looked exactly the same. There was a small scar under his right eye, and the expression on his face was one of pure terror. There was a bullet hole under his left breast.

"You know him?"

"I think so. Yes."

"Questions?"

"His eyes. I thought they were blue."

Lowry chuckled. "You don't miss a trick, do you?"

Emma wasn't sure what that was supposed to mean, other than that the intention was insulting.

"He had blue contact lenses."

"Oh." A weak response, but the best she could manage. She could hear Lowry breathing, hear the ticking of the clock too, even hear her blood surging through her body.

"So with that little caveat, I've got your approval." Lowry wasn't asking, he was demanding.

"He was the man who approached me, he forced me into the car." Emma didn't stop intentionally. Her voice gave out.

"I'm going to need a little more than that," he insisted, and she felt him move closer. Felt his breath raise the hairs on the nape of her neck.

"They mistook me for Dawn." His naked hostility was the antidote she needed. "Detective Fitzsimmons took an extensive statement."

"Always better to hear it from the horse's mouth."

"Isn't it," she retorted. And finally had the strength to turn and meet his eyes.

"Why don't you tell it again," he said, as if he was only being reasonable. Lowry's hand extended to take in the room, the M.E. who had managed to move away from the two of them, giving them all the privacy that sterile place could afford.

"Fine. Dawn phoned me and asked me to meet her. I was waiting at the corner of Carroll and Third Avenue, and the next thing I knew these two men drove up in a black town car, they both stepped out, and this man came up to me, he asked me where Smith Street was. Then he grabbed me. His friend had a gun."

"What type?"

"I'm not an expert," Emma said.

"Funny, I thought you were."

Fuck you, Emma thought but didn't say the words. It felt wrong to utter a curse, to rise to his bait, here. Lowry did a half turn and his rubber soles squeaked against the floor. She saw he was on his way out.

"Lieutenant."

He stopped moving, had expected it, she supposed. Why else come all this way. Turning, he gave her a short-fuse smile.

"Yeah?"

God, he was smirking. He really was despicable.

"Could I see her?"

"Her being who?"

If looks could kill, he would have been dead, piled up into a mound of carbon chips on the floor.

"You know who I mean. I'd like to see Dawn's body."

"Sorry." He wasn't. "That's for next of kin."

"Please," Emma said.

He smiled thinly. "Why would you want that?" he asked.

"I'm not leaving until I see her," Emma said.

He cocked his head, considering the threat. "Suit yourself," he finally said. Then he jerked a shoulder and the M.E., Hobart, pulled open drawer 3.

The white-blond hair fell away on either side, her forehead, her eyebrows, her eyes open, her expression defiant, the pink lips pressed tight. Emma could make an educated guess about the way she'd died; there was extensive bruising on Dawn's neck, her eyes were distended, and her skin had that telltale bluish tint. She'd been strangled.

She tried to put it together—the bullet hole in his chest, the imprints around Dawn's neck.

"The preliminary examination indicates asphyxiation as the cause of death," Hobart said, giving the drawer a final tug, which exposed the rest. Dawn was so thin, really emaciated, her breasts mostly muscle, sculpted ribs right above the stomach, a hollow that was scooped out between jutting hips. There was a mole above her navel, and her pubic hair was threaded with gray. Emma wanted to cover her up, to carry her away. But it was too late, there was nothing she could do to protect her friend. This was only the beginning of the indignities, the autopsy, the embalming. Emma told herself the body was not the spirit, Dawn was gone, long gone, and yet she still wanted to reach over and ask for forgiveness. I should have protected you from this, Emma thought. I should have done something. "I'm so sorry," Emma said aloud. She meant for everything, for every minute where she'd failed Dawn, betraying her in small ways, sharing a laugh with colleagues or ducking her when she knew a request was forthcoming and she would rather, much rather, be home.

In large ways too, Emma knew, for years they'd been such close friends. When Dawn had fallen in and out of love repeatedly, Emma had been her confidante. Dawn would call her up to analyze her misery late at night, but then Emma had married, had a child, she'd had to back away, deflecting the apparent need. There had been times of tension after that, but they had finally worked through those.

Emma's gaze came to rest on what she'd avoided for so many years. After all, Dawn couldn't see her now. She stared at the T-shaped scars on both wrists.

"That'll do," Lowry said.

Only then did she realize: she was crying.

Outside, waiting for the elevator, he asked, "You need to take a private minute?"

Emma shook her head. She felt in her pockets for Kleenex and came up empty-handed. Her nose was running, there was nothing for it, she had to wipe it with the back of her coat sleeve. Emma felt like a child, doing it. Lowry extended a handkerchief.

"Don't worry, it's clean," he told her. His voice held no invective. Emma took it gratefully.

They got into the elevator; an intense, mournful sort of quiet reigned. He broke it with an offer of a TicTac.

"No, thanks."

His jaw cracked down on the candy.

Upstairs, he led her into a room with a sign warning SECURITY STAFF ONLY. The time clock was ticking away. There was a nine-inch TV in front of three orange plastic chairs and a couch. Dog-eared magazines were strewn across a shabby coffee table.

"Sit," he said, indicating where. "I'll be back in a sec."

Emma didn't ask him where he was going or why. She did as she was told. Frankly, her legs were giving out. Making a mute survey of her surroundings, she read the names on the time cards, then looked down at the magazine in front of her, *Soap Opera Digest*. "Ruth Leaves Tod For Danny," blared the headline. *People* magazine lay next to it. "Teen Queen Ramone Rates Gold." Underneath the headline—Pru Ramone, the star of Will's movie, clutching her Golden Globe.

The door opened. Lowry, returning, setting out a plastic evidence bag. Inside, there was a handgun.

"Familiar?" he asked.

She stared at it blankly.

"Well?" The kindness he'd offered was gone, in its place truculence.

"I really can't say."

"Try."

So she did. He'd bullied her into it. Shutting her eyes, Emma attempted to conjure up the past. He'd flexed the weapon, sticking it into her ribs. Emma tried hard to find the gun, but instead she saw the sneer, saw the flash of metal. Emma's eyes sprang open.

"Why does it matter?" Emma asked.

"I think you know."

The gun had a wooden handle, it was small, the sort of weapon that felt tidy in your hand. "I absolutely don't. My saying it looked the same, what would that do for you?"

"A .22 Smith and Wesson," he said. "Marketed for the ladies. Home protection. Keeps you feeling safe all day and all night long too." And he sat, on the couch, much too close for comfort. "So how about we work on that story of yours."

The smell of mint did not disguise something else. She realized that when he'd gone out, he must have had a drink. Or else she'd missed it before. There was definitely the distinct odor of alcohol under the fruity freshness.

"I don't understand. Work on it?"

"You and I both know that those two, Miss Prescott and her gentleman friend, weren't exactly strangers."

Emma stared at him. "Of course they were."

"Look, I appreciate loyalty same as the next. It's rarer and rarer, times being what they are. I'm sure you and your boss were close. You want to protect her after the fact."

"You are so wrong about this," Emma said.

"I think not." And Lowry actually managed a look of complete self-satisfaction. Emma shifted away as far as she could, scrunching her slim frame into the corner.

"What I'm indicating here, little darling, is how everything comes out in the end, and all you've done, coming up with this tall tale, is wasted my time, made me work twice as hard at disproving what's already bullshit. Now, is that nice, wanting to waste man-hours, not to mention taxpayer dollars? How about you save us all that time and money, do the good people of Nassau County a favor. Do your dead friend, Prescott, downstairs one too."

Emma let out a small, desperate laugh.

"You see this as funny?"

"Absurd. I made up this story to defend Dawn's honor? I must have quite an imagination, not to mention a penchant for self-abuse. You think I liked her so much I was willing to crack myself in the face, throw myself in the bay, then crawl out across the levee and faint to make it look good?"

"Hey, I don't know what the two of you cooked up. But don't act like I'm a novice. I saw what you did with Nevins. Trying to slam me for brutality, trying to make it seem like it was my fault the fucker beat his ex to death, lit her and her kid on fire. Seems to me, someone who does that doesn't quite have a conscience."

"Excuse me! This has nothing to do with defense tactics."

His turn to laugh, harshly. "Little darling, listen, your friend Prescott wouldn't be the first woman on God's earth to like a little juice. Maybe bad boys were her weakness, and this time she met her match. The faster you clear the air, the faster it becomes yesterday's news."

"You're crazy," Emma said, rising to her feet.

"Not so fast," Lowry said. His hand sprung to her shoulder, and he shoved her back down hard. "I'm not done with you yet."

"But I'm done with you."

In response, his hand pinched her flesh. She grabbed at it, trying to pry his fingers loose. Lowry grinned, but then he had a good hundred pounds on her. Letting go, she balled her hand into a fist, punched at his arm. Like a gnat, she decided. The next thing she knew he'd squash her, then flick her away.

Lowry leaned in close. "The Quality Inn, in Hempstead, the two of them having a little festival of love. The clerk swears they couldn't keep their hands off each other when they were signing in."

"I don't believe a word of it."

"No?"

Reaching inside his shirt pocket, he withdrew a handful of Polaroid snapshots, dropping them on the table. It was impossible not to look at Dawn, caught in different angles of repose, including a close-up of her hand wrapped around the barrel of the gun. A ladies' gun, he'd insinuated. Now she knew why.

"Dawn hated guns," Emma said firmly. "She wouldn't have one in the house."

"Really? Another thing you're sure of?"

"Positive."

"Her father tells me different. Says she won awards when she was a teen, for marksmanship. But who knows, maybe you weren't aware of this about her, maybe you're just eager to try and help her out, now that she's gone. I guess it doesn't hurt to give you the benefit of the doubt."

How was he doing that? Emma pointedly looked away and heard the flutter as he gathered the photographs up.

"Lovers' spat that turns ugly," Lowry said. "Mr. No Name's got a short fuse, so he goes for her throat, maybe she opens her big mouth one time too many. I have some personal experience on that subject, so I guess I don't find it all that hard to imagine."

"I can't believe you'd try to float this," Emma said bitterly.

He squinted at her, like she was some curious specimen. "Hey," he said, "I'm just doing my job."

Emma sprang up, and he didn't try to stop her this time. She was at the door, her hand on the knob.

"Your friend had a history of emotional instability," he said. "She was a head case, pure and simple. Tried to kill herself more than once."

"How can you even think to use that against her? Jesus, she went after you because it was her job. It wasn't personal."

"No?" He grunted to show how little he believed her.

"Dawn was murdered," Emma said.

"So what did she tell you about those scars?" he countered. "Did Prescott claim she punched her way through a plate-glass window?"

"It's not pertinent," Emma insisted.

"How about you let me decide that?" Lowry smirked, adding, "Anyhow, don't trouble yourself too much, the senator's been more than forthcoming."

Emma felt her body shaking, she was that angry. She stepped out the door and pulled it shut, hard. But it was only a thin wooden barrier, not enough to protect her from him, or from what he was threatening to do to Dawn.

She leaned against the wall, and couldn't help seeing her friend, Dawn, sitting next to her at the bar at Lucky Al's. Was it really almost fifteen years ago? That rundown dive had been their regular, post-court-date stop. Dawn would have a boilermaker, Emma a pint of Guinness. Dawn would drink hard, Emma would nurse two and be done with it.

"Truth," Emma said.

"Come on. Dare me. I need the challenge."

"You always try to squirm out of it. Not this time. No begging off. No changing the subject."

"I would never," Dawn said, throwing a "you-ought-to-know-me-better" look. Emma did.

"The scars, you didn't really shove your hand through a plate-glass window."

"I was framing a picture, the glass broke."

"Bullshit. Everyone knows you tried to kill yourself."

"Everyone being?"

Emma waited the requisite amount of time.

"All right, if you must, you must," Dawn said, extracting a pack of cigarettes, banging on the bottom, retrieving one, lighting it, and taking a long, steady pull. "Thing is, if you want to kill yourself for real, you make good and sure. Like smoking these death sticks, that's a definite one-way ticket."

Emma couldn't help flinching; only two years before her mother had died from lung cancer, a fact Dawn was more than aware of.

"Sorry," Dawn said reflexively.

"You were saying," Emma responded, knowing that this indirect jibe was likely another way of diverting her attention and throwing her off the scent.

Dawn smiled, something she did infrequently. She had a nice smile, Emma decided, slightly tentative, as if she was afraid to make a full commitment. Emma's own, a full-blown toothy thing, was embarrassingly wholehearted and emotional in contrast.

"Mitchell Glass," Dawn said, threading a finger across the scar on her right hand, looking down at it dubiously, then turning back to Emma. "Mitch and my own stupidity. I was a sophomore at Radcliffe and I thought the bastard was going to ask me to marry him. What the fuck did I know? Son of someone my dad did business with, we'd met once before college, and then we reacquainted ourselves, and the rest was history, as they say. My dad treated Mitch like he was the goddamn Second Coming. It didn't even matter that he was of the Hebrew persuasion; after all, he was progeny of a Citibank chairman. New Year's Eve was when I was sure he was going to propose, and sure enough he did. He proposed that we no longer see each other. 'The spark's gone' were his exact words. I was crushed, didn't tell anyone, not my friends and certainly not my parents. Every time they asked what we were up to, hint, hint, hint, I made up an elaborate story. One night, I couldn't think of anything else to lie about, so I went into the bathroom at the dorm and slashed both wrists. About a minute later, my roommate walked in and found me."

"God, I'm so sorry."

"Don't be," Dawn replied. "It's all good."

Emma shot her a skeptical look.

"My parents committed me. Not to Maclean, that was too close, plus they knew half a dozen kids there. They sent me to Menninger's in Kansas for my rest cure. Hoped that whoever came and went wouldn't gossip about the wayward daughter. My mom visited every few weeks. She'd sit there, rubbing her hands together, looking like she had indigestion, not like her daughter was bonkers. As for Ham, he didn't bother with visiting. That wasn't his thing. The whole time I was there, he wrote me one letter, saying how disappointed he was that I'd tried to take the coward's way out."

"That was it?"

"The entire extent of his affection for his only daughter. That's my dad, empathetic to a fault."

The shaking had subsided by the time Emma reached room 2. Entering, she found Fitzsimmons was glued to his *Newsday*. He looked up, then rose to his feet. "You okay?" he asked.

"Fine," Emma said. But she was wrong, her eyes were welling up with tears yet again. Fitzsimmons put his arm around her shoulders in that practiced, professional, completely neutral manner that certain policemen and health-care professionals wore like a second skin.

"It really sucks," he said.

Which was exactly how Liam would have put it.

* * *

Sinking into the passenger seat, Emma stared out the window. Lowry seemed to believe that Dawn had brought this on herself. Now that she'd managed to get far enough away, she realized the obvious. Lowry was trying to hide what had actually happened. Dawn had been taken out here to Nassau County to be killed for a reason. Now Lowry trying to tell her what to think. Emma saw the dead man's face, set into a glassy-eyed grimace. He'd seen his own death coming. Emma thought of how he'd stepped aside, letting her sail past, saving her life and quite possibly condemning his own in the bargain. She was sure his muscular companion was the real culprit, taking care to adjust the bodies, to make it seem like a murder-suicide. He must have known he could count on police cooperation. But why would Lowry do something this damaging? Why would he chance so much?

Whatever it was, it clearly had to do with Arthur Nevins. He was the only reason Dawn and Lowry had a history.

Nine years ago, Arthur Nevins had been convicted of murdering his estranged wife, Julie, their six-year-old daughter, Kara, and Julie's aunt and uncle, in their Glen Cove home. The house had been set on fire in a futile attempt to mask the murders. Back then, Lowry had been a lowly homicide detective; nailing Arthur Nevins had been the springboard that launched him into full public view; three commendations later, he'd been promoted to lieutenant.

Nine years ago, at 3:17 A.M., the first call had come in—a fire out of control—at the end of a very private cul-de-sac. By the time the engines arrived, flames were licking around every corner of the small ranch house. But the firemen were aided by the lack of wind that night, and the heavy rains that had fallen for the last few days. They managed to contain the fire, then put it out just as the sun came up.

Julie Nevins's body was found in the kitchen, her daughter's upstairs in the bedroom, the aunt and uncle's in the garage steps away from their car. It took forensics to discover that Julie hadn't died from the gunshot wound in her chest. A blow to the head had done some damage, but then she'd been strangled. The three others had been shot, execution-style, at point-blank range.

It wasn't too hard to figure out the motive, what with the

acrimonious divorce, the threats, and the order of protection Julie had taken out. It was only a hop, skip, and jump from Glen Cove to Arthur's Brooklyn apartment. In the basement, in a black garbage bag, they found two empty gas cans. Digging deeper into the pile, they discovered the gun. Ballistics made it a match. Arthur was in custody by then, as a suspect. Only hours later, he confessed.

It was all there, on videotape, Arthur reading a statement in a robotic voice. Lowry claimed the statement had been given freely, that there was no coercion on the part of the police, Arthur had simply wanted to clear his guilty conscience.

"Freely, shit," Arthur had told Dawn. "That cop's a fucking lunatic. Sticks this gun to my head like we're in the Wild West, says, 'You got two choices, brother, you tell it like this, or I blow your brains out.' You see the light in his eyes, you'd do the same. I'm no virgin, I know what goes on."

And there it was. The Nevins case had been Dawn's first assignment at her new job as lead attorney for New York Capital Crimes. She'd done her best to prove Arthur's story and offered up the lineup of character witnesses. All to no avail.

Emma saw Arthur Nevins in his current incarnation, his shaved skull catching the reflection from the harsh fluorescent light as he sat opposite her, separated by the wall of triple-paned bulletproof glass. He presently resided in the separate wing for death row inmates, at Clinton Correctional.

Nine years later, Dawn's appeal was based on the issue of "cruel and unusual punishment." Going over the groundwork, reinterviewing the principals, this was all part of the preparation. Had Dawn come across something new and not shared it with Emma? That night, when Dawn had pressured her to show, she'd said, "I'll tell you about it when I get there."

A promise that couldn't be kept. If only I'd forced Dawn to explain, Emma thought.

They were nearing her house, pulling off Ocean Parkway, making for the Ditmas Park enclave. This had once been farmland; then the Victorian gentry from Lower Fifth had decided they needed a summer colony and built themselves little pleasure palaces. Now it only took forty-five minutes to get there via the IRT express. The neighborhood had gone through good times and bad. Once it had been a haven for middle-class Jewish families, but then, in the late sixties and early seventies, landlords had started busting blocks, filling up buildings in the surrounding area with funky tenants in an effort to promote white flight and drive down the prices. It had worked. A little too well. Plenty sold and some of the great homes lost their sheen. But others refused to cave. They weathered the bad years, and Ditmas Park recovered. After all, it was an unusual spot. Where else could you find a ten-bedroom gingerbread mansion on a quiet residential block, only a short subway ride away from Manhatttan?

Lately, as housing prices in the rest of the borough had skyrocketed, these houses had appreciated. Many were now selling in the high six figures. And in keeping with the surge in upscale ownership, there had been a rash of renovations, including historically accurate nineteenth-century paint jobs in four clashing colors. Emma didn't care for that particular aesthetic, but these were the homes with the best-kept lawns and the perfect wicker porch furniture. Hers, in contrast, was the eyesore.

Pulling up, Emma saw that the Dumpster was full to overflowing, and her roof had a new blue tarpaulin raincoat. The paint on the outside of the house had been sandblasted, exposing naked wood. The motley collection of cars belonging to the illegal immigrants who made up her contractor's crew made it seem like she was throwing a party.

"I'll walk you inside," Fitzsimmons said firmly.

"Watch your step," Emma warned.

"You weren't kidding," he said a minute later as his foot broke through one of the rotting boards on the porch steps. Listing to one side, he cautiously raised it. "So what did they call this, a handyman's special?"

"A fool's paradise." No point in engaging him in the story of how this house had been deeded to her, as a sort of penance, by an old friend. Although, being a cop, he would probably have found it intriguing to note that the last owner had been found shot to death in the kitchen.

"Looks like a lot to take on." Fitzsimmons shouldered the bag that held the scant belongings she'd brought home from the hospital. She'd left the house keys, along with her purse, in the kidnapper's car. Suzanne had spent hours on the phone making sure her credit cards were stopped and her bank cards canceled. Not that Emma thought it likely they were after her money.

No one had mentioned the purse, or her wallet, turning up at the motel. Of course, its existence would have put a definite crimp into Lowry's version of events. Clearly, changing the locks was a priority, as was hiring an armed guard for 'round-the-clock protection.

Was that a joke?

Yes. And no.

The door opened to reveal her contractor.

"Mrs. Price," Paul Angeleno exclaimed. "Your friend said you were at the hospital." She watched as his eyes skated over the bruise, then decided to pretend it was nothing worth commenting on. "You okay now?"

"Never better."

"That's so good."

Behind Angeleno, on the floor, she saw a huge bouquet of irises, tulips, and hyacinths, wrapped in clear plastic. "Those just come. Want I should take them upstairs?"

"I'll do the honors," Fitzsimmons said, scooping up the oversized burden.

Up to the second floor, where Emma discovered her bedroom just as she'd left it, an unrepentant mess. There were piles of half-unpacked boxes, and the bed had the covers thrown back, trailing across the wooden floor. On the rug, her clothing was separated into three distinct piles: clean, lightly soiled, and funky to the max. There was certainly no obvious place to set down his burden.

"Follow me," Emma said and backed up, going next door to her office. Here, minimalism ruled. The room was furnished with a desk and a task chair. The desk held her laptop, a phone, and an answering machine. Beside it, there were several cardboard file boxes holding the briefs and statements from the three cases she was working on currently. The windows, facing the west, were bare, so that the sunlight poured in.

"I haven't really gotten settled yet," she explained.

"Just moved in?"

"Yes." Actually a good six months ago, but she surely wasn't going to mention that.

"Here you go," he said as he removed the greeting card, adding, "But I think you really should reconsider staying here. What about a friend?"

She shook her head.

"If there were two of these guys to begin with, that leaves one still hanging around."

"I'm calling a locksmith. And there's a burglar alarm installed."

"You think that's going to stop this guy?"

"Then you believe me!" Emma knew the rush of gratitude she felt toward him was completely disproportionate, a product of everything she'd been through.

"Never said I didn't."

"Then talk to someone, explain that Lowry's going about this all wrong."

"Thing is, ball's kind of in his court." Fitzsimmons was hedging, she knew how it worked, even his admission that her story was credible could be read as a betrayal. If only Laurence had been here, she thought, not for the first time. Make it about the thousandth.

"What do you think those men were after?" he asked.

"I wish I knew."

"But you and Lieutenant Lowry know each other."

"Yes." She was going to tell him how, then hesitated. There was something she couldn't read in his face. Something that unnerved her.

"Something wrong?" he asked a little too quickly.

"I'm exhausted."

In answer, the buzz saw hummed downstairs. "Let me take you somewhere else," he insisted.

She shook her head firmly.

"I'm going to come by and check on you later then." Lifting a card from his pocket, he scribbled a number on the back. "My cell."

Finally, he backed out. She listened to Fitzsimmons's steps recede down the stairs. Then the front door shut. Leaning down, she took the card from the cellophane wrapping and lifted it out, reading the inscription: "From Will and his friends at Brighton Beach Productions, wishing you a speedy recovery." It was typed. No signature. He'd undoubtedly gotten the PA to call in the order.

Turning to her desk, she saw the answering machine blinking violently. Thirty-seven messages. Emma stepped over and hit the playback button.

"Emma, it's Dawn. I'm here. It's twenty after. Sorry, I'm running late. When I tried to leave, Millie threw a fit." *Click.*

There was a twisting inside. Dawn was alive, the recording the evidence, but knowing better came right on the heels of that. Emma let out a gasp as Dawn's voice emerged again. "The corner of Carroll and Third. I'm here under the Acme sign. It's nine-forty." *Click.*

"Emma? Emma, are you there? It's ten."

"Emma, it's after eleven. Are you screening? Emma? Emma! Now I'm getting worried. Call me as soon as you hear this. Please." *Click.*

Emma felt as if she was literally about to jump out of her skin. What next? The answer was Laurence, his deep voice a surprise. "You'll be happy to know I behaved myself. Didn't make a scene. Didn't do one thing in character. I was a good boy, and now here I am, lying in this king-sized bed, missing you."

"Missing you too," she said aloud. God. She wasn't going to start crying again, even if no one was there to bear witness to her weakness.

"Hey."

Whipping around, Emma found Fitzsimmons standing in the doorway. He smiled apologetically and held out a piece of paper.

"Must have dropped out of the bag," he ventured.

Moving to grab it, she saw it was the prescription for antibiotics she'd been given at the hospital.

"Dawn left four messages on my answering machine," Emma said.

"It proves I'm telling the truth." Her finger lifted above the replay button, but she saw no look of surprise on his face.

"You heard them," she said.

Fitzsimmons didn't bother to dispute that. And she realized she'd never heard the doorbell ring. It didn't take much to realize he'd probably closed the door, stood there waiting, then climbed the stairs cautiously.

"What were you hoping to find out?" she demanded.

"I don't get you."

"I think you do. Telling me you believed my story, what was that about?" Stuffing the paper into her pocket, she added, "I want you to leave."

"You're wrong about this," he began.

"If I am, I'm sure I'll figure it out," she said firmly. And moved toward him so that he had to retreat into the hallway.

"You've got my card," he noted.

"Yup."

She followed him right to the front door, shut it firmly behind him, and double-locked the locks. Looking through the window, she made damn sure his car pulled away.

Emma remembered how she'd shoved the prescription down to the very bottom of the plastic bag, underneath the pile of ruined and shredded clothing. The bag had been placed on the floor of the car, right next to her feet. She hadn't touched it again. There were two possibilities: Either he'd palmed it when he took the bag from her as he carried it into the house, or he'd gone and looked inside while she was at the hospital, thinking to use it as insurance. Why? To prove what?

She couldn't imagine. Staring out at the street, Emma saw Dawn opening the door of her own home to the man who would murder her. None of the news reports had indicated there were any witnesses, or any sounds of a struggle. True, it was late at night, but the bar on the corner stayed open, and Emma knew that section of Bergen Street. If Dawn had screamed, someone would have heard. Had she really gone willingly? Had she shut her front door, locked it behind her, and left her only child alone? Dawn was an avowedly overprotective parent. For her to do this to Millicent seemed totally out of character.

Yet, without a doubt she had. What had they used to convince her, if not brute force?

Emma was afraid she knew. It wouldn't have taken a whole lot of digging to make a connection between Dawn Prescott and Emma Price. A simple search of the Palm Pilot that was at the bottom of Emma's handbag would have culled the address and phone number. All they'd have to have done was punch in P for Prescott. And then, how easy for them to rectify their initial mistake, they could have used Emma as the bait. "Your friend's in trouble. She asked us to get you."

You're being absurd, Emma told herself. How can you possibly think you're in any way responsible? Yet she did. Her guilt gnawed at her, and she knew there was only one way she could hope to assuage it.

# Chapter Three

"How's my lady Dawn?" Arthur had asked
only a few months before. It had been a frigid mid-January day in the
Adirondacks. Outside, the snow was piled to either side of a narrow
path carved through the parking lot. On the walk from the guard-
house to the front of the prison compound it had towered a good six
inches above her head. But in here, on death row, weather was super-
fluous, days passed in twelve-hour blocks; lights on, then lights out.

"She's good," Emma replied.

"Good? Never is and never was. That woman is wired. She live on
fossil fuel or what? Better get to fattening her up, otherwise she ain't
never gonna get a man to stick, men don't like a body that scrawny.
I told her as much."

Emma just bet he had. Suppressing a smile, she passed the draft of
the appeal brief to the guard on her side of the glass divider. He flipped
through the pages, ensuring that no weapons or contraband had been
secreted, a joke, considering what was available to every prisoner on
the inside, providing they had the necessary funds. The guard shoved it
through the slot. His counterpart on the other side then did exactly the
same thing before finally dropping it in Arthur's lap.

Arthur loved to rag Dawn, loved to get her going, about her
weight, her love life. Emma? He seemed to know better than to start
in with her. Funny, she thought, because most people would have considered Dawn the more intimidating of the two of them. Not Arthur.

As for his preoccupation with Dawn's physique, Emma was pretty sure it went back to his own transformation. On the night of his arrest, he hadn't exactly been a tower of power. At just under six feet, Arthur had weighed a mere one hundred and sixty-eight pounds. Worse, he'd had the kind of face that women loved, a pretty-boy pout, with just enough tint to make it clear he was ethnic. His record till that night had consisted of two years in juvie for car theft. Suddenly, he was being sent up to do major time.

In the nine years since, Arthur had acquired a wrestler's beefy neck and etched musculature. His nose had been broken during his time in detention; a bump showed where and gave his face a slightly lopsided look.

Admiring the heft of the pages settled in his lap, he said, "I'll be back to you."

Emma knew he would. He'd have read it by day's end, and when his computer time started, he'd start firing off the e-mails. Arthur had received a bachelor's inside and was working on a law degree. This year, he was doing distance learning, taking Torts from Albany Law School. There was nothing he liked better than fine-tuning the argument. Or, at least, imagining he could.

"So how's your son doing? Still in love?" he asked Emma.

"Yes."

"See, I told you this one was golden."

Another one of Arthur's areas of expertise, but then there was no way else for him to live but vicariously. She had to give him a lot of credit: Most of her clients were nursing serious drug habits. Arthur had had the strength to resist, thus far.

On her last visit, Emma had mentioned Cleo, Liam's new girlfriend, describing, in descending order, the pierced eyebrow, the fetching laugh, and the passion for punk music. "This one's a keeper," Arthur had insisted. A dubious claim: Liam's track record at fourteen was hardly stellar. Girls had come and gone so quickly, Emma finally gave up trying to remember their proper names. Oddly enough, Arthur seemed to be right, at least for now. Cleo was still his lady love.

"But you got to be careful," Arthur went on. "No matter what charms this Cleo has, you keep an eye out. No one knows how to protect a boy better than his mom."

"How would you suggest I go about protecting him?" Emma asked.

"You're the one who gets paid for digging up dirt," he noted.

"That's not exactly true," she countered.

"All I'm saying is, a guy's brain stops working the minute his dick's involved."

"He's fourteen, Arthur."

"So? You're telling me what? I was younger than that."

"Fine, I'll take it under advisement."

"Fancy way of saying mind my own business."

True. He laughed. "So how's your other one, the queen bee?"

"Good."

"Glad to hear it." But, for a moment, his expression darkened.

She couldn't help but wonder if they were both thinking about his own daughter. That photograph the judge had allowed into evidence had been horrible. It had showed her small charred body on the M.E.'s slab.

Arthur reached forward, tapping his manacled hands on the partition. The guard moved toward him, as if this was a sign he was attempting to break through and make a run for it. Her client's face was distorted, the nose and chin larger than normal. It looked as if he was drowning. Emma wanted to reach through and pull him back to shore.

"Take care of those two kids of yours," he told her, then sat back, shooting the guard a wry, contemptuous smile.

Two hours later, the locksmith had come and gone. The burglar alarm was set. And the phone in her hand was on automatic redial. It was continually busy. Clearly, she was not alone in attempting to reach the senator. The clock on her bedside table said seven-o-eight. Lifting the open container of sesame noodles from its perch on top of the boxes, she checked and found there was one last bite. Finishing it off, she dropped the gritty chopsticks back inside and set the container onto the floor with its partner, the empty fried-dumpling box. Pulling open the drawer of the bedside table, she rifled through the mushrooming pile of takeout menus and spare change, digging out the channel changer. It was time for ABC and the pre-Oscar countdown.

As Hollywood's elite paraded down the red carpet, Joan Rivers shouted "dahling" and air-kissed her victims. Was it possible that Joan had gotten even more plastic surgery? Her eyelids seemed to have dissolved back into her skull, while the flesh on her cheeks was pulled so tight it was, quite literally, transparent. "Stahrs, stahrs, stahrs," Joan gushed.

It was so shallow, so mindless, so authentically all-American, the idea that you could blanket yourself with glitz and, by doing so, add something that was critically missing in your own drab life. Emma was mad at herself for giving in, but for long moments, her mind went blank as she followed the stars' progress. It was a blessed relief, nothing she was going to see in the next few hours was going to upset her, the one guarantee was boredom, her only question how long it would take as Hollywood congratulated itself to excess.

Inside the theater, the cameras panned the crowd, focusing in on the great and near-great. The announcer intoned, "Rock czarina Pru Ramone, only seventeen and nominated for Best Supporting Actress. With her, the brash New York–based producer of *Baby Mine*, Gregory Chavitz. Next to him, Will Price, up for an award for Best Editing in a Major Motion Picture." Emma's eyes passed Pru and lodged on Will; then, as the camera drew back, she saw Liam, seated next to him, and a flush of pride welled up. He wore the iridescent blue Presley jacket they'd bought for this occasion at Second Hand Rose. He'd actually asked her to come along, to help him decide. Liam's hair was in a spiked up-do, dyed with dashes of red.

The camera moved on to lesser and greater idols. And, as it did, Emma was left with a much more painful image of Dawn, only a little over a year ago, standing in the middle of the international arrivals terminal, opening her coat to reveal the sleeping body of her infant adopted daughter. "Meet Millie," Dawn had said, showing her off. There was that dark thatch of hair, the head lolling to one side, while Dawn inexpertly cupped it.

"Oh God," Emma said aloud, her sorrow primed with guilt.

On the screen, Billy Crystal told jokes at the academy's expense, then the announcer was back. "And now, the nominees for Best Actress in a Supporting Role."

Here it was, the traditional teaser, the first award was always major, followed by mind-numbing hours of self-reflexive back-patting. And Emma was sobbing yet again. What a wimp, she told herself. Wiping her eyes with what she hoped was a slightly soiled Kleenex, she caught the camera zeroing in on the five nominees; the four actual professional actresses smiled deliberately, while Pru Ramone, in keeping with her reputation as punk bad girl, scowled. The envelope was ripped open by last year's winner in the Best Supporting Actor category, who waited a beat before reading the name.

"Pru Ramone."

The camera was on Pru as she stared blankly forward. Then Will leaned over to whisper something to her; Chavitz did the same and tugged her up. "Little old me?" she mouthed and suddenly went into action, kissing Chavitz, then Will, then Liam, who blushed and looked absolutely smitten.

Pru made her triumphant march to the dais. Standing there, she raised her hand to her forehead, shading her eyes and surveying the audience. "Wow," she said. Then, "Fuck." At least that was what Emma made out, using her best lip-reading skills. Pru had on a nontraditional Oscar outfit: a micromini and a tank top; in between, a pancake-flat stomach, the bellybutton pierced. Her ears bore a vast collection of studs and hoops. "Sorry, I didn't prepare anything. This really rocks, though. Thanks go out to my posse, Emilee, Jackie, Masha, and Saint. Thanks to my adoptive parents, Mark and Lydia, who raised me, and to Chav, who has just always, always been there for me, he's like a fucking godsend. Oh yeah, and special thanks to one truly uncommon friend who knows just how much he matters." She lifted the statuette high, then paused. "Mom. This is most definitely for you." She seemed about to cry. Then, as she was half-turning, Emma was pretty sure she said, "This shit rocks!"

One for Will's side, Emma thought. As for Pru, there was no

question that her wraithlike body was desirable, or that her face was exquisite. She was young and wildly successful, all at the tender age of seventeen. It was more than enough to give a woman of forty-plus pause.

The doorbell rang. A second later, there was a crack of thunder, then lightning flashed across the sky.

"Changing the locks on me," Laurence said when she opened it. "Hope you weren't intending on sending a message."

"What are you doing here?" Because she had expected him back on Wednesday, though even as the words tumbled out, she regretted them.

"You want me to go?" There was humor in the question.

In answer, Emma dove into his open arms.

Upstairs, he sat next to her on the bed, his luggage stowed in one corner, his suit bag hanging in the closet, his fingers threading across the damage. Her face. Then her body.

"I feel better than I look," she insisted.

"That's supposed to comfort me?"

"Wasn't your son upset about you leaving early?"

"I stayed put for the service. Did my duty. Shaun's a big boy. He'll get over it."

Laurence held his palm up, covering the bruise on her cheek; she felt the warmth radiate.

"Hey," he said and pulled her in close. "I should have been here," he added. She found herself weakening, about to agree, and refused to go that route. Instead, she pulled away. "What did I say?" he asked.

Emma shook her head.

Reaching out, he tucked a stray hair back behind her ear.

"Nothing," she insisted. For a long while, they sat like that, immobile on the bed, then she disengaged completely, pulled her knees toward her, crossing her legs Indian-style. "Tell me about the wedding."

"You're kidding me, right?"

"No. Shaun's your only child. It's important."

Important to be diverted from what was currently preoccupying her too. She saw he understood. Watched him physically change gears, and loved him for that, for doing whatever she needed. "The spot was all Shaun's doing. Carved ice swan and all, costing more money than God ever had. The bride's parents acting like fools, their little girl's marrying a surgeon, looking so goddamn pleased with themselves, like they'd just gone off and won the damn lottery."

Emma kept quiet, it was his own son he was busy critiquing. He and Shaun had had words before he left. She knew she was the cause, and didn't want to know more than that. Didn't ever want to have to take sides in this. It was the sort of conflict that was bound to blow up in your face. You never stepped between a parent and their child.

"He looked happy enough," Laurence admitted.

"That's good then," Emma noted mildly. "So, his new wife's nice?"

"Too nice if you ask me." Back on his high horse again, meeting her eyes in what amounted to a dare. She refused to rise to it. "You think I'm being too hard?" he ventured.

"I'm reserving judgment."

"Since when have you ever done that?" Pursing his lips, he waited. Thought he could outwait her reticence, Emma whose opinions were always literally tripping off her tongue. Not this time.

The clock on the table behind him said it was just past midnight. If Will had triumphed, she'd read about it in the morning paper. That would be soon enough. She saw Laurence about to ask her a pertinent question and leaned toward him, kissed him, then slid her tongue inside his mouth, experimentally. He didn't respond at first, so she moved her hand down his chest, finding the place where the shirt was tucked properly into his pants, then she dug down even deeper until her hand touched bare skin, her brain humming all the while. Laurence pulled back, just a little.

"Sure about this?" he asked.

"Positive," she said. This wasn't about making love, it was about muting everything else. It was sex, and sex was the best way she knew to stop thinking.

He was unspeakably gentle, uncovering her to discover more damage, kissing the bruises as he did, tenderly, working his way down, then back up her body, while she shut her eyes, trying to concentrate, and then forgetting to, tears starting at the corners, forcing the memory back, until finally the pleasure took over.

"Wait," she said, and went to the bathroom to insert her diaphragm. Laurence followed her inside the spare, utilitarian space, barely room enough for the two of them, a private, public moment. He brushed his teeth, then splashed water on his face, then turned her way and she realized that she loved him so much. She couldn't think how it had even happened.

"You okay?" he asked.

"Yes."

No. Laurence lifted her. She watched the faded rose wallpaper on the sagging walls, the chipped blue tile behind the tub, the shower curtain showing a map of the world, and then she gave in, gave up, saw Laurence instead.

"Hello there," he whispered, inside her now.

In the bed, afterwards, Emma's free hand dabbled with his scant chest hair, then flattened out over the hard knot of stomach muscles, achieved through the use of diligent situps.

"Well?" he ventured. His way of saying "We've digressed long enough."

"I don't know how to talk about this without losing it," she admitted. Getting out of bed, she went to the window. The rainstorm was over, puddles glistening under the streetlights. Her block was more suburban than urban. So quiet at night, with the old maples planted every few feet, with the private houses dark and shuttered, all of them equipped with state-of-the-art burglar systems, because although it looked like Any Town, USA, it wasn't, by a long shot. There were clues, the sirens moaning in the distance, and the three African-American teens decked out in urban hip-hop majesty, walking advertisements for Phat Farm and Sean John, walking down the middle of the street, eschewing the sidewalk, and cursing as they went, a chorus of voices. "Bust a cap on her ass, you know what I'm saying?"

He was up, next to her, cupping her shoulder in his hand, making her turn his way. They had spoken only once that day, and that was before the news about Dawn broke. But she assumed that was part of the reason he was back. It was in the afternoon paper, and on every news channel. Emma realized she was avoiding explaining where she'd gone, what she'd put herself through. And not because she thought he'd ask why she'd felt it necessary to bear witness, he'd understand why implicitly. Still, talking about it would make her remember every piece keenly, talking with him would make it hurt even more.

"They're not giving out a whole hell of a lot about what happened with Dawn," Laurence said. "That's the senator's doing, I'm guessing."

"Or Lowry's," she suggested.

"I saw he was in charge." His eyes were lively with intelligence. But he was waiting for her to push him on it.

"Lowry's making it into a murder-suicide," Emma said. "Which it's not."

"Then that won't wash for long."

"How can you be so sure?"

"Because the evidence will point some other way."

"Dawn's father is speaking to him. I'm afraid it will help his cause."

Laurence asked the silent question, How?

"Dawn tried to commit suicide. It was a long time ago," Emma added. "She was in college."

"Light years ago," Laurence agreed. "So the father told Lowry about that?"

"Yes. The only thing I can do is try to get the investigation taken away, get someone impartial to really look at the evidence," Emma said.

"To do that, you're going to have to prove incompetence."

"I know."

"Then we've got our work cut out for us." Us? He patted the bed. "Come here," he told her.

He was offering more than comfort, Emma knew. He was saying he was truly her partner. She came toward him slowly, sat with a shrug of her body. She felt grateful, no question about that. And he knew better than to touch her, quite yet.

"It just doesn't seem real," Emma said. "And it should. You see someone dead, it should sink in. But it doesn't. I keep going over it and over it in my head. What I could have done differently."

"That's how it always is," Laurence said. There was a tightness in his voice, a dryness. "Jimmy D. We'd watched each other's backs since grade school. We were coming back up Adam Clayton Powell from this party, a sweet sixteen for a girl we both knew. First thing you see is the flash of light, then you hear the crack, then you go facedown, out of habit. Next thing you know, your friend is lying there, bleeding to death, and you can't even find a goddamn phone that works to dial EMS."

It was her turn to put her arms around his shoulders. So generous, giving her this, now.

"You're not meant to forget, but you have to go on," he said. "You spend a lot of time saying how things should have been different, but in your heart of hearts all you feel is grateful, grateful it wasn't you. And that's not wrong. That's just how it is. Maybe it's what makes you change course, become a cop, but then again, maybe not. It could be you're just practicing resistance, avoiding the map your dad set out for you, or it could be you're giving something back. Who the hell knows, in the end. Sometimes life just twists you around."

"I wasn't a great friend to her," Emma said.

"How do you figure that?"

"There were things she needed."

"And? 'Cause you couldn't give them to her, that made you a failure as a friend? You stuck with her, talked back if you had to, gave her parameters, Prescott wasn't the easiest to get along with." He reached out, cupping her face in his hands, forcing her to give him her complete attention.

"Look, the woman never made anything easy. People she worked with couldn't stand her, even if they respected her. You stuck with her. That counts for something."

"I suppose."

"You have to sleep. If you don't, morning's going to come crashing down. You won't be good for anything."

Even if he was saying it to pacify her, Emma knew it was true. She let him pull her back.

"Who drove you out by the hospital?"

"That officer who took my statement."

"Fitzsimmons?"

"You said you knew who he was."

"I do."

Emma was up on an elbow, telling the rest. "He brought me back here, and did this end run. Shut the front door and waited, as if he was gone. Then snuck back to spy on me."

The pissed-off look on Laurence's face gave her comfort.

"I was listening to the messages on the machine. From Dawn. You. Suddenly there he was, holding out my prescription, which was most definitely dug out of my bag at some point to use as collateral."

"Then he does have a brain in his head after all," Laurence muttered.

"You said you knew him. How?"

"I get around."

Shutting down the question. Apparently, the time for confessing was over. He lay on his back, hands folded under his head, and closed his eyes. Emma envied his ability to rest whenever and wherever he had to. Planes, trains, and automobiles, she thought, not to mention strange beds, well-lighted rooms, even airport terminals. He'd take catnaps and wake completely refreshed.

In a few minutes, Laurence would be fast asleep. By the end of the night, he'd have managed to grab all but one of the pillows, the blankets, and even the sheet if she wasn't strong enough.

But then he surprised her, saying, "Someone sent your friend Dawn on that fool's errand, and she knew enough to know she shouldn't be off on it alone. Let you in for a world of trouble, let herself in for it too. It wasn't just for company, that call." He reached out, clicked the light off. Then Laurence pulled her close, into the crook of his arm. "You got to give that woman credit, she was ferocious. Sank her teeth in, and wouldn't let go till the job was done. Truth is, you can't ask for a hell of a lot more than that from anyone."

His eyelids slid shut again. His breathing thickened. And just like that, he was gone. Abandoned, Emma thought, turning on her side, watching the shadow cast by the streetlight as it burrowed into the room. It fingered the pile of unopened boxes, then slid across the rug, caressing the dress shoes Laurence had placed just beside the bed. As it snaked up, touching the edge of the sheet, Emma made Dawn a promise: she would find the man who'd done this, and make him pay.

That brought a smile. Very nice, she thought. Avenger Emma. If only she'd been provided with a useful special power, other than pig-headedness. Grabbing the sheet, she wrapped it tightly around her body, making a snug cocoon. Then laid her hand atop the curve of his hip. A gentle snore erupted from Laurence's side of the bed. Kissing him lightly on the shoulder, she shut her eyes and drifted off to sleep.

# Chapter Four

Emma got to work a little before nine. There was no one in reception, no one in the offices on either side of the long hallway. Turning the corner, she heard Brian Pinsky's familiar voice coming from conference room A. The door was partway open. "I can only encourage you to speak with Dr. Schneider," he was saying. "Look, it's not mandatory, but it's useful, plus it's free. Schneider's a good guy, I want every one of you to take advantage."

Just then, Laurie Anne, the receptionist, popped her head out and did a double take.

"Emma? What are you doing here?"

"Where should I be?" she countered.

"We just thought you'd want to stay home . . ." Laurie Anne looked immediately apologetic. Emma felt ashamed of her own defensive outburst.

Colleagues flocked out to greet her. Brian at the rear, grabbing hold and giving her a bear hug. She realized the odd barking sound emanating from him was a muffled sob. When he finally released her, she saw his face had turned red, perhaps from the force of this pent-up emotion. Please, she begged him silently, don't lose it, because if you do, how will I manage, and the last thing I want to do is start crying again, here.

Brian's hand went out, pushing back the hair that she'd brushed forward to reveal the mottling around her bruised cheek.

"Jesus!"

She pulled away, her hand smoothing her hair back, re-creating the mock veil.

"What are you thinking?" He was chiding her.

"I couldn't just sit home and do nothing."

Thirty-nine pairs of eyes homed in on their target. Emma forced herself to try to meet each individual set. Some looked away immediately, as if embarrassed, while others registered sympathy and concern.

"Let me get you some coffee," Laurie Anne said, and went scurrying off. There was an edgy, uncomfortable silence in the interim. The cup was offered to her, and she took a sip, wondering if that would defuse things.

"How are you really doing?" Brian asked, sotto voce, as she swallowed.

"Coping. And you?" She swiveled her head, to greet them, one and all. When she returned to Brian, she realized his face was sheet-white. With Dawn gone, he was de facto head of New York Capital Crimes. What a way to get the promotion he'd been angling for.

Emma couldn't have sat home, but being here, in the room filled with her coworkers, she felt Dawn's absence even more keenly. If it had been a day like any other, Laurie Anne would have grabbed her at the front desk to provide her with an assessment of the boss's mood. When Dawn was content, the hive hummed; when she was out of sorts, there were furtive groups ringing the water cooler, or jammed into the unisex bathroom.

Ever since she'd adopted Millicent, Dawn's mood had lightened. She was not an easy person to work for, but she was happier than she'd been in all the years Emma had known her. And of course, she was an excellent attorney, one who could easily have made partner at any of a number of prestigious Manhattan law firms.

"I heard they dragged you out to the Island for the ID," Peggy Bass, one of her assistant investigators, said. "Talk about sadistic."

"I wanted to go," Emma insisted.

"Sure, I get you," Peggy said, putting out her hand, patting Emma on the shoulder. She was their resident firearms expert, as well as a card-carrying member of the National Rifle Association. Emma made a mental note, later, to ask Peggy about the gun Lowry showed her.

"Could you believe the story they ran in *Newsday*?" Peggy said. "Claiming that man was her boyfriend. How can they write such crap?"

"They were quoting Lowry."

"You'd think they'd be a little sharper, wouldn't you? I mean, consider the source. Prick that he is. We've just been trying to figure out what to do to discredit him. Have you spoken to Dawn's father?"

"No."

"Actually, I talked to him this morning," Brian said. All eyes scuttled back. " 'Lovey-dovey.' That was the quote they used from the motel clerk. How ridiculous is that?"

Emma noted the immediate change of subject. Brian must have his reasons, she decided. "Meanwhile her supposed inamorato couldn't tell the two of us apart," Emma noted.

"Idiots." From Peggy.

She could have been referring to either Lowry and his cronies or the two thus far nameless assailants. Emma chose to go with the latter.

"They might have been rank amateurs, but they still apparently got what they were after." Emma surveyed the room, adding, "Does anyone have any idea what this meeting Dawn set up could have been about?"

"I checked her calendar," Brian said. "No red flags. And nothing for Saturday night, either."

"Is there anything that seems odd, after the fact? Some remark she might have made in passing?"

No response, other than a shaking of heads.

"If Dawn didn't tell you what this was about, chances are she didn't tell anyone," Peggy noted. "You know how close-to-the-vest she was."

Emma did. "Let's try to take this step by step," she said, thinking out loud. "If all of you could make a log, write down whatever you remember Dawn saying to you in the last few weeks, even the most banal interchange. I'll go through everything." She smiled, adding, "It'll give me something to do." Turning Brian's way, she saw a flash of discomfort, or was it displeasure? Had she co-opted his leadership position? "If that's okay with you," she offered.

"Why wouldn't it be?"

He honestly sounded surprised at the question.

As her coworkers filed out, there were hugs and words of support. Then she and Brian were alone. "Your office?" he suggested. Once inside, he shut the door tight against inquiring eyes.

"This has been an absolute nightmare!" he exclaimed, and promptly collapsed on the beat-up leather couch, putting his legs up and propping his head on his arms. Therapist alert, Emma thought; it was the position he assumed before he let loose with whatever complaints he had stored up from the day. They were always funny, often vicious, and, more than likely, earned. "I tell you, the phone doesn't stop ringing. Everyone wants me to make a statement. CNN. MSNBC. Even the major networks. If Dawn could see it now, she'd be livid. All we ever wanted was media attention, and they wouldn't give us the time of day. Now they're breaking down the fucking door to get a comment." Rolling onto his side, he admired her from afar. "You look like shit, by the way."

"Thanks. So do you," she countered. He didn't, actually. Brian's pride of appearance was part of his charm. "I was trying to reach Dawn's parents but couldn't get through. What did the senator say?"

"Ah yes, dear old Dad."

The harshness of his tone took her aback.

Brian stood and moved toward her, leaning in as if to share a confidence, then he pursed his lips apparently thinking better of it. His hand went out to push her hair aside. "You know," he said, "I could do something with that."

Flinching, she withdrew. "Brian, answer the question."

"Emma!" he responded in an annoying imitation. "Listen, you can't go around like that and not have people stare. This isn't the time to go au naturel."

Emma batted his hand away.

"The senator advised me that he's planning a service in due course."

Emma cocked her head to indicate she knew there was more. And Brian reached out, caressing her chin. "Let me work on it," he said.

"No."

"Sweetheart, give me a sense of purpose."

Or a way to practice purposeful avoidance, she thought. Still, Brian did have that second life as an entertainer. During the run of his one-man show at La Mama, Brian had transformed himself nightly into divas of the sixties, bittersweet monologues in drag, beginning with Jackie O when she was Jackie K, and ending with Janis. It was actually quite good. Funny, wry, and moving, as well as totally outrageous.

"Fine," she told him.

"You won't regret it," he insisted and started rummaging through her purse. He pulled out her scant supplies of makeup.

"God, where did you find this stuff?"

"Clinique bonus time."

"Which century?"

"Brian, makeup doesn't have an expiration date."

"It does, my dear. Your mother obviously neglected the essentials."

"She taught me how to bypass the cutoff valve and get a furnace to start. Also how to hotwire a car."

"Your mother sounds like my kind of woman."

"I'll take that as a compliment." Meanwhile, his fingers smoothed away the wrinkles on her face; it was absurd that she was letting him do this. An odd way of taking solace, Emma thought, but that was obviously what it was.

"Your mom boosted cars?"

"She'd misplaced the key, and she didn't want to go back inside, it was freezing, and a long walk. She pulled the plate off with a screwdriver she kept in the glove compartment and twisted the wires together. Voilà, just like in the movies."

"And to think, my mom just baked brownies."

Emma wished that he really could transform her. Then the bruise would disappear and, with it, all it signified. Brian handed her the compact mirror and stepped back, as if he had worked that magic for her, but she still saw the bluish-brown mark lurking under its camouflage.

"Well?"

"Well?" she countered, because they'd come to an impasse and he knew as much. Brian met her eyes evenly. "I just can't believe this is happening," he said, and then he was crying.

"And here I was trying to comfort you," he noted. Reaching for the Kleenex she kept on her desk, he dabbed his face dry. "Would you think that I'd be so broken up? It's crazy, isn't it?"

"No."

"Yes it is, there wasn't a day went by I didn't lock myself into my office to escape from her. She made my life a living hell. Every night I'd go home and have to be talked out of quitting. You know that, Em. She was the most impossible person I've ever met. Tony told me I was a masochist for staying. I had plenty of alternatives."

"You love what you do," Emma insisted.

"True." He shook his head hard, as if to dislodge the sentiment. "She may have been a bitch on wheels when she was roused, but our Dawn was one hell of a lawyer." He paused, and she sensed it was coming, whatever he'd been keeping from her. "Promise not to get crazy."

Emma tensed. When people made this sort of request, they were always about to tell you something you didn't need or want to hear.

"I can't promise anything," she reminded him.

"Well, you can swear up and down that you knew Dawn as well as anyone. But remember two years ago, when she was dating that Aryan?"

"Swede. Rolfe was Swedish."

"Was he? Are you positive?"

"Yes," she said coolly.

"All I'm saying is, he shows up at the Christmas party and no one up till then had even heard of him. Come to find out they've been significant others for over a year. I see you giving me that look, but it's entirely possible she kept this guy from you like she did Sven."

"Rolfe."

"Whatever. Anyhow, she could have been hiding this bad seed. Why not?"

"And he was blindfolded every time they saw each other. That was why he thought I was Dawn."

Brian's eyes met hers. She saw he was searching to discover what part of what she was saying was true. It stunned her. Did Brian really believe she would lie to protect Dawn's image? Would she make up something as outlandish as her own kidnapping? How could he think that?

"So the senator thinks they were dating?" Emma said bitterly. "He knew his own daughter that well."

"Darling, it's purely supposition."

"Excuse me, I have work to do."

"Emma, don't be angry. I had to ask."

No, she thought, you really didn't. She began to shuffle papers, turned on her computer, and basically refused to give him the time of day. Brian got the message. He crept out of the room, shutting the door with a subterranean click.

She was finally alone.

It felt absolutely horrible. Piles of unfiled documents on her desk seemed further evidence that her life was completely unraveling. How many times had Dawn stepped in, closed the door, and sat down to discuss the progress of a case, how many times had Dawn cast her eye judiciously over the disorder. "I don't know how you can think with all this mess around," she'd chided.

"To each their own," Emma had countered.

They had been polar opposites—blond, blue-eyed, statuesque Dawn, and Emma, with her auburn hair and brown eyes. Indeed, Emma thought, if her hairdresser hadn't convinced her to go blond in an effort to hide the gray, she would never have been in this fix at all.

Only a month ago, Emma had arrived extra early to discover she and Dawn were the only ones in the office. Stopping by the coffee machine, they'd made themselves a palatable two cups. And Emma had offered a recounting of her absurd trip from Brooklyn into Manhattan. She'd stood on the platform with a neighbor who had proceeded to tell her about her unraveling marriage; then been accosted on the train by a homeless man who railed against her outfit; arriving at work she'd been waylaid by the security guard, Brett, launching into a complaint about the antics of his teenage daughter . . .

"People love confiding in you," Dawn said. "It's because you listen. I don't seem to have that problem."

"Lucky you," Emma had quipped.

"Not really. I wish I was like you, I wish people trusted me. I don't mean to be unapproachable."

Emma thought of saying something trite, like "You have other good qualities" or "Don't beat yourself up." And winced internally. She chose silence instead, something she'd done a lot in their friendship. Dawn was prickly, you never knew how she'd take things. And now it was too late to tell her how much she was admired and loved.

Opening her office door, Emma found the corridor empty. She ducked out.

Dawn's office was neither the largest nor the nicest. It overlooked the site of the former Twin Towers, and scaffolding from the new buildings had risen up, past Dawn's seventh-floor window. They'd signed the lease six months before 9/11 and there had been no question of reneging. While downtown stank of PCBs, they moved in. The day had been balmy, their mood somber, and the smell pervasive, seeping in through the walls and sealed windows. Dawn claimed this office immediately, the only one with the full-on view, and none of them offered even a feeble argument, no one bothered to attempt to save her from her own nobility.

Typical.

Dawn's desk was sparely decorated, the computer, an in-and-out box, and five framed photographs, all of Millicent. Emma could hear Dawn, sitting at her desk and telling Emma how becoming a parent was literally the best thing she'd ever done. On days when the babysitter called in sick, Dawn had brought Millicent to work. She'd cooed, cuddled, and pronounced her child "delicious" as she made popping sounds, mouth to Millicent's bare stomach. Initially cynical, Brian had dubbed it "Dawn's Hallmark phase," adding, "Just wait till that child grows a personality."

But he had been proven wrong. Millicent was a toddler now, and Dawn had been even more deeply infatuated. She finally had someone to love, someone she could give herself over to unconditionally.

Switching the computer on, Emma waited for it to boot. The desktop was a photograph of Millicent with her mop of black hair and her dark eyes, beaming from a backpack strapped onto her mother's back. Adopted from China, the child was now a two-time orphan.

Dawn's computer files were meticulously kept, an anal retentive's masterpiece. In alphabetical order, with all drafts erased, a far cry from Emma's own desktop, which was overloaded and constantly freezing for want of memory. Organization didn't help, though, when you didn't have the slightest idea what you were looking for. Opening the Nevins file, Emma found many of the same documents she'd looked through the night before at home, along with the final draft of the current brief. Dawn was attempting to redraw the rules by asserting that in order to convict someone of capital murder, the standards should be raised above the usual charge to the jury, which was to find the defendant guilty "beyond a reasonable doubt." She argued that, in capital cases, the standards had to be more rigorous. In order to put a defendant to death, there could be no doubt at all in the jury's mind.

They were waiting, right now, for the court's decision.

If Dawn won, then there was a chance of retrying the case, of vacating the verdict and starting again. Or the court could simply set aside the death penalty phase of the argument, leaving Nevins incarcerated for life, without possibility of parole.

That would be their Pyrrhic victory.

Opening Dawn's daily calendar, Emma backtracked, but Brian was right, there was nothing even remotely suspicious. However, there were two meetings scheduled for that very day, one with the Brooklyn D.A., the other with Arthur Nevins's parents. The appointment in Brooklyn was at one that afternoon. She knew what that was about, a case that was coming to trial. As for the meeting with Mary Nevins and her common-law husband, perhaps Dawn had intended to give them an update on the progress of the appeal. This case was the one place where Lowry and Dawn's lives had intersected. Right now it was also the only thing she had to go on.

Pulling open the top desk drawer, Emma noted that here, too, order reigned supreme: small plastic containers with rubber bands, paper clips, and push pins; a glut of pencils that had been filed to indecently sharp points; a stamp pad, with Air Mail, First Class, and Special Delivery stamps lying next to it. Everything looked brand-new; either they were or Dawn was so anal she had washed the ink off the stamps with a solvent.

In the small, circular well there was a silver earring. Lifting it out, Emma noted that it was in the shape of a wing, like the ones tacked onto the sides of Mercury's hat. It looked a lot like one from the set her mother had given her in honor of graduating from high school. That set came with a matching brooch. Turning the earring over, she froze. The initials, stamped on the back, were ALM, the initials her mother's friend, the silversmith Alice Laycock Morris, had printed on Emma's own set.

There was a knock on the door. Emma felt guilt flooding her. "Yes," she called out. Sticking his head in, Brian said, "Here's where you've been hiding out. It's the senator, on line two."

Nodding, Emma instinctively shoved the earring deep into her pants pocket.

*I'm so, so sorry. I can't even begin to imagine how you must feel.* Those words would have been offered, if only he'd given her a chance. Instead, there was frost in his voice as Hamilton Prescott insisted, for the fifth time, on his rights as a grandparent. "No one will let this stand. You won't get away with this. No judge is going to give you Millicent. Over my dead body."

"Excuse me, Senator," she said. "I'm still not completely clear on what we're talking about."

"I think you are."

"No, really, I'm absolutely at a loss."

But he stormed on. "You pretended to be her friend, manipulating her in this way. You knew how weak she was. How easily led."

"Excuse me, are we speaking about your daughter? Easily led?"

Emma had understood the outlines of his claim, that somehow

she had been made Millicent's guardian, which could only be some sort of horrible mistake. Or a joke. Apparently, more of the cosmic sort than the traditional type, equipped with a punch line.

"Don't act innocent."

"You've got to believe me, I had no idea."

"Then of course you'd be willing to sign a document that says you cede all rights to the child?"

Emma was ready to agree, except that the words stuck in her throat. Make that my craw, she decided. His tone had prompted her resistance, that and his completely inaccurate assessment of his only daughter.

Emma looked at Millicent pulsing on the computer screen, at Millicent in Dawn's arms in the photo to her right, by the phone. In both, she was waving at the photographer. Emma. In each, Dawn was giving Millicent a look of unequivocal devotion.

"Hello!" The peremptory bark raised Emma's hackles. "Are you there?"

"The will hasn't been probated yet. How did you find out?"

Silence. He was undoubtedly regrouping.

"You think I shouldn't know what's in my own child's will?"

"All the same, I haven't seen it."

He gave a derisive snort. "A likely story. It was drawn up by one of the attorneys in your office."

Emma was about to ask, Who? Then she realized. Brian. The talk they'd had earlier that morning. His odd reticence about it.

"We're blood relations, and you? What claim do you pretend to have? That you were involved with my daughter in some way? That you and she were intimate . . ." He spluttered to a stop, breathing heavily, then slammed down the phone.

It took her only a second to realize what new accusation was being leveled at her.

Emma found Brian in his office.

"You could have told me about Dawn's bequest," she said. "You knew she'd made me Millicent's guardian, didn't you?"

A sheepish look, then the weak excuse: "Dawn told me the two of you had discussed it."

"Brian!"

"Okay, maybe I assumed that." Then, half turning as if to confront an invisible audience, he added, "No one would name a person as the legal guardian without asking the party or parties involved. It only stands to reason."

"So when she put my name down, you didn't bother to ask if she'd spoken with me about taking on the responsibility."

"Dawn knew the way it worked as well as anyone."

He was right, of course. There was no point in blaming him. How could Dawn have done this, though, how could she have assumed that Emma would be ready, willing, and able to take on rearing a third child? It wasn't like she was doing such a bang-up job with her own two. And now, because of how Dawn had died, because of the senator's attitude and her own free-floating sense of guilt, Emma had to think seriously about this request, instead of rejecting it out of hand. She wouldn't have put it past Dawn to have thought of that possibility too. "What a mess," Emma said, but she couldn't help adding a rueful laugh.

"Call him back," Brian suggested. "Tell him you were in shock. Now you realize what's been asked of you. Give him the kid to raise."

"Believe me, I want to," Emma said.

"So what's preventing you from doing it?"

"His response, for one thing."

"What did he say?"

"He accused me of being his daughter's gold-digging lesbian lover."

Brian giggled. "Very trendy of you," he said.

"Plus, he believes I've taken advantage of his will-o'-the-wisp daughter. That I've forced her to rewrite her will to include me."

Brian offered a skeptical look.

"I kid you not," Emma said.

"Dawn?"

"Dawn."

"He wasn't really being serious?"

"I don't know." Emma didn't add what was coming to mind, Lowry's insinuating the senator had offered him private information about the state of his daughter's mind, its apparent instability.

"Look, about the will, I'm sure Dawn assumed what most people assume, that the worst wasn't going to happen."

Emma gave him a skeptical look. "Dawn never did one thing in her life that wasn't entirely thought through to the bitter end."

She had a point. He knew it too.

Just then, the phone buzzed. Brian pressed the intercom button, and Laurie Anne's cheerful voice announced the next surprise of the day. "Is Emma there? Mary Nevins is here with her husband. She says she'd like to talk with her."

Conference room A's plate-glass windows overlooked Broadway. Mary Nevins and her common-law husband, Rafael Perez, took seats on one side of the long, narrow table.

"Something to drink?" Emma offered.

"No. Thank you very much," Mary said. She met Emma's eyes for a moment. "We weren't sure we should come, what with the news, you know. What happened with your Miss Prescott. I can't even start to tell you how sorry the both of us are. She was just one big-hearted woman."

Emma nodded.

Though in her early fifties, Mary looked to be at least ten years older. She was a light-skinned, heavyset African American, her red hair straightened and styled. The outfits she chose were always too cute by half for her age, not to mention her Lane Bryant dress size. Today was no exception. Although the colors—ochre and mauve—were muted for her, the cut of her dress was decidedly not. It hugged her body, accentuating the ample curves. There were dimples in her cheeks and undoubtedly everywhere else.

Rafael said not a word, which was also typical. He wasn't Arthur's dad but the stepfather, coming on the scene three years in. Still, he'd raised the child as his own.

"I'm assuming Dawn wanted to brief you on the progress of the appeal," Emma said.

Mary flushed. "My oh my, I was thinking Miss Prescott had told you. She said she would."

"Told me what?"

"It was Arthur's doing. Me, I've been nothing but grateful to you and Miss Prescott, looking out for my boy the way you have."

Emma's blank look seemed to rattle her even more. She blushed.

"You got to understand. It's really not up to me or Rafe. It's his call. We just got to follow along with him." Wringing her hands, she turned to Rafael, who was mute, as usual. "I guess maybe I didn't make it clear enough. I thought Miss Prescott, she understood why we were coming by. Maybe she thought it was something she could talk us out of, but what's done is done."

"I really don't follow," Emma said.

"My boy, he's got himself another lawyer. We only stopped by to pick up the files."

"But we're in the middle of working on the appeal."

"I know all that. I tried to talk to him about it, but he says it's what he wants. I got to go along with that." Mary slid the card out of her wallet, pushing it tentatively across the tabletop. Looking down, Emma read, "Jason Samuels, Attorney at Law."

"Your son hired Jason Samuels? How can you afford it?"

As soon as she'd asked, she felt bad. But it was a reasonable question. Samuels was the ultimate criminal defender, but his clients always paid. And paid well for his services. He certainly loved publicity, not to mention punditry. Samuels would appear anywhere, at any time, providing the cameras were on him. He'd represented members of the Brighton Beach Mafia and Park Avenue widows. His last case had involved the latter. He'd represented Annabel James, wife of a megabucks Wall Street financier, who had contrived to kill her husband with the help of her lover, by offering him certain sexual favors. The kinky details had been splattered all over the popular press.

And he'd gotten her an acquittal, though her lover was not so lucky.

"Mr. Samuels, he's an old friend of Arthur's."

"Jason Samuels?" It was the first Emma had heard of this.

"They went to grade school together."

"I don't remember you mentioning him before."

Backpedaling and not meeting Emma's eyes again. "Grade school, it's a long time back."

"What exactly did you tell Dawn?"

Mary opened her mouth to reply, then looked over at Rafael. She got a nod of encouragement for her trouble. "Like I said, maybe it wasn't clear."

Or maybe, Emma thought, it was.

"Look, all I'm telling you is, Mr. Samuels, he's the one who came looking for Arthur. Said his conscience got the better of him."

That Jason Samuels had a conscience was news to Emma.

"I can't tell you how bad this feels," Mary said as she reached into her purse and withdrew a notarized document. Dated Wednesday of last week, it was signed by Arthur, a request that all the files pertaining to his case be turned over. "Mr. Samuels said for us to take what we could today and drop it by his office." Standing hurriedly, she added, "We'll just wait out by the door, we don't want to disturb you any further. Whatever you got, Rafe here can carry out. We brought the car along, we got plenty of space for it."

# Chapter Five

"What's your interest?" Fitzsimmons demanded. He and Laurence Solomon were alone in the locker room at the sixty-first. Fitzsimmons had already changed into his civvies; he was wearing a T-shirt featuring a portrait of Tommy Boy—some wannabe white rapper, was Laurence's assumption, knowing Fitz's predilections.

"For a friend," Laurence said, throwing him a bone. "Doing them a favor."

"This friend's got a name, I'm assuming?"

Dancing around, when they both knew what they knew. All that bullshit they wrote about being brothers under the skin, Laurence thought, here they were, case in point, same graduating class out of the academy, but a ten-year gap in age separating them, not to mention skin tone.

After graduation, they had never been assigned to the same precinct, which, as far as Laurence was concerned, was a very good call. The times when they'd had to work shoulder to shoulder had been enough to irk him. Fitz loved to assume he was a homeboy, loved to use slang in the most original way he could, thinking he was *down* with Laurence.

Like there was only one way to be black and he knew all about it.

The place they'd actually spent the most quality time together was over at the Fourth Street basketball courts. Okay, so that was a cliché in itself, he acknowledged, being that the game was what brought him and this wannabe gangsta white boy into the most direct contact, but really who gave a shit, as long as they were playing, playing hard, and he and Fitz were on the same team, because when they weren't, he couldn't help but get his back up. Fitzsimmons was a grunt, not enough talent for finesse, which he more than made up for with hard work, dogging you all the way up and down the court, in your face, pretty much the entire time, playing like the pest he was, stinging you with little jabs to the face, you spending too much time trying to swat him back while he made himself a menace with his persistence, pretty much showing his true colors as a royal fucking pain in the ass.

"I was acquainted with the victim," Laurence said.

"Prescott? You two close?" A little grin, insinuating the rest, then Fitzsimmons slamming his locker shut, shrugging on his knapsack, like they were more than through.

"There's no call to say that."

"No?" Fired back at him, making him remember what had gone wrong, and how fresh the wound was. Last fall, in late November, still warm enough to play outdoor ball, Fitzsimmons had drawn him to guard and there was the height advantage, not to mention skill, so, of course, Fitz got overzealous, slapping at his body instead of the ball, sticking a hand right up in his face, managing to cut him, right above the eye, which was when Laurence saw fit to finally retaliate, leveling a punch to his midsection.

They were pulled apart, Fitz talking a whole load of trash. At the end of which he'd stuck on, "Niggah, what's your fucking problem?"

There was a moment, frozen in time. Glaring at Fitzsimmons, Laurence caught himself, pulled himself back from the brink, because of what he would have done; where this was going was someplace so filled with rage. Suddenly every fiber of his being was focused on how he was going to teach this "no account" white boy a lesson.

Fitzsimmons must have realized, because he backed up a step, then another, then walked lamely off the court and away. Now he was about to do the same, tucking his Knicks cap on his head, lifting his Sean John jacket.

"I think it ought to be enough, me saying I have a personal interest."

"You do?" Fitzsimmons turned his way pugnaciously. "Coming in here, not telling me what you want, trying to play like I don't know what you're about with this. You think I'm stupid, right? I know you've been dating that Price woman."

"And?"

"Look, all I'm doing is my job. You ought to be aware of that."

"How does your job entail treating her like she has something to hide?"

"You ought to know better than to ask me that." He tried to shoulder past Laurence, who held his ground, held him there for a moment longer. "Man, you have the shortest fucking fuse," Fitzsimmons added. "If it was your case, you'd do what I did. You'd take the opportunity."

"To do what?"

"God, I have to spell it out?" Sighing, like Laurence was slow. "Your girlfriend ends up in a lot out near the bay, bruises on her body, signs of hypothermia from being a charter member of the Polar Bear Club. First place we go is the boyfriend. Seeing as how you were out of town, I guess you're in the clear, but there's always the possibility of her having more than one."

Laurence knew he was being baited, tried to reason with his own, reflexive response, which was to slam Fitzsimmons against the wall. Instead, he offered, "That's supposed to be funny?"

"I don't know, how does it sound?"

So Fitzsimmons was going to drag this out, make it personal with him.

"You've got a professional responsibility," Laurence insisted.

"How'm I not being professional?"

"She said you heard the calls from Dawn. I'm assuming you brought that to Nassau's attention."

"You go on and assume away," Fitzsimmons told him. He swept by, was at the door, then stopped, turning Laurence's way. "You know, you might not believe it, but when you made detective so fucking fast, people weren't exactly jumping up and down for joy, said how you didn't deserve it, how you hadn't put in the time, but I didn't agree, not that I liked you, mind, but fair is fair. I knew you well enough to know you did what you had to to get there. I saw you operate at the academy, you rubbed it in, how you were smarter than the rest of us, but, okay, maybe that's how you had to be. I mean, what the fuck do I know about it?"

Exactly, Laurence thought.

"Being that way, it's okay in school, people think maybe you don't know any better, but out here, in the real world, being humble counts a little more. Okay, so maybe the rest of us are jerks, but we're the ones watching your back."

Then he was gone, Laurence hot on his tail, out to the street, getting there in time to catch Fitz shooting past in a black Ford Explorer with the New York Knicks vanity plate—N UR FACE—on the back of it. Ain't that the truth, Laurence thought, pretending this was about him eating some humble pie. Bastard giving him advice, sure, like that's what went on between them, him being arrogant, pot calling the kettle black . . . bullshit was what it was.

Getting into his car, Laurence jerked the key into the slot, turning it too fast and pumping down. The car screeched shrilly in response. He backed up, peeled round the corner, and just missed clipping a passenger van filled with senior citizens, the driver raising his middle finger in protest, screaming out the window at him, "Why don't you look where you're fucking going?"

Good goddamn question, Laurence thought. Why didn't he just.

# Chapter Six

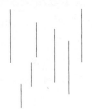

By five, Emma had doubled the suggested dose of ibuprofren caplets, her way of fending off a pounding headache. Her stomach responded by doing a series of flip-flops. At Rite Aid, she sprang for a bottle of extra-strength Maalox, then returned to the office to pore over the Nevins documents.

She could find no mention of Jason Samuels.

"Going home?" It was Brian, sticking his head in.

"I was thinking about it."

"Making progress?"

"None whatsoever," Emma admitted. She stood, gathering her purse and belongings.

"By the by, Dawn had a meeting scheduled with the Brooklyn D.A.'s office. She was seeing Matthews."

Emma nodded noncommittally. She couldn't help but feel funny about going into Dawn's office, even if it was her right, not to mention her duty, to snoop.

"He called to offer his sympathy, and mentioned it."

"Would it have killed her to tell us something," Brian mused, then added gloomily, "Oops, didn't mean it that way." Pressing his hand to Emma's shoulder, he added, "Get some rest."

Right, Emma thought, rest, what a concept!

\* \* \*

Stepping onto the subway, she took up her SRO berth, leaning against the doors. The train clattered out of the station and promptly crawled into the tunnel, where it stuttered to a stop. They waited, and waited, and waited some more, until the air-conditioning went out and the lights flickered off. They sat. And sat some more. Starting up after an immensely long ten minutes, the train made it to the next station, where it stalled out for good. In the end, what was usually a forty-minute trip took just over two hours to complete.

It was after eight when she dragged herself up the front steps. Opening the door, Emma let out a gasp of amazement. In her absence, a pulverizing sort of progress had been made. The hall was stripped of wallpaper, and there were gashes in the walls that exposed the wiring and plumbing. Stepping into the living room, she found dust drenching the covered clump of furniture. The house was deathly quiet even though Angeleno's van was still parked in the driveway. Perhaps he was resting on his laurels.

"Hello," she called out. And heard an answering grunt. Lifting the plastic that covered the swinging door to the kitchen, she pushed through and found the contractor seated on a pile of planking, partaking of a cigar.

"I was waiting on you," he said, tipping the ash unceremoniously onto the pile of new wood. The stink from the cigar permeated the room. Emma had made one rule, no smoking in the house. She understood that he was breaking it and that he was, undoubtedly, making a point. The look of belligerence on his face was another clue, of course.

"My wife, she tells me, that's my trouble. I'm just too nice a guy," Angeleno said meaningfully. "Too trusting. Know what I mean?"

She saw this was a rhetorical question. Her patience was completely exhausted. For a second, she contemplated losing her temper, but there was no way she could, the man was holding her hostage, it had taken her months to get him to even come to her house and begin the job.

"We had ourselves a guest this afternoon," Angeleno said.

For tea and crumpets? Was he going to tell her who? What this was about? Or was he going to wait for her to guess, then winnow down the list? "I'm sorry," Emma said, because apologies were part of the price you paid. "I'm just not following you here."

He stood, took another hard puff, and asserted, "We made ourselves a verbal commitment, you and me, did we not?"

"As to?" God knows, she'd been doling out cash on demand for what, two and a half months plus.

"What was it, that cop friend of yours, sticking his nose in?" he said, reaching down to scratch his balls, then jerking his pants up. Lovely, Emma thought. "You got questions, you're supposed to bring them to me. Don't go making trouble. I know what he told you, how you catch us up unawares, how maybe you're going to see what's really going on. Now me, when I do business with people, I got to know I have their trust."

"Mr. Angeleno, what is it I'm being accused of?"

"Like you don't know." His disgust with her so excessive he couldn't help but drop the cigar on the floor, then stamp it out with his heel. "That inspector, he got a hard-on with me. All up in my face, and for what? How'm I s'posed to know who he is, come to find him snooping around inside the house?"

Emma's blank look must have gotten to him. He cocked an eyebrow. "Well," he said. "Don't you have nothing to tell me?"

"What inspector?"

"We come in back from lunch and one of my guys goes downstairs to the basement to take a piss, and he finds this guy, says he's inspecting the wiring, goes and flashes a badge, gets all up in his face."

"How did this man get inside?"

"Said you gave him a key." Angeleno gave her an extremely meaningful look.

"I didn't give keys to anyone other than you and Laurence," Emma insisted. "Not to mention that the lock was changed yesterday." She almost added, "Capisce?" but managed to resist.

His eyebrows lifted to express his further incredulity.

"You locked up when you left, right?"

"What are you doing, accusing me now? You ought to know better than that."

She did. After all, she'd arrived home more than once during his tenure to discover her back door unlatched; ease of entry and exit seemed to be one of his less endearing traits. She had told him repeatedly to lock up, but before this, it hadn't been nearly as important, although the back of the house was hidden from the street by thick shrubbery and a brick wall. It was easy enough to sneak in and test the door without anyone being the wiser. That morning she'd been insistent. "Please, when you go out, make sure to lock up, and set the alarm."

He'd undoubtedly done neither one.

"Look . . ." The bravado had fled a little. "Maybe there was a little mix-up about who did what, I don't know." It was as much of an admission as she was going to get from him. "The thing is, as soon as he shows, half my boys are out the back door, thinking he's INS. So what is it?" he asked, his tone suddenly a little too friendly. "This the guy that beat you up?"

"Could be," Emma allowed.

"Thing is, this is likely gonna put a crimp in the scheduling."

What a surprise. This from the man who had sworn he would have the house completely finished by the time the moving van pulled up to the door. That was, Emma ticked back, six whole months ago.

"What did this 'investigator' look like?"

He shrugged.

"Dark hair? Blond?"

"Dark."

"About your height?"

"Yeah, more or less."

Angeleno was hardly statuesque. Emma took a breath, then asked the $64,000 question. "How about his voice, anything funny with that?"

"Yeah, now you mention it."

Not funny at all, Emma thought, feeling her heart sink.

"It was kind of high-pitched. You know that guy that used ta call in on the Howard Stern show? They had a bit with him, right? Called him High-Pitch Eric. It was kind of like that." Angeleno peered at her. "So what is it? You got yourself a stalker? Another boyfriend?"

"Nothing like that," Emma said.

"All I got to say is, these days, you have to look out for numero uno, you can't go trusting anyone, people, the world over, they're fucking loons."

Words of wisdom, Emma thought as she lifted the phone.

Laurence promised he'd be there within ten minutes. In the interim, she got Angeleno to swear his fealty. He sat in the kitchen with a new cigar in hand, this one unlit.

"No accidents on my watch," he promised.

And Emma headed for her bedroom to pack up a few essentials. Digging down under the pile of mismatched bras and Jockey French-cut briefs in her top dresser drawer, she found her father's old switchblade, ridiculous to imagine that it was going to afford her any protection, but it was the only weapon she owned.

Beside it, in the drawer, she found her mother's wooden jewelry box. When she popped the lid, a ballerina twirled in a threadbare tutu to a scratchy theme from *Swan Lake*. Her mother had never worn makeup, and despised dresses, but she loved wearing jewelry, the bigger and bulkier the better. Emma had gotten rid of much of it, only a few choice pieces were left, none of them to her taste. Nor was the wedding band, an old family heirloom that Will had once slipped on her ring finger. Lifting up the shelf to reveal the separate compartment, she found the brooch, but the felt jeweler's bag that had held the matching earrings was gone. Emma slid the one she'd found in Dawn's desk out of her pocket.

A match.

There was no doubt of that.

On the way to their last interview with Lowry, Dawn had stopped at the house to hitch a ride with Emma. "I'm here. One of your guys let me in," she'd yelled while Emma finished her shower. Yes, she'd had time to lift the earrings, but why on earth would she?

The phone was ringing. Emma dropped the lone earring into the box, shut it, and pushed the drawer closed.

"Mom? I just saw it on the news about Dawn. Are you okay?" Liam's voice was full of anxiety. "I'm coming home. We're flying back tomorrow."

"I'm fine," Emma said. Meaning, you can wait, though the thought of having her children close gave her a sudden rush of joy.

"Don't pretend," Liam said firmly. He sounded like such an adult.

"Let me speak with your father," Emma said, her voice husky with emotion.

"Don't try to talk me out of it, either," Liam insisted. He waited for her to agree.

"I won't," she swore. Only then did he hand off the phone.

"Hey," Will said, a little too jovially. "How's it going back East?"

"Is Liam right next to you?"

"Affirmative."

"For Christ's sake, go someplace private."

"Where would that be, exactly?"

Emma had tucked the phone into the crook of her neck, the switchblade was out of her pocket, used as a drumstick, tapping time on the top of the dresser. She heard fumbling on the other end, static, and finally, "Okay, I'm out on the patio, what's going on?"

"The guy who attacked me, I'm pretty sure he was at my house earlier today. I'm going to Laurence's."

An audible hesitation before he said, "Don't worry, the kids can stay with us as long as you need them to."

A horn beeped. Laurence had arrived.

"What's the timing tomorrow?"

"The plane gets in at three P.M. We should definitely be home for dinner. You should come."

As if this was a casual invitation, his to extend. Emma and he both knew it would be a first, her actually sitting at the dining-room table in his new house, supping with his new wife and infant daughter. What a cozy sextet.

"Okay," she agreed, thinking these were desperate times and, after all, desperate times did call for desperate measures. She guessed that was likely to be just one of the array of arguments Will was going to have to employ when Jolene was informed that her nemesis was invited to dine. She would have paid good money to be a fly on that wall.

# Chapter Seven

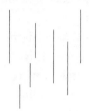

They were driving down Flatbush toward Laurence's current home, a three-bedroom duplex in Clinton Hill. And he was weighting down the car with silence. Almost a quarter mile had passed, without one question posed, one comment made.

"I didn't know this was going to rattle you so much," Emma said.

"Who says I'm rattled?"

"Something's eating you."

"No." He shot her a look. "Nothing."

"Laurence, come on."

"Come on where?" he countered.

His anxiety was physical, his fingers drumming on the wheel; for additional commentary, he pushed the down button for his window and the cool air rushed in. "Motherfucker," he cursed, swerving around a slow-moving driver in his path and running a red light.

"You're obviously pissed off at someone. Or something."

"No I'm not."

"Come on."

"I . . . am . . . not . . . angry." Each word marking its territory. "Why does every woman in the world think there's a subtext when you're quiet? Why do all of you suppose that there's some inner brilliance we haven't graced you with?"

"Oh, I forgot. Men don't think," Emma said. "They've got cotton upstairs, instead of a brain."

Turning, he stared at her, hard. "Exactly!" he finally offered, deadpan. "Should we stick to Flatbush Avenue or cut over?"

"Cut over," she said mildly.

He took umbrage at this too. "What, the way I'm going wasn't working out?"

"Hey," Emma said. "You asked, remember?" She reached out to touch his leg; a tentative peace offering. Laurence kept his gaze locked on the road, veering past a slow-moving truck, narrowly avoiding injury as he swished through a yellow light.

She watched him breathing, hollowly, in, then out. Wait, she told herself, and did, but it seemed like a very long time to her. When he did turn her way again, the anger had dissipated, and in its place there was tenderness. "Look," he said. "I just think it's my fault, common sense dictates keeping an eye on you. Which I wasn't exactly doing."

"You were at work, I'm assuming," she countered. "Besides, who would think he'd come calling. The guy must be out of his mind. He should be twelve states away by now."

"Maybe," Laurence acknowledged. "Then again, you're the only one who knows what he looks like."

Emma had figured that one out all by herself. Her turn to stare, moodily, out the side window.

"From now on I'm not letting you go anywhere alone."

"What? You're going to be my bodyguard?"

"Is that so bad?"

Chivalrous of him to say that, but impractical; besides, they both knew if someone wanted her gone, they'd find a way.

Laurence reached out, caressing her arm. She smiled thinly. They were almost at his place. She tried not to think further than that, tried to stay right in the moment. And failed miserably. Looking his way, she read the intensity of his desire to protect her. It scared her, more than she was willing to admit.

It was crazy, all of it. "I finally spoke with Dawn's dad," she said.

"How was he?"

Sidestepping that for the moment, she said, "Guess who gets Millicent? Yours truly."

"Come again?" Scanning her face, he saw it was no joke. "God-damn." He was so astonished, it had even affected his driving; instead of rushing through the green light, he stayed put. The driver behind had to sit on his horn.

"The senator wasn't amused."

"I'll bet not. You told the man it was a mistake?"

"I don't know that it is."

"What else?" he ventured.

"Dawn put me in the will as Millicent's guardian. Brian drew it up and cosigned it."

"You're saying she never mentioned it to you? Not even a what if?"

Emma nodded. Perfect timing, she thought. They'd pulled up in front of his house, the usual spot, in front of the hydrant.

"She couldn't have been thinking straight," he noted, as if for the record.

An hour later, Laurence was snoring broadly. If only she could have blamed that for her sleeplessness. Emma borrowed one of his shirts and went out, shutting the door before she turned on the light. This duplex on a street in Clinton Hill cost him more than he could afford. Laurence had rented it, without a mention, taken her here on the day he moved. The upstairs had three bedrooms: One was a study, one was theirs, and one was for her two children to use. A signal to her of his honorable intentions, a sweet sign.

Which left it up to her, Emma thought. She loved him a great deal, but was that going to be enough to bridge their substantial differences? The black/white divide was what everyone saw, from the outside. But that wasn't what really separated them. That hurdle was the easiest to leap over, in some ways. They were truly different people in almost every respect. His living room was a case in point: a fireplace stacked with wrapped Duraflame logs, no muss no fuss, that's my man, Emma thought. There were photographs of his son, Shaun, on the mantel, and of Laurence standing next to him against the backdrop of a Florida beach, father and son looking equally buff.

That was it for family; she'd met his brother Ralph twice. As for his dead parents, they were packed away inside a desk drawer, in an envelope marked "personal." Next to them, photographs of Shaun's mother.

He kept things so very close.

She sat on the leather couch, facing the forty-inch plasma TV. The floors were full-grain oak, covered with two coats of poly. At night, they reflected the streetlight that stood in front of the building. There was not one magazine out of place on the coffee table, no dust on the mantel, no mess anywhere to be found, while her life—well, look at it—one part of it spilled into the next. And yet, without quite saying as much, he expected a commitment. *Let us set sail together, in this not quite seaworthy boat.*

And then what? Emma imagined him attempting to reorganize her life and times. It seemed inevitable that he would fail miserably. Wandering into the kitchen, she poured herself a beer. With that in hand, she went back up to the third bedroom, which doubled as an office. Shutting the door tight, she turned on the light. Reaching into the file drawer, she pulled out a sheet of paper (from the file marked "scrap," not to be confused with the other two paper files, "parchment" and "laser ready"). February seventeenth had been a Wednesday. Emma stroked her memory, culling details. Dawn chatting over coffee, then the two of them watching the videotape of Arthur Nevins's confession, which Emma pretty much knew by heart.

The camera focused on Arthur in an interrogation room, a voice-over from Lowry indicated the date, the time, who was present. Then Arthur read from the paper in front of him.

"I came in through the back. I only meant to talk to her right then, about the kid, about seeing her. Julie got all up in my face, as soon as I walked in, said, what was I doing there, and that she was gonna call the cops. I told her all I wanted was a sitdown, but no, she was going for the phone, telling me I had some nerve sneaking up on her. She had the phone in her hand, I grabbed it away, next thing I know, I was using it on her. I guess I didn't think too much about it, then she's lying on the floor."

There was a pause, Arthur staring intently at the paper in front of him, not raising his eyes to his interviewers, not looking even sky-wards, toward a possibly forgiving God.

"It took a while for it to hit, then I realized Julie was dead. I was going to leave, that was it, going to leave her there and maybe some-one would think how a burglar broke in, the way I had, coming in the back door, breaking through the screen to open it. Then I heard their car coming, it was her aunt and uncle, they were pulling right into the garage, and I guess that was when I thought about how it was going to look, how there wasn't anyone but me, and how they were going to know it.

"I had the gun with me. I just went out there and shot the both of them. Then I came back. Shot Julie too."

He stopped. Sat there, still as could be. And this time, he looked up, somewhere distinctly separate from the camera's eye, as if he was looking past whoever was holding it, past the room and all the rest of what had happened, to someplace better.

There was an odd crunching sound as if someone was eating. Emma had always attributed it to the quality of the tape. Arthur had never mentioned anything happening at that moment, but something must have, she knew, because there was a physical response in him, his shoulders definitely sagging. Then he went on to tell about his daughter, how he'd pulled the blanket over her sleeping body, then taken care of her as well.

After that, he'd found the gas cans in the garage and set the place alight.

"You're not being reasonable," Laurence said for the umpteenth time. He was wolfing down his usual modest breakfast on the run, a power bar and a triple espresso. That morning, he'd nicked himself in that tricky spot, right under the curl of his right nostril, now a tendril of blood trailed down. Reaching for a napkin, Emma blotted it. Other-wise, not a whisker out of place, she noted, Laurence had put on a perfectly pressed white button-down shirt, a navy tie, dark blue linen trousers, and black shoes that were barely regulation. She wore the outfit she'd picked out, in the minute she had to jam clothing into her bag, a pair of tan cotton trousers that she'd attempted to iron, a short-sleeved T-shirt in pink that was, thank God, unstained, and the black jacket off the pantsuit she'd worn the day before.

There was a honk.

"I absolutely am," she insisted. "I'm being as careful as I can be."

He gave her a look that called that into question, then walked her out to her ride with the "TLC" license plate, which didn't exactly stand for "tender loving care." The driver, Rubinovsky, Ivan, pulled out with a squeal from tires that were undoubtedly low on pressure, not to mention virtually bald. Inside the pine-scented Lincoln Town Car, Emma uncoiled, leaning forward when they hit Flatbush to tell him the change of plan.

By her watch, it was a little before eight. If she was lucky, she'd be just in time to catch Jason Samuels.

# Chapter Eight

Samuels owned a four-story brownstone on one of the most expensive streets in all of Brooklyn Heights. The house backed onto the Promenade, a strip of land that stood between the houses and the water, built atop the Brooklyn-Queens Expressway spur. From there, and undoubtedly from Samuels's upper two floors, you could take in the entire southern tip of Manhattan, including the South Street Seaport and Lady Liberty out in the harbor.

There were two buzzers on the door, both with Samuels's name on them. Emma tried the top one. Minutes later, a woman's voice responded.

"I have papers for Mr. Samuels."

"Just a sec."

After which the door was pulled open to the full length of the chain. The woman on the other side looked even better than she had in the huge wedding photo that had appeared in the Sunday *Times* Style section. Her face was, of course, familiar, not because it had launched a thousand ships but simply because for years she'd been a high-fashion model, gracing the glossy covers of *Vogue*, *Glamour*, and *Marie Claire*. She was razor-thin and towered over Emma. "I'll take them."

"Sorry, I have to see Mr. Samuels. He has to sign," Emma said, tapping the manila envelope.

"You're from?"

"New York Capital Crimes."

"One minute."

As she waited, Emma turned toward the street. Busy Wall Street types were on their way to work, along with students heading for the two local private schools, St. Ann's and Packer.

The door opened: turning, she found Jason Samuels. The tan he sported could have been the product of a Caribbean getaway; though the orange tint hinted at a chemical application. All the rage these days, Emma thought.

Samuels was dressed for success, a natty light gray suit, purple tie, and lavender shirt. "Papers?" He held out his hand.

Emma didn't offer him a thing. First, he looked puzzled, then annoyed.

"I wonder if I could have a word with you in private," she said.

"About?"

"I have some information. I think you might find it extremely useful."

"Information concerning what, exactly?"

"Arthur Nevins."

He looked her over more critically, not to mention skeptically. "Do you have a name?"

"Emma Price. I'm the lead investigator for New York Capital Crimes. Trust me, I wouldn't come to see you unless I believed it was important."

"Trust you, eh?" A laugh, then a check of his Rolex watch. "I'm due in court," he added. "You'll have to be quick."

He led her into the hallway, lifting a half-filled cup of coffee off the side table, and he told her, "This way." They went through a door that led to a flight of stairs, down to the garden level. This was the waiting area for his home office. It contained a hardwood bench and two equally uncomfortable-looking Bauhaus leather sling chairs, between them an oval table strewn with magazines. He showed her into the inner sanctum, which overlooked the garden with its teak patio set and cobalt blue Weber grill.

"Sit, if you like."

The office was paneled and featured three glass cabinets. One held a collection of baseball memorabilia; another, fine ivory figurines; the third, exquisite glass paperweights. Between them, hanging in rows, framed newspaper stories recounting his accomplishments; they made for some odd bold-face reading—"Wall Street Wizard Walks"; "Caviar King KO'd"; and his most recent triumph enlivened in the *New York Post*'s inimitable purple prose, "Heiress Claims: I Was His Sex Slave." Looking from them back to him, Emma wondered what she could actually hope to get. In her 3 A.M.—fevered imaginings, she had been more than a match for Jason Samuels, but the cold morning light was, to say the least, illuminating.

"So what have you got for me?" he asked. She'd taken a seat, which was a mistake. He didn't, just stood, watching her.

"I'd like to offer my services."

"Come again?"

"I've been working on the Nevins case for over three years. I've vetted all the witnesses, done the legwork. I'd really like to stay involved."

Samuels laughed. "This is your way of asking for a job? Quite the come on."

"It worked," Emma pointed out.

"A little disloyal, though, isn't it, asking me for work at a time like this?"

"I'm doing it for the client," Emma lied. "Arthur Nevins has to be my first priority."

"Really? And why should I be impressed with the job you've done for Arthur?"

"What's that supposed to mean?"

"Only that my client would be loathe to have me hire anyone from your office, in any capacity."

"Are you saying we mishandled his case?"

"I don't think that's reading between the lines," Samuels said.

"What did we do wrong, according to you?"

He laughed. "You're the investigator, right? If you don't know, then you can look into it. Now, if you'll excuse me, I have an appearance." He jutted his chin, pugnaciously, making it clear her time was up.

Emma had invented many scenarios, but not this one. He was going to scapegoat Dawn.

"You intend to argue incompetent counsel?"

"I don't believe I have to make you privy to my strategy."

"It won't work," Emma said. "Dawn Prescott did an excellent job."

"Really? Then why were you so eager to sign on with me?" His eyes sparkled. "Or was that just a strategy? You wouldn't have been trying to pull a fast one on me, would you?"

He moved around the desk, standing quite close to her, certainly much too close for comfort.

"If you and Arthur were so close, why did it take you all this time to have an attack of conscience? Where were you nine years ago?"

"My, my, you don't expect an answer, do you?"

"You don't do pro bono work," Emma countered. "Charging your usual fee?"

"Out." The way you'd say "scat" to a cat. He drew even closer, and she could smell his morning on him, aftershave, the faintest hint of coffee. Emma didn't flinch.

"It doesn't bother you that the last attorney representing this client was murdered?" she demanded.

"Murdered? Please! Ms. Prescott was mentally unstable. Plenty of those who've had dealings with her will attest to that under oath. Now, if you don't leave, I'll have to call the police." Reaching for the phone, he added, "It would be my sincere pleasure."

# Chapter Nine

Laurence watched as Emma shut the gate, then turned, staring up at the façade. She strode around the corner, and he followed at a safe distance, saw where she was heading, waiting till she left Starbucks and headed to the car service.

Was she stubborn? Hell, it wasn't even a question worth asking. Sure Laurence had offered her the crash course in taking care of Emma, told her go to work, stay inside, and when you're done for the day, give a call, I'll come pick you up.

Emma had assumed he was headed in to work. Laurence surely didn't bother to disabuse her of the notion. He'd taken the last of his personal days because there was nothing more personal than this.

Laurence followed the late model Lincoln Town Car till it got to Tillary and headed over the bridge. Then he made a U-turn, stopped at the light, and watched as a brother played traffic cop, waltzing out into the middle of the street, causing a wailing of brakes, a celebration of middle fingers. Unperturbed, he took his own sweet time crossing, while the commuters cursed and fumed. Horns made a chorus to send him on his way. And through it all, the boy didn't even bother to flick his eyes over the danger, didn't give it the time of day. He wore the look of the moment, a leather tricolor jacket, green, purple, and yellow, with a hoodie up top, diamond-encrusted bling bling in one ear, in the shape of a cross, and fine Cons that looked like they could lift themselves and rocket into outer space.

It drew a smile from Laurence.

Laurence had done it himself on occasion, strolling across the street, holding up traffic, not even bothering to give the drivers the goddamn time of day, shoving back against what was bearing down on him, the whole weight of history piled on top of the daily abuse you got.

Emma thought he didn't get it. But he surely did. Got why she was refusing to follow what he'd laid down, the common-sense rules of behavior. No point railing against her for it. No point at all.

The sky was blue, the air crisp, not that it was nearly warm enough for sunning yourself, which was fine, he wasn't heading out to the Island for pleasure.

# Chapter Ten

The Gap window next to Emma's office featured Pru Ramone demonstrating just how fine you could look in a pair of low-rider faded blues. Her punctured belly button was prominently displayed, along with her drum-tight stomach. A selection of solid-color tops were highlighted as well: a black sleeveless Gap T, a tan skintight off-the-shoulder shirt made of stretch material that emphasized her perfect breasts and her lack of a bra, and—last but not least—a purple velvet bustier. They'd certainly managed to capitalize on her Oscar in record time, Pru being the "It" girl of the moment, another one of those perfect embodiments of everything America loved to stand for, the melding of art and commerce into one sexually charged package.

Emma remembered a time, not too far in the past, when there had been actual separations between the two. Back then, rock stars would likely have disdained hawking clothing, while actors and actresses spoke lovingly of their craft, only has-beens deigning to pose for Blackgama in mink.

Those were truly the good old days, she decided as she pushed through the revolving doors. Pausing to consider whether she deserved a Starburst, Emma did a double take. The headline on the *Post* posed the question "Insanity Defense?" Underneath this, they'd stuck a particularly unflattering photograph of Dawn.

Emma inhaled the story as she ascended. Apparently, unnamed

sources claimed that Dawn Prescott had been a resident of Silver Hill in Westchester. She'd taken the cure there twice. That, plus the stay at Menninger's, made her a three-time loser. And, to add insult to injury, her parents were refusing comment.

Was this Samuels's work? More to the point, was it true?

Emma made a mental assessment of the years she and Dawn had spent working in Jersey for that state's version of the Capital Crimes division. There had been a lengthy gap in between, Emma taking time off to marry and raise her first child, perhaps then, Emma reasoned, but no, she told herself, they'd always kept in touch. They'd spoken at least once a week, even during the tensest times in their friendship. She found it impossible to believe that Dawn would have hidden this from her. During Dawn's tenure at Capital Crimes, the only time she took off was for vacationing, and every trip was supremely well documented. Dawn returning with fistfuls of photographs taken by fellow travelers showing her rafting down the Colorado or rappelling off the face of a craggy peak in Glacier National Park.

If she had been hospitalized, and that was a big if, it had happened before they met, Emma decided.

Opening the glass door, she saw Laurie Anne was busy reading. Emma knew what was capturing her complete attention.

Pushing open Brian's door, Emma found him bent over his desk, similarly engrossed. Looking up, he met her eyes.

"Unconscionable," he said, shutting the newspaper and pushing it aside. "Whoever leaked this should be drummed out of the health-care profession."

"You believe it then?"

"Don't you?"

She let that slide for a moment and took a seat. "I talked to Jason Samuels this morning. He intimated that there would be something coming that would make his job a whole lot easier."

"You're saying he's the one who planted this?"

"Why not?"

Brian squinted, toting up the internal figures. "It makes sense," he agreed. "Samuels loves to skew perceptions. This plays right into his hands. He can use this against Dawn and the entire office." Dropping his voice, as if they might indeed be overheard, he added, "The problem being, even if it isn't true, people will believe it."

"Why? Dawn was a wonderful litigator."

"Yes. I agree, but this has nothing to do with her intellectual capacity." Lowering his voice, he added, "Emma, we all saw the scars on her wrists."

"What about it?"

"No one thinks she put her hand through a plate glass window."

Emma nodded. "Okay," she said. "But that was back when she was in college."

"So she told you about it."

"Yes," Emma admitted. "Which is why I think she would have told me all the rest."

"Maybe," Brian agreed. "Then again, maybe not. People don't like to be considered weak."

"Still," Emma argued, "wouldn't the adoption agency have looked into her background?"

"And? You've already admitted she attempted suicide. That should have been enough of a deterrent if they actually cared. She had money and connections. That often seems to clinch the deal. Take Angelina Jolie, how many children has she been allowed to steward?"

"Dawn wasn't exactly a celebrity," Emma said.

"No, but she was a Prescott," he countered. "So, you and Samuels had a nice little chat?"

"Lovely."

Brian gave her a steady look. "You could have clued me in to your plans. I would have liked to tag along."

"It was a spur of the moment decision," Emma told him.

"I see." He clearly didn't. He sighed the way a disappointed parent would, when told of his child's reckless behavior. Sitting back, he clasped his hands, then said, "I think I know who could have come up with this one for Samuels. Hector Calderon."

That brought her up short. "Calderon? The guy who was lead investigator before me? I thought he was out in LA. That was what

Dawn told me when she offered me the job." Emma didn't add the rest, that Dawn had only called her up knowing that Will was finally gone. Her offer to Emma had been both providential and tactless. After all, her marriage to Will and the birth of her first child had effectively severed their original partnership.

"Hector's been back a little while. Called me up for lunch a few weeks ago, that was when he mentioned Samuels."

"But this is so vindictive," Emma said. "Why work for Samuels?"

"You can't measure that when you're doing a job, you hand over what you find," Brian countered. "Still," he added, "I would venture to guess that damaging Dawn Prescott wouldn't have been a sticking point for him."

"All Dawn told me was that he'd had a better offer," Emma said. "I've talked to him several times, he's been nothing but cordial."

"Hector was always a perfect gentleman with me, but he most definitely has a temper. Used to be a boxer, still coaches the Golden Gloves. He was an old hire, like myself. He and Dawn seemed to hate each other on sight. The day he left, they were having words. The whole office heard, especially his final pronouncement. It was, and I quote, 'Get out of my face, you fucking cunt, I hope you rot in hell.'"

Just then Brian's phone buzzed. He stared at it balefully, letting the machine pick up and raising the volume so they could both hear. "Brian, are you going to try and give me the runaround all morning? I'm going to get your comment on this, whether you like it or not. I would appreciate you being a mensch and not forcing me to come down there."

Emma recognized the distinctive voice. It belonged to Kip Mason, a Metro reporter from the *Times*. "Seventeen calls in the last half an hour," Brian said, echoing her own disgust as he added, "If only we could get this sort of attention when we needed it for a client. Instead, you have to literally insinuate yourself into their consciousness in the hopes that you'll get a fair hearing."

"I can't believe Dawn's parents won't defend her."

Brian shot her an incredulous look.

"What?"

"It's totally to the senator's advantage to stay quiet with this, if he has a custody battle looming. How best to prove his daughter incompetent without looking like a complete ass." Rubbing his chin, dressed with elegant, closely clipped stubble, he added, "You think it's Samuels, but why couldn't the senator's camp have leaked the story through the proper channels? It's almost quaint, a man willing to taint his daughter's reputation so he can save his grandchild from being brought up by a decadent lesbian."

"A father wouldn't do that."

"I beg to differ, a father most certainly would. By the way," Brian added, "the service is this afternoon. Senator Prescott hopes you'll be sensitive to the family's wishes in this, and not attend."

Right, Emma thought. Not in this or any other lifetime.

Dawn was being honored, then buried in the town where she'd been born fifty-one years before. The irony was hard to escape, since Dawn Prescott had done everything she could to get out of Dodge, make that Greenwich, Connecticut. She'd spent her entire adult life trying to undercut everything Greenwich stood for: money, power, and—the fruit of both—conspicuous consumption.

Pulling off the Merritt Parkway, Brian drove past familiar scenery featuring tasteless McMansions big enough to house a ten-child family. They had been built next to similarly huge, though stolid, Tudors and colonials. The town boasted several Hollywood celebrities, as well as Will's boss, producer Greg Chavitz, as residents. But the real money belonged to Mayflower families and Wall Street honchos. There were also the usual high-end surgical specialists and bankruptcy attorneys.

"The bigger the home, the smaller the family," Brian quipped as they passed yet another regal monstrosity.

News vans had parked opposite the church, and a phalanx of police were stationed at the entrance. As they drove past, Emma dipped her head toward the floor.

"They'll think you're giving me a blow job," Brian noted. "If only my mother could see me now."

Then they were in the parking lot, and it was safe to come up for air. She did, but discovered her breathing was ragged.

"Don't worry, Hamilton Prescott the Fourth isn't going to make a scene, WASPs don't do that."

"Think again," Emma said. Whose funeral were they attending, after all?

"Darling, who do you think she was rebelling against?" Brian reminded her.

Point taken.

It was a white clapboard church, wearing the ultimate Presbyterian countenance, so modest, so blandly utilitarian. The day was brisk and windy. Emma wrapped the scarf tightly around her neck, raising it up to cover her mouth. With a huge floppy hat that obscured the rest of her face, she had constructed a minimal disguise. Still, in this crush of people, she couldn't imagine the senator would spot her. Or even necessarily recognize her, if he did. They'd only met a handful of times, and back then, she'd been a brunette.

Once inside, she and Brian headed for the upper gallery.

From there, Emma had a true advantage, overseeing all that took place directly below. Mourners were finding seats, or chatting in hushed groups. The closed coffin was center stage, masked by a huge arrangement of white calla lilies.

The members of the extended Prescott clan took up the first two pews, blond to ash blond for the women, and only a notch darker for the men. Emma spotted Ruth, Dawn's mother, and then saw Millicent who was clambering up to get a better look at the crowded church. She was by far the youngest in attendance, only a month past her second birthday. Emma wondered why they'd brought her—was it some idea of offering her closure? Millicent's black hair was impossible to miss in the sea of natural and dyed blonds Ruth bent over, tugging her granddaughter down, to no avail. She got a protesting screech for her trouble. Hamilton was a few feet away, standing in the center aisle. Emma watched him turn, take in the trouble, then reach over to slap his granddaughter's behind.

He'd assumed that would silence her. Wrong! Millicent broke out into wild, hysterical sobbing, which only grew more and more intense as first her grandmother, then grandfather, tried to quiet her. The minister crossed the altar and the rest of the audience fell silent, so her hysteria was even more noticeable. As he tapped the mike and it crackled in response, Millicent screeched, "Mommy!"

That did it. Ruth scooped up Millicent, carrying her protesting body down the aisle and out the side door. It slammed shut in their wake. A second later, Emma got up, making her way past Brian.

"The sort of loss that seems both unfair and unbearable," she heard the minister say as she shut the door behind her. The walkway was empty. Up ahead, there was one lonely policeman, standing at the entrance to the parking lot.

Circling the church, Emma found a small, gated playground. Ruth was there, seated on a bench with Millicent glued to her body. As Emma watched, Ruth's hand went out to cautiously rub her grand-daughter's back. Emma lifted the latch and pushed gently, but the gate made a squeaking sound. Ruth turned, and their eyes met. Emma couldn't help feeling a flush of shame. Ruth pulled Millicent even closer, twisting her own body as if to hide her. In case, Emma thought, I've come to spirit her away.

"Ruth, I just want to talk," Emma said.

Millicent's crying became a hiccough, then disappeared completely. She pushed at Ruth, broke away, and raced to Emma, clutching her legs. Her hand went up, and Emma lifted her, hugged her close, kissed her; doing so, she felt her heart constrict. Millicent grabbed onto the sides of Emma's face with both hands and pushed hard as if making sure she was real.

"I'm not going to run off," Emma said to Ruth. "You don't have to worry." But it was sweet, holding Millicent. Still, Emma slowly disentangled herself, setting the child down.

"Would you like to go on the slide?" she asked.

A nod.

"Here we go, then." Walking over, letting Millicent climb up the four tiny steps, and sail down. Once was never enough at this age,

Emma noted, as the child raced around to the ladder and grabbed onto the molded plastic sides.

Emma backed away to where Ruth stood. "She doesn't understand," Ruth muttered. "At least that's a blessing."

"Ruth, I can't tell you how sorry I am."

Ruth glared at her.

"I tried to explain to the senator." Emma found it impossible to utter his Christian name. "Dawn didn't consult me about the guardianship.

"Really." Ruth studied Emma, a head-to-toe assessment that seemed to find her lacking in most every way. "Withering" was the adjective one commonly associated with that look, Emma decided, but rarely had she seen it done in such an artistic and practiced fashion.

"But if she wanted me to take responsibility," Emma added, "I feel I have to consider why."

"Ah. Here we go." Ruth pursed her lips and shook her head. "My daughter wanted so many things, how does one keep track?" Turning to Millicent, she said in a demanding voice, "That's enough. Time to go."

" 'Gain," Millicent said.

"No!" Firmly, and with apparently better results this time. Millicent relented, crossing the rubber safety mat to her grandmother's side, then letting her grab a hand and rush away. Emma was left wondering what she could add that could undo the damage. Ruth paused by the gate. Turning to Emma, she said, "This will kill him. Her wish too, I assume." Then the gate clanged shut.

Emma didn't have the energy to follow them back inside that packed church. Besides, Dawn had claimed to want a Viking funeral, more than once.

Waiting, Emma leaned back on the hood of Brian's car and shut her eyes. It was cold, but the sun created the illusion of warmth.

"Hello."

Caught in the act, she sprang up. Fitzsimmons had that little secretive smile on his face that people often got when they'd been watching you and you hadn't known. The second time was definitely not the charm, Emma decided, her annoyance at being surprised growing as she took in his dark blue suit that was inches short in the sleeves, his cuffs riding out. Undoubtedly a lender, she decided petulantly.

"Taking a breather?"

"Yes."

"I don't blame you. It was getting close in there." To illustrate, he tugged at his tie, loosening it. At that moment, the church doors opened. The mourners began to stream out. "Looks like the fun's over," he noted.

"Fun?"

"Just a turn of phrase, okay?"

It wasn't okay. Not at all. Emma felt herself about to say something she might regret; she tried to tamp it down, but oddly enough he saved her from herself. "You and Solomon, now that's one for the record books. I would have picked him for being exclusively Afrocentric. How'd the two of you hook up?"

"None of your business."

"Just trying to make conversation," he said.

She pointedly ignored him. Eventually, he sauntered off.

The crowd scattered, car doors slammed, and life went on . . . Brian waved to her from across the lot, his eyes were red, his cheeks flushed. A few yards away, she saw Fitzsimmons get into a black Nissan Pathfinder and wait. Lowry was wearing his dress uniform. She watched him awkwardly lift his overlarge body up inside, then slam the door. Only then did the Pathfinder pull out, joining the funeral cortege.

# Chapter Eleven

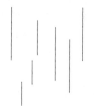

Merrick looked about the same as any other Long Island ticky-tacky suburb to Laurence—small houses, barely set back from the main road, no one walking anywhere at all, just cars and more cars. There was snow on the ground out here, icy patches on the asphalt, trees throwing their bare fingers up to grasp onto the sun. As for the Sunrise Motel, it looked like any other sleazy place, two stories of plywood construction that you could most likely huff and puff down. The kind of place where you could hear everything right through the walls. Only no one had heard anything that night. Of course, there had been only two guests registered, Prescott's party and one other who happened to be lodging at the opposite end low-slung building.

The Sunrise sat between a Burger King and a 7-Eleven. The giant-sized Grape Big Slush sign, complete with straw and purple plastic liquid bubbling over, pivoted above Laurence's car as he made the turn. Today, there was only one other vehicle parked in the lot. Merrick wasn't exactly a vacationer's paradise.

The motel office had a nice view of the Sunrise Highway. The clerk, a kid who looked too young for working papers, ignored him, busy with a handheld Nintendo. Laurence slid his ID forward and cleared his throat.

Glancing down at what had been offered, the kid said, "Room 9, it's out back. Say, when are you guys gonna be finished so we can clean that sucker up?"

"There's a big demand?" Laurence asked.

"Sure. We're expecting a convention any day. The boss told me to ask, aw'right?"

Aw'right, Laurence thought, scrawny kid, pimples on his face along with sprigs of hair. "Were you working on the night Prescott checked in?"

"Nope, that was Christian."

The room was at the back of the motel, last on the right. From there, you got a scenic view of a condo, the brick homes basically shoehorned together. Laurence undid the crime scene tape as carefully as he could, then pressed in the code to the police lock. It paid to have friends wherever you went, and he did in Nassau. Kyle Russo, a pal of his from South Brooklyn, had taken early retirement from NYPD, then signed on out here where he lived, working for the county. First time in his life, he said, he was making decent money. He'd even gotten Laurence what was in the case sleeve, copies of the crime scene notes and sketches, even a couple of Xeroxed photos.

Pulling out his tape measure, Laurence reconstructed. Lowry's notes were cursory, but the C.S.I.'s made up for them. "Female is on her side, ligature marks on her neck, her right arm holding the weapon. Male subject is on his back, entry wound apparent directly under the left nipple, exiting cleanly . . ."

After he read this, plus the M.E.'s report, it took no time to see what was wrong with Lowry's take. The bullet wound in John Doe was just too clean. If Dawn had actually been in a life-and-death struggle there in bed, shoving the gun against his chest that way, there would have been all sorts of trauma inflicted on the body, but the hole was even smaller than the bullet. The only time that occurred was when the shot came from a certain distance. Once the inquest was convened, and the M.E. testified, there was no way Lowry's version was going to hold. Not unless there was evidence pointing to Dawn being able to levitate the gun, then shoot it from afar, undoubtedly using her finely developed paranormal powers.

Leading back to the obvious, someone else had been there in the room. Someone else had staged this little event. And that someone else had a definite face, if not a name. One that, right now, only Emma had seen.

Back out at the desk, he asked to look at the register.

Room 9 had been rented several times in the last month. Every week to Mr. and Mrs. Smith, and once to a Robert Walker. Walker and the Smiths had paid cash. "You remember them?" Laurence asked, tagging the Smiths first.

"Why?"

"It's a murder investigation," Laurence pointed out.

"You're the first one asking."

No surprise there. Laurence brought his steady look to bear, waiting for the kid to flinch, which he inevitably did. "Look, I'm not supposed to tell, okay? They tip me extra for it."

"As long as they're not involved, it won't go anywhere else."

"Believe you me, they're not involved," he blurted out. "I mean, Mrs. Robbins, she was my third-grade teacher. And Mr. Smith, he's Mr. Gold, teaches human sexuality at the high school."

"I get you," Laurence said, moving his finger down to Robert Walker's name. "How about this one?"

"Walker. Paid cash. That's what it says."

"You remember what he looked like?"

"People come and go." Hedging. His eyes inching back to his handheld device.

"What are you playing?"

"The new X-Men game. I got one life left, I can't fucking beat this level."

Probably had the game for what, a good twenty-four hours, Laurence thought. Patience was not exactly this generation's forte.

"Says here he checked in two weeks ago. That's not exactly ages ago. How about you give it a little more energy. Dark hair? Light?"

"Look, I didn't pay much attention. He wanted the fucking room, okay?"

Considering the amount of attention he'd gotten from him, chances were the kid had barely looked up. Still, Laurence decided it was definitely worth pursuing, even if it meant wresting the damn Game Boy away.

"How about the way he talked?" Laurence said.

The kid paused, apparently willing to forgo Doctor Octopus for a pivotal second. He looked curious, almost intelligent. "Yeah, come to think of it there was something about his voice. It was you know, kind of gay."

"As in?"

"Hey, I don't know exactly. High, I guess."

"Thanks," Laurence said.

"No problem," the kid countered, already losing interest, clearly unaware that he'd just made himself into a witness, not to mention a target.

# Chapter Twelve

Emma had just managed to sequester herself inside her office, behind the closed door, when her cell phone buzzed.

"How was it?" Laurence asked.

Unreasonable to be angry at the flippant way he'd framed the question; still, she couldn't help responding with a "How do you think?"

"That bad?"

"Worse." Sitting, she found herself hoping he'd say something else for her to pick on. Of course, that could have consisted, right then, of him simply clearing his throat.

Instead he uttered a name, sounding a little too pleased with himself as he did. "Morgan Blair."

"Am I supposed to know him?"

"The dead man's name. And I have an address to go with it. Over on Delancey."

Hard to be angry now.

"Who is he?"

"An out-of-work actor," Laurence said.

They drove through the winding streets of Chinatown, and he told her the rest.

"Born and bred in Salt Lake City, nice Mormon boy gets the acting bug and applies to Juilliard. Comes East for school, but drops out after a year, then works as a waiter. That's the last the IRS knows."

"Lowry's guys told you all this?"

"Professional courtesy."

"Who identified him?"

"An ex-girlfriend. She works right downstairs from the late Mr. Blair's apartment." Eyeing her critically, he added, "You had a pretty busy day yourself." He was cueing her, but she wasn't at all ready to discuss any of it, not even Fitzsimmons's hostile jibe. She felt oddly light-headed. Looking away, she saw a typical Chinatown scene, a street cramped with pedestrian traffic, behind them the shops displaying their wares, layers of salted fish and produce, ducks crisped to a golden brown. She realized her mouth was actually watering. She hadn't eaten a thing since breakfast, and for that, she'd downed a cup of strong coffee.

"Could you pull over a sec?" she said. She bought a bag of greasy pork buns, then rapidly inhaled them. The dizziness abated. Sometimes, Emma thought, there really were simple solutions at hand.

Glancing at Laurence, she noted that the look he'd had on his face was still there, he was just a little too pleased with himself.

"What aren't you telling me?"

He flushed. "Nothing."

"All this information, suddenly at your fingertips."

"Yes."

Scrutinizing him, she tried to think what it could be.

"You didn't go out to the Island to dig around yourself by any chance?" she asked.

He didn't say no.

"I thought you were back at work?"

"I had a personal day to take."

"And?"

"I dropped by the Sunrise to see about a room." He turned her way. "All I can say is the M.E.'s report definitely gives the lie to Lowry's version."

The relief was immediate. "Good," Emma said.

"Plus, the day clerk at the motel remembers a guy coming in two weeks ago, renting that exact same room. His voice was the marker."

Laurence's hand went out to touch her knee, a physical reminder of how this could be very good news indeed. "I asked my friend out in Nassau to go over the details with the clerk. Then, bring it to Lowry's attention. Once the Lieutenant admits there was someone else in the room that night, there's a logical next step."

"Here's betting he does everything he can to avoid taking it."

"Then we push back."

It was meant as comfort. "Lowry was at the funeral," Emma said. "Fitzsimmons apparently gave him a ride."

Scanning Laurence's face, she saw there was discomfort. "What's the story with you and Fitzsimmons?"

"No story."

"Laurence, come on, the guy doesn't like you. He made it more than obvious."

Laurence's expression was impossible to plumb, like trying to figure out what was going on in the ocean depths without benefit of sonar. Good luck navigating this, she thought, and turned away.

117 Delancey was a traditional Lower East Side building. Six floors high, with a fire escape that was painted lavender, hanging in front. BLUR, "a store for male plumage," took up the main floor. The shirts in the window display had been hung austerely, one of the means stores used to imply that their wares are much more than clothing, raising them up to the rarefied status of objets d'art. Things had changed so much, Emma thought; when she had been younger, dress was seen as a way to rebel against your parents' generation and their out-of-date values, hippie had bled into glam, punk, and disco. Now there was little separation between old and young. Both seemed to view clothing as a desirable status symbol. Even at work, where younger staffers were barely paid a living New York wage, there were discussions about what bargains they had gotten at brand-name designer sample sales. This from people who sported highly developed social consciences.

BLUR's wares were exclusively fine shirts, cut from a delicious assortment of fabrics, in prints and solid colors: violet, mustard, olive, swirls of paisley, subtle stripes, half the garments were rayon, the other half silk. Emma felt the cool, slithery fabric and lifted a sleeve to check the price. $600. For a shirt.

What a bargain!

The sole salesperson was a black-haired, striking-looking woman perched on a stool at the very back of the store. Her hair was super-long, cascading down, witchlike, almost to her waist. Her choice of makeup included plenty of eyeliner on both the upper and lower lids, while the powder on her cheeks was white, giving her a purposeful Kabuki look. She was clearly a mixture of two races, if not more, certainly she had Asian forebears. And European roots as well.

"Jane Appel?" Laurence asked, flashing his ID.

"You're the one who just called about Morgan? Look, I don't know what I've got to add. I pretty much told the other guys everything I could think of."

"Sometimes it can be the questions that make all the difference," Laurence noted.

"You think?" She looked as if she doubted it.

"This is Emma Price, she's working the case with me."

Appel took Emma in, barely.

"You told me over the phone that you were fairly certain about Morgan Blair's involvement with Ms. Prescott," Laurence continued.

"Ms." She laughed. "That's nice. They teach you that sort of thing now at police school?"

"I came up with it all on my own," he said, smiling.

"Maybe you should talk about it to those other two guys who were in this afternoon."

"You mean Lowry and Fitzsimmons," Emma ventured.

"Yeah. One of them kept trying to impress on me how he was some big honcho. Captain? Major? Hell if I know. They sure didn't bother with the Ms."

Emma gave her a commiserating look.

"Then again," taking in the obvious, "that could be why the two of you got matched up."

Emma leveled an "Exactly."

"Anyhow, like I said on the phone, I don't believe for a second Morgan was dating that woman. She wasn't his type. She was way too old. Morgan never even looked at a girl over thirty. I guess maybe it's partly because his mom was so young when she had him. He said, women of a certain age out and out gave him the creeps. He had a few issues with his mom," Appel added, and her expression dimmed. "This all seems so bizarre. I mean, last Friday, he was just fine. All buzzed about this shot he had. No fucking cares, not one in the world."

"Shot?"

"Morgan was up for this big part. Made it through the second round of casting, and he was pretty sure he'd aced the scene they made him read."

"In what?"

"A movie, that was all he'd tell me. The rest was for later, you know, didn't want to jinx it by getting too specific. He was superstitious about that sort of stuff." The doorbell rang, a customer entered. "Can I help you?" she called out.

"Just looking," the man said.

The man really was just looking. Lifting a sleeve, he surveyed the price tag, then did an abrupt about-face. The bell tinkled after him.

"The shirts are gorgeous," Emma said.

"Thanks."

"You designed them yourself?"

"That's what it says." Touching the logo behind her, in the corner, hard for forty-plus-year-old eyes to make out, in elegant script, Emma squinted to read, "Appel Designs Inc."

"How's business?"

"Great, actually. This is just basically for fun, the store. I've got Federated carrying the line. I'm doing just fucking great," the last thrust off as a bitter aside.

"How long since you two broke up?"

"Jesus, centuries." Appel blinked, and Emma saw she was holding back tears. "A year," she added. "Just about to the day. Right after Valentine's Day last year."

"His idea or yours?"

"His," she admitted. "Morgan just didn't feel ready. He wanted to stay friends. Guess what? I did. He made that part easy."

Especially, Emma thought, when you were still in love. When proximity of some sort was better than nothing at all. She put out her hand, touched Appel on the shoulder, did it gently and quickly, so that if she didn't want to recognize it had happened, she didn't have to.

"That's how us males are," Laurence said. "Trapped in eternal adolescence."

"Isn't that the truth." Appel laughed. "Those other guys, all they wanted was his name. The rest, they seemed to care less about, didn't give a shit who Morgan was, what he was really like. They thought they had everything figured out."

"Your friend was murdered," Laurence said. "I'm trying to find out why. And what he might have gotten himself into."

"What about work?" Emma asked. "He had to make money somehow?"

"He did odd jobs for me," Appel said. "Other people too, he was a great carpenter."

"So what about auditioning?" Emma said. "Morgan had an agent, I'm assuming."

"Craig Klose at William Morris. Got him just in the last few months. Craig would most definitely know what he was up for."

The bell tinkled again, another potential customer, this time a well-dressed woman.

"Thank you so much," Emma said.

"It's just that, I don't know, he was really a nice guy, he knew his own shortcomings, he would have been the first to admit them. You couldn't help liking him. You would have too, if you'd met him. He was so totally charming. It made you forget what an asshole he could be."

Emma flashed on Morgan Blair, stepping aside, to let her pass, to let her live.

"I know just what you mean," Emma agreed perhaps a little too forcefully. Appel gave her a searching look. "Don't worry, we're going to figure this out. We're going to find out what happened to him."

"I haven't got all day," the woman said in an officious tone of voice.

Rising from the stool, Appel made a face only Emma could see.

"I'm sorry, I was just finishing up here," she said. Pausing, she touched Emma's arm, "Thank you," she added softly.

"I liked her," Emma declared.

Laurence was already on his cell. "New York, New York," he said into the phone, then "William Morris Agency." In an aside, he added, "Would it kill them to hire an actual human being for once?"

In the car, he drove in his usual distracted, aggressive manner. Emma knew better than to even make a peep. On the phone, he bulldozed his way past the personal assistant to the personal assistant, and on up, until he was told that Craig Klose was out on the other coast and wouldn't be back till late in the day tomorrow, they would relay his name and number, Klose would be sure to call just as soon as he could.

"The endless brushoff," he said. "What do you have to do to get these assholes to pay attention?"

"Say you're Denzel?"

"Ah, never thought of that." Shaking his head at the stupidity, he added, "What I don't get is how people forgive themselves for spending that kind of money on a shirt."

Emma heard echoes of her own father, asking the same question about the profligacy and waste he saw around him; he had been a true believer, a Communist. That he made no real money was of no concern to him.

Just then, Laurence cursed at the traffic that had all but come to a halt, and turned off Delancey onto Ludlow. There was her grandfather's store, Cohen Textiles, displaying bolts of brightly colored cloth in the window, bargain swatches in the cardboard bin out front. A woman wearing a headscarf and fur was fingering a bright pink sateen.

Her father had brought her here twice to visit her grandfather, a dour man, dressed in black, complete with payos and beard. "He never forgave me for anything I did," her father had said bitterly. Then he'd hugged her close and whispered, "But you, you'll never disappoint me."

Fathers and daughters, Emma thought. She had undoubtedly let him down on numerous occasions, but she'd never doubted his love.

Unlike Dawn, who'd declared again and again that what her father thought of her didn't matter. Her insistence being the ultimate proof that it had.

# Chapter Thirteen

Emma buzzed again. And again. Finally the door was pulled back, roughly. She found herself face to face with her nemesis, Jolene Pruitt Hayes Price, who was holding her squalling infant, Winnie, in her arms.

"Look at this!" Jolene demanded, before Emma had even made it over the threshold. Sweeping back Winnie's overabundant blond locks, she revealed a stunning red welt. "That child of yours is a monster!"

"Wait a second, Jolene," Emma said, attempting to enter. Jolene stood there, barring her way.

"Wait a second for what? So she can make good on the job?"

"What happened exactly?"

"Brigitte was upstairs, taking a shower. Will and Liam are out getting dinner. I was in the kitchen with Winnie, heating up her baby food. I turn my back for one goddamn second and your little witch goes after her, throws a bowl at her head." Jolene made a furious uh-huh sound in her throat, echoing an interior peanut gallery.

"I'd like to talk inside," Emma said as civilly as she could manage.

Jolene stepped back, barely. Emma had to brush past, and as she did, she heard Jolene mutter a subterranean curse.

"What was that?"

"I'm not having her here another second, she's pathological."

"Pathological? She's two and a half, for God's sake," Emma retorted. "Kids act out."

"You call it what you like," Jolene countered icily.

"Come on, Jo. You've got to see this is hard, having to share her father." Oops. Jolene's face had turned a bright, bright red.

"I have to see? Why the fuck do I *have* to see anything? Her father? When Will didn't even want to have a child with you in the first place? Now you want me to feel sorry for her? Maybe you should have thought of that when you got yourself pregnant."

Emma raised her hand to slap Jolene silly, then took a breath. It was how she'd managed to avoid meting out physical retribution to both her kids. It worked. Though Emma immediately regretted not giving in.

Jolene let loose a bitter laugh, then turned her back and stalked up the stairs, with Winnifred Pruitt Hayes Price pressed to her wounded breast. From above, a door slammed.

Emma went to find her daughter. Katherine Rose was in the kitchen, huddled in the corner, her body a tight little ball. Her tears were the silent kind, filled with penitence and anxiety. Bending down, Emma whispered, "Katie?"

"Mama!" She literally leapt into Emma's arms for the hug, and held on extra tight. Her crying escalated now that she had a proper audience.

"Shh," Emma said, rubbing her shoulders and feeling an influx of complex emotion. Yes, there was reason to chastise Katie, to explain the dimensions of this wrong, because Emma had no doubt that her youngest had done this. It sounded exactly like the sort of out-of-control behavior Katherine had been exhibiting lately. Still, her blame was tempered by her understanding of the complex emotions that ruled her youngest child. Not to mention, there was a reason they dubbed this "the terrible twos."

And then, of course, there was Jolene's comment, still reverberating. "Will didn't even want to have a child with you in the first place." Call it playground rules, Emma thought, call it whatever you like, but don't pretend it's easy or painless. Don't think that you're going to escape unscathed when you fall in love with someone who happens to have a wife and children of his own. You claim to love him, then admit that he comes with plenty of baggage and be gracious about it.

"I miss you," Katie insisted. Her use of the present tense gave Emma a pang as did her daughter's fingers digging in to exact their pound of flesh.

"Me too," Emma told her. "I'm here now." Katie lurched back, giving her mother a searching look.

"No!" she insisted.

Ah, the *no*s. One day, she and Liam had actually counted the number of times Katherine had uttered this word. Seventeen minutes later, they'd passed the two hundred marker.

"Jojo's bad," Katie added. "She hit." Her finger touched her cheek and Emma saw the evidence. A red spot had been left behind. They were twins with matching bruises. Both inside and out, Emma told herself with a pang.

"Ouch," Emma said sympathetically, leaning in to touch foreheads.

"Dinner!" Will was making the announcement from out in the hall. He sounded so hearty, so jovial, so clueless.

*It was so fucking typical of him.*

"We're in here," Emma called out.

Minutes later, Will was upstairs, trying to broker a truce, while Emma organized dinner. Liam had followed his father into the kitchen, seen the mess, and immediately retreated. He sat at the dining-room table, with an uncharacteristically somber expression on his face. Every now and then, she felt his eyes on her. He'd noted the bruise immediately, how could you not? She guessed that he was having second thoughts about believing her version of how she'd received it. Liam was nobody's fool.

And barely a child, she noted. Had he grown in the last five days? It seemed as if he had, an incipient beard had sprouted on his chin. She felt her heart lurch inside her body at the thought of losing him to the world, to his own life, and then wanted to laugh at the absurdity, because, really, he was long gone. He had a very serious girlfriend,

Cleo, whom he spent every minute either talking on the phone to or IM'ing.

Katherine Rose, meanwhile, was omnipresent. She twined her Pad Thai into a braid. "Look, Mommy," she said, shoving it toward Emma. "Eat!" she demanded.

Right then, from directly above their heads, there was the sound of breaking glass; close on the heels of that, a door slamming. Then slamming again, the click of a lock. A baby wailing; this time, Emma guessed, in terror.

"Jo, come on," she heard Will call.

Nothing.

Finally, the stairs creaked. Will emerged, looking sheepish and more than a little forlorn. Here he was, supposedly at the pinnacle of his career, an Oscar winner—it was ironic, wasn't it? Because Emma decided he had never looked quite so pathetic and miserable.

"Sorry," he said. It was clearly meant as a general apology. Or perhaps, she thought, a comment on the state of the world as Will knew it.

Will puttered in and out, carrying condiments, juice, cups, hot sauce, anything to avoid talking. When he sat, he asked conciliatory questions of his children: "How's that green curry?" or "Some more sticky rice?"

Finally, there really was no escape. Dinner was over. The kids were in the other room, oddly content. It was just the two of them, cleaning up the mess.

"What's going on?" Emma asked, but of course she'd already guessed. He'd caved, given in, and told himself it was for the sake of the marriage. Maybe he was right, but Emma couldn't help feeling that it was cowardice, or worse. Your children should come first, she told herself. Then amended that, because he had three children now, had to weigh the needs of his youngest one against the other two. And she gave him credit: he'd been the one to insist that Katherine Rose accompany them West, he never missed one visit with her or with Liam. Emma had argued against it, saying what was the point, she would never be able to attend the awards or the parties. To which he pointed out, neither would Winnie. It had seemed absurd, his attempt to spread the wealth as equally as possible, but she understood all too well. After all, it wasn't the children he'd abandoned, it was Emma.

Will stared into the sink, at the suds in the water, but nothing there was going to help him. Not unless he shrank to pea size and floated right down the drain. "Emma . . ." He turned, spreading his arms to show the length and breadth of his troubles, troubles he'd made for himself, she noted. "It's not a good time for Jo. I tried to explain things to her, but she feels she really won't be able to cope with having the kids here this week."

"We made a deal," Emma said.

"I know we did, but what can I do?"

Asshole. But she didn't dare say it aloud. Will had always been a coward. It was why he'd gone running to Jolene for comfort in the first place. Indeed, Emma told herself it was as much her own fault as his, she had believed he would do this for her, he would be there for once. She should have known better. Every time she let herself believe he was dependable, he disappointed her.

Emma swept the broken plate into a dustpan, sponged up the tomato sauce that had dripped down the side of the high chair, hid all evidence of her daughter's frustration. She felt so sad for Katherine Rose, who would never get the attention she craved, and wrongly believed her tiny rival was to blame. Emma knew better. Will was incapable of really focusing on anyone else for very long. He was so charming, so warm, you fooled yourself into believing it was your fault when he failed you.

The only way to win was to give up.

"Have you ever run into an actor named Morgan Blair?" she asked. It was clearly a relief to him that she was changing the subject.

"Can't say I have." Will smiled his most charming and ingratiating smile. "Is he someone I should know?"

"He's the man they found with Dawn."

"That guy was an actor?"

"Apparently. I talked to an ex-girlfriend of his this afternoon. How about an agent at William Morris named Craig Klose?"

A whistle of admiration. "Craig? That's who represented him?"

She nodded.

"Then he was either incredibly talented or amazingly well connected. Craig is a shark of the first order. He only deals with A-listers. He's got Pru, Oreg, even Mike Raines, the director. Klose is the one who basically put the deal for *Baby Mine* together."

And the rest, Emma thought, was history. A gritty, downbeat, pretentiously titled movie about an abusive mother whose teenage daughter takes her prisoner and teaches her some interesting life lessons. "Unflinching," raved Ebert and Roeper. "Four thumbs up." Kirsten Rogers, a bona fide star, had the bigger part, playing the mother, but newcomer Pru was the one receiving the attention. Not to mention the Oscar.

"You've met him?"

"A number of times."

"His office said he'd be coming back tomorrow."

"For the party. You're invited. It's at the River Café. Greg loves touting Brooklyn. You'll come, won't you?"

"I don't know." Hardly in the partygoing mood, not to mention that her being there was basically going to seem like a slap in the face to Jolene. Then again, that made it, at the very least, intriguing.

"I'd really like you to come."

"Why would that be?"

Will had wiped his hands on the dishtowel and moved in to close the deal. She assumed he was going to apologize even more profusely, and then, without any real prelude, he kissed her, hard, wrapped his arms around her and pulled her close, tenderly. Not on the cheek, either, right smack on the lips, and there was tongue involved. He tasted so familiar, her body responded in a purely habitual way. The warmth pooled inside as his hand slid up under her shirt, and even though she recognized the illicitness, the stupidity of doing this here, in Jolene's brand-spanking-new kitchen, she also had an even stronger desire. Come walking in now, she begged silently.

Then he cupped her breast, the way he always did, possessively, and it was over for her. She pulled away, gave an uneasy laugh, said, "What the fuck do you think you're doing?"

"What do you mean?" In his best, small boy's voice.

"You're married. And to someone else, by the way."

"It's just, with this whole thing happening, when I think I could have lost you."

*You did lose me.* But Emma held her tongue. As she watched him shape-shift, she had a startling revelation. She actually felt sorry for Jolene. Backing toward the door to make good her escape, she saw where she was—another woman's kitchen, with copper pots gleaming from cast-iron hooks in the ceiling, Mexican tile on the floor, a Sub-Zero refrigerator, a blue porcelain Viking stove—all this for a woman who, according to Liam, never cooked a meal. Yes, Jolene was to blame for a lot of what had befallen her. She was selfish, self-involved, and mean-spirited. In attacking a child who had no real ability to defend herself, she had shown her true colors. Emma disliked her intensely, but she wanted no part in whatever was being played out between these two. Will had chosen someone else, let him try and work it out. Or not.

"I take it you want Liam to come to this party?"

"Of course," he said, a little too eagerly.

"What time does it start?"

"Eight."

"I'll see if Laurence can make it."

"Laurence?" It came out unbidden, along with the look of surprise and discomfort. Gotcha, Emma thought. Then his expression hardened.

"Great," he said, sounding pained. "I'll add his name to the guest list."

Back at Laurence's apartment, it took hours of hysterical crying, heavy pleading, and back rubs before Katherine Rose gave up and fell asleep with Emma's hand crushed in her own. Extricating herself from the Vulcan death grip took careful work.

Finally, Emma managed, getting up and tiptoeing out.

Passing the bedroom where Liam was bunked, she heard him talking on his cell phone.

Knocking, she got the answering, "Yeah?"

"Go to sleep. You have school tomorrow."

"Okay. In a minute."

She listened as he chatted on. "Yeah, it was unreal," he was saying. She recognized the tone of voice, relaxed, informational, loving. She knew he was talking to Cleo. Emma remembered when she'd been his confidante, and couldn't help feeling a pang of sadness.

She could knock again, make a point of shutting him down, but not tonight, she decided. He needed to talk more than he needed a good night's sleep.

Laurence had taken the sofa bed in his living room by default. His reading glasses were perched on the bridge of his nose, a new affectation, one that he tried to minimize the use of, with decidedly mixed results. He'd ordered veal, which he detested, because he refused to have her read the menu to him, and refused to wear the glasses in public.

"So you'll go with me?" she asked. "Craig Klose will be there."

"I prefer a talk at his office. Not as many distractions."

"I don't want to go alone."

"Don't then."

"Don't go at all, you mean."

"What's wrong with that?"

"Liam wants to go," she tried.

"And your daughter most likely wants you home. So?" He was toying with her. She wasn't about to tell him of the close encounter with her ex. Still, it seemed as if his senses were fine-tuned enough to pick up any subtext.

"Aren't you even the least bit curious?"

"Nope." Smug. Satisfied. Throwing it back to her.

"You don't want to star search?"

"How about you tell me which one you're trying to stick it to by going. Your ex? Or his child bride?"

She was transparent, at least, to him.

"Both, I guess," she admitted.

"How about I sleep on it. It's past one." And Laurence promptly turned on his side, tucked the pillow in as a barrier, and went right to sleep, with the lights in the room still blazing.

# Chapter Fourteen

Laurence had made her swear she would have an escort. Unfortunately, the only one available was Marc Tannon, her least favorite intern at the Albany office. An eager second-year law student at Albany Law, Marc always wanted to prove how indispensable he was. He prattled on about this, the subject closest to his heart, on the drive to Dannemora. At least Marc required very little in the way of response. Dozing off, Emma came to, every now and then, and offered one of her three mainstays—"Um-hmm," "Really?" and "That's something, all right!"

Cook Street was Dannemora's main drag. As such, it offered a scenic view of the razor wire–topped walls of Clinton Correctional. Leave it to the powers that be to compound the harsh punishment by putting death row in this prison. Frigid. Bleak. And about as far from most of the inmates' loved ones as you could get.

They passed Stewart's, Nick's Liquors, and the Cook Street Café. Snow was piled waist-high. Outside town, it was a landscape of severe beauty; once on the main drag, it was simply depressing. As was the reality of life in Dannemora, where most of the residents depended on the correctional facility for their livelihood.

"You might as well wait here," Emma said. "Get yourself some lunch." She pointed to the café. "Go with the grilled ham and cheese. And avoid the coffee."

"I'd really like to come."

Fat chance of that, though to give the man credit, he never stopped asking.

A blessed relief to get out of that car and away, even though the cold smacked her in the face. She was waved through the main gate and into the staff parking lot.

The prison was red brick, characterless, its sole unique feature the exercise ground inmates called "the courts." These were buried under deep drifts, but in spring they were fenced off into individual, workable plots of land. Inmates grew vegetables and flowers; the ground was dotted with handmade benches and chairs, as well as more personalized items, mailboxes, whirligigs. And of course, no death row inmates were allowed access.

After passing over all metal objects, her keys, a pair of turquoise studs, and two bracelets, Emma walked through the first of two metal detectors. Doors rolled back, and she was led down the maze of corridors, the smell of the prison confronting her, rank with sweat and industrial-strength cleaning fluid. Past cellblocks A and B, to get to C, where she stepped through the second metal detector and was let into the visiting room.

The guard who'd accompanied her took up his station by the door. Waiting for Arthur could take all the time in the world, since it depended on what mood the staff was in. Not to mention Arthur. Emma had cleared her visit with the warden, who had undoubtedly informed him. But he could still refuse to see her.

She began to think he would. Half an hour passed, and the door leading into the room on the opposite side of the bulletproof glass didn't open. Standing, Emma felt ridiculous. Where was she going to go in this twelve-foot-by twelve-foot box? She could leave, of course.

She sat down heavily instead. Time inside was a completely different animal—there was no point being anything but patient. Still, she couldn't help it, she began playing the game she'd used to divert Liam when a bus came late, or a line moved too slowly, counting back from a thousand in intervals.

Reaching zero she started again.

After which, she tried being Zen. Not something she'd ever been too good at, the whole be-here-now, live-solely-in-the-moment thing. Although, Emma thought, you sure do achieve Zen-ness when someone's holding a gun to your head. That stops time cold.

Finally, she accepted that he wasn't coming, and got up, approaching the guard. Which was exactly when the door on the other side opened and Arthur emerged. Stepping up to the glass, he tapped his hands against it in greeting. "Hey, girlfriend. Where you heading in such a hurry?"

Sitting back down, she replied, "Nowhere special."

"Sorry I kept you waiting, we had a little strip search going on." Throwing a look behind him, at the guard, he added, "Some people getting their thrills."

"I wasn't sure you'd want to see me."

"Surely do. First off, I got to say how sorry I am, hearing about Miss Prescott."

"Thank you," Emma said.

"You holding up all right?"

"Doing my best." His tone was genial, as if they were still the best of friends.

Emma flushed. "You know your mother's spoken to me."

"I do," he said agreeably.

"Jason Samuels? How did you come to hire him? You never even spoke with us about being dissatisfied." Not to mention the question of payment. Perhaps Arthur's mother had managed to win the lottery.

"I got no choice in this. Got to go with my best interests," he said. "I know it's harsh, but that's how life is. No need for you to take it personal."

"But I do," Emma said.

Leaning in, Arthur countered with, "And I say there's no call for it."

"Arthur, just tell me why you're switching now, we're right in the middle of the appeal."

"It was the right thing," he insisted. "You got to go with your gut instinct sometimes."

"Then Mr. Samuels approached you?"

"Did he say different?"

"No."

"We went to high school together," Arthur pointed out with a patent lack of sincerity.

"I thought it was grade school," she countered.

"Look, I'm not saying you knew any of what happened," he told her. "You and me, we always had a decent understanding. And I don't like to speak badly of those that have passed."

"Then this is about Dawn? What did Samuels say she'd done? Whatever it was, he was lying."

"You know that for a fact, do you?" Arthur cast his eyes over her, scornfully. "Baby girl, you ought to drop this right here and now."

"You're threatening me?"

"No. No threat in that," he said blandly. "Just some good advice." He began to get up, motioning to the guard.

"Don't do this to me," Emma begged. "Don't walk away."

He shook his head at her foolishness. "To you? Do this to you? Jesus, girl, you think I give a good goddamn about you? You got a hell of a lot of nerve trying to run that by me."

"Dawn was murdered," Emma said. "And the man who did it is still out there."

"Not according to the county police. What's wrong, you don't trust them to do the job?" He shot her a meaningful look. And that was it. He was gone.

She had come all this way and gotten nothing, Emma thought bitterly. Arthur's hatred of the county police was not exactly news. Basically, he'd stonewalled her.

Outside, the sun had slid midway down into the western sky. It was after two, and she still had to make it to Albany, catch the plane back. What had she been thinking when she agreed to attend that party? It was the last place on earth she wanted to be tonight.

Of course, it had been all Liam could talk about over breakfast.

Looking left, then right, she discovered no sign of the car or Marc Tannon. Calling his cell, she got a recording, and left a message indicating her exact location, then stepped inside the Cook Street Café.

She had warned him against the coffee, but sometimes there was no other choice—better the devil you knew, Emma thought as she ordered hers black.

It was busy inside the café, every table occupied. Making a circuit of the room, she saw no sign of Marc, but the man with the Yankees cap definitely looked familiar. He was likely a guard, Emma thought, thick-necked and barrel-chested, but then she reconsidered. He had a wicked tan; there weren't a lot of prison guards who could afford a midwinter island getaway. Just then, he turned her way, gesturing for the waitress. Hector Calderon hadn't aged a bit, she decided.

"Hector?"

He looked up, squinting. "Hey," he said, clearly fumbling around in his memory bank to remember just how they knew each other.

"Emma Price. It's great to finally meet you in the flesh." She slid into the chair opposite, without waiting for the invite.

"I got your messages. Sorry, I've been crazy busy." He tried on a syrupy smile. "So how'd you know it was me?"

"There are a couple of photos of you hanging around the office."

"She didn't take them down and burn them?" The waitress arrived with his burger, meat so gray it defied adjectival evaluation. "Just kidding," he added. Dosing the patty liberally with ketchup, he took a bite, then wiped his mouth clean, grunting. "Food in here still sucks."

"You're up here visiting?"

"Sure. A regular vacation paradise."

"Who are you visiting?"

"A client."

"Arthur Nevins?"

"Not at liberty to say," he said.

"I hear you're working for Samuels."

Hector chewed thoughtfully, took a long draught of soda, wiped his mouth, and settled back in his chair.

"Why did you leave Capital Crimes?"

"Prescott never told you?"

"She said you'd had a disagreement."

"The queen of understatement." Harsh, Emma thought, and he

seemed to know that, shoving his chin out pugnaciously, as if expecting to be upbraided.

Emma quieted the urge to defend Dawn. In her most nonconfrontational tone of voice, she said, "You obviously wanted to take another approach to the case."

"No kidding."

"I wish you'd tell me about that. I'd like to help."

He seemed to consider her offer seriously. That lasted for all of about two seconds. "Water under the dam, right?" Dragging his wallet out, he raised his hand to get the waitress's attention.

"You don't think I would want to help a former client?"

"Not up to me to make that call."

"Try me," Emma said, because he was standing, apparently itching to escape. "What have you got to lose?"

"Now, that's funny," Hector countered. "Try you? Why should I? You and Ms. Prescott, you two were thick as thieves, according to my sources."

"She's dead," Emma said. But her voice shook, betraying her.

"Yeah, she sure is." Something like regret showed on his face. "Wish I could help you," he added. Then he was up and heading for the door. Emma pursued. Outside, she grabbed his sleeve. He looked down at her hand, then lifted it, thrusting it away. "I'll work on giving you the benefit of the doubt," he said. "Tell myself you're just as ignorant as that cunt you worked for. Not that you deserve it, but I'm just such a standup sort of guy."

"Fuck you," Emma threw back.

"Sweetheart," he replied, smirking. "If that's what makes you happy."

# Chapter Fifteen

There were some things Laurence didn't get rid of, Spartan though he was, like these family photos that showed his dad and mom, impressionably young, dressed for an Abysinnian Baptist Church Social. What he liked about this particular shot was the way his mom was turned toward his dad, like a supplicant, with the look of unparalleled devotion on her face, the same one that she wore during every family dinner, listening to the man pontificate, not realizing that basically he was a blowhard. Love is blind, Laurence thought, as well as deaf and practically dumb. That was his mom, a woman of very few words, though some well chosen, the master of the sneak attack.

Next to that photo was another he'd kept, showing the entire extended Solomon clan. They'd been at a reunion in Carolina, on a cousin's parcel of land. Laurence was nine, his brother, Ralph, fifteen. Laurence stood in the foreground, fourth in the line of younger cousins, most every one of them smiling but him. He looked too damn serious for a boy his age, brow knitted, lips tucked tight, while Ralph, directly behind him, had his head tipped forward, the reason being Ralph had been working hard to crack him up and he'd resisted, dug his heels in, to the point where it seemed like he was outright miserable, just in time for the click of the shutter.

Laurence took a long look at them both, then stuck them away in the file marked "personal." Underneath them was the wooden cigar box that had held his father's best Monte Cristos. His dad had liked to sit, smoking one, watching TV, comfortable in his favorite La-Z-Boy chair. By the time the man died, there had been a dent in it, conforming exactly to his body. That was how he was, Laurence thought, the sort of man who tried to bend the world to fit around him; the sort of mission that was bound to end in failure.

Inside were keys, marked with tape. Some were to his parents' house way uptown, others to his first solo apartment, on 121st and Amsterdam, others to the one right next to CCNY, on 137th, where he'd lived with Shaun's mother. Half his romantic history laid bare, through the keys he'd been given by girlfriends, those who had either forgotten to ask for them back or hoped that if they didn't, something might come of it. Each one was marked with the name and address, because it didn't do to trust that sort of thing to memory, memory being about as unreliable as any eyewitness account.

Here they were, the keys to the back door of Emma's old house on Bergen. Palming them, he snapped the lid.

Strolling across to Bergen took a good half hour. He passed where they were going to erect the new stadium for the Nets. Knicks fan or no, he had always kept an interest in the team, watching Dr. J as a little kid, doing those astounding midair turns, then dunking the red-white-and-blue ABA ball in the basket. It always seemed like a mistake when the Doctor came out to do color commentary and there was this old guy, with salt-and-pepper hair.

Laurence passed Bethel Baptist, hit the corner of Nevins, traveled the extra block and a half, and there it was. Emma had gotten the four-story brick row house in the divorce agreement, but when she'd been deeded that old white elephant in Ditmas Park, she suddenly had one home too many. It had been a smart move, cutting her expenses and selling the place where she could make the most profit, though most would have done anything to avoid living in a house where someone had been shot to death. Laurence liked to tell himself that was the ultimate judgment on her marriage to Will.

Dawn had snapped the place up before it even went on the market and paid in cash. No broker, no muss, no fuss.

He stepped through the gate and listened to it click shut, then climbed the stairs, wondering if his luck would hold. The key slid in, and he held his breath a second more, until the locks tumbled. Pulling on his gloves, he turned the knob and stepped inside, avoiding the pile of mail on the floor. Leaning over, he sifted through it carefully but found only bills and advertisements.

The difference between when Emma had lived here and now was astounding. Dawn had clearly spent another small fortune putting in brand-new birch floors. Her taste was like her, he decided, cold, elegant, every stray touch of personality something a decorator had advised. There were fluted glass vases on the end tables next to the sofa, with wilted flowers in them. The coffee table was glass, no baby-proofing on the sharp corners, not exactly child-friendly.

When Emma had told him Dawn was adopting, he'd assumed it was a joke. She was pretty much the last person on earth he'd thought would have the capacity to look after a child's needs.

He'd been wrong, first to admit it. Glad to admit it, even.

The metal dining-room table was ringed with six matching chairs, another glass vase in the middle held orange flowers. Metal was the unifying theme in this room. The hutch was white enamel on top of metal, looked to him like one of those things you found in an old-time doctor's office, only instead of scalpels and stethoscopes, it held plates and glasses.

He thought back to how it had looked in here when he'd first met Emma, like funkytown: a couch that sagged in too many places to count, and, dead center, a mini basketball hoop where he and Liam had worked out their differences.

The kitchen was so clean now, you could pretty much eat off the floor. Not that much eating went on here. Dawn didn't enjoy food; she liked to move it around her plate during a meal, so it was odd how she had to have all of this, the new double fridge, the Wolf stove. He looked through the window at the deck. Emma had put a baby pool on it, which was gone for good, the furniture was under its winter cover, but he'd sat on the Adirondack-style chairs, had a drink out there once, when Dawn invited them both over for cocktails. As nice as those chairs looked, they were perversely uncomfortable.

That was how he'd felt about her too, truth be told.

Respected her. But never liked her.

Not that he'd say that to Emma.

He walked up to the second floor. Here was where Emma had gone into labor with Katie. He'd rubbed her back when she needed it, taken her down to the hospital, her cursing like a sailor for the entire ride. The mouth on that woman. "I can't fucking believe I did this again, what the fuck was I thinking?"

At the hospital, she'd begged for drugs. That midwife had laughed. "You're kidding me, right?"

Too far gone for them to deaden the pain.

Then.

And now.

He knew how she was hurting. It wasn't just the fear of what might happen, it was knowing what had, having that weigh on you.

He understood. Jimmy lying there, how long had it taken him to realize? Seemed like years, watching his best friend die. Some nights he did it all over again, woke in a cold sweat, doing what he'd done then, trying to flag down the passing cars, trying to find a working phone, trying to get help where there was none.

Only so many times you could say you were sorry.

In Dawn's bedroom, the covers were half off the double bed. A pair of slippers sat waiting on the floor, a white bathrobe hung over the back of the rocking chair. Dawn had gotten up, gotten dressed, and left, Dawn who kept track of every little detail and worried that baby to death, hadn't even put a shout out to her next-door neighbor, Irma, to look in, which said to him that what had gone down had gone down fast. Too fast for her to think of anything other than that she had to step out, shutting the door and locking it tight. Had she told herself the baby would be fine, the nanny bound to show herself in, and till then, it would have to do? Had she been brave? Afraid? Or both? He wondered how much she had known, how much she had guessed, or if it all was a surprise. It always was, he supposed, no one thought they were going to die, till they did. Life was something you clung to, because, hell, it was better than the alternative. Or, at least, it was known.

Laurence had gotten the phone log from a contact at the bureau. Only two calls had been received that night, one from her parents in Greenwich, the other from a phone booth on the corner of Third Avenue and Bergen, that call coming in only a few minutes before she'd dialed Emma to ask for her company.

Laurence thought that the way his dad had gone was a gift, his heart giving out on the daily walk to the newsstand, death coming to him from one decisive jolt. Faulty wiring. Whereas for Dawn, the end hadn't been quick at all, she'd seen it coming, fought against it, all that clear from the M.E.'s photos.

Millicent's bedroom was next to Dawn's. A huge framed poster of *Where the Wild Things Are* hung behind the crib. The hooked rug featured the full alphabet. The bookcase was packed, floor to ceiling, with children's books: *Goodnight Moon, Pat the Bunny, Good Dog Carl.* That one always stumped him. Trying to tell kids Rottweilers were their best friends—maybe in the white-is-right, sanitized kingdom. As for getting educated, what you had to do was take a four-block walk to Jose's, a full-service establishment where you could pick up either a lucky number or a bag of weed. The dog Jose kept guarding the back door was a Rottweiler, looked just like Carl except for its metal-spiked collar, the foam that dripped from its mouth, and the psycho way it tried to nail your ass, pulling the entire length of its chain.

Up the stairs, to Dawn's home office, where the desk and file drawers were cleaned out. Into the next room, which used to be for storage but now was supposedly for exercise. An Elliptical Trainer, as fine as the one at his gym, easy to imagine Dawn pumping away.

Laurence stepped up on the pedals and saw she'd folded back a *New Yorker* to the "Talk of the Town" page. As he lifted it, the pages fanned, and a piece of notepaper dropped out. On it, the word, "Rosalita," underlined three times.

From downstairs, he heard the front door open and shut.

The stairs creaked, and a man's voice called out, "Dimitri." Who was that supposed to be?

"There you are." Then, "Psst." The damn cat, Laurence thought. Getting the cat to follow him downstairs, or else shooting it up. The cat had diabetes, Dawn had gone to some lengths to explain, and he'd pretended to listen, all the time thinking what a waste, paying good money to keep something that useless alive.

The stairs creaked. Dimitri's companion was on his way up. Laurence looked around for a hiding place, not even a closet in here, plus movement would just alert whoever it was to his presence. Best to tone down his breathing, try not to move at all, hope that whoever it was was stopping a flight below.

"Oh my," the voice said, and there was a sigh. The man was in Millicent's room. Laurence heard the sound of drawers opening. Then it was quiet. Laurence tortured his breathing, letting it come out ridiculously slowly in little, level puffs. Finally, from down below there was a dry, racking cough that turned into something else. Sobbing. Growing in volume. It went on for quite some time.

Eventually, it stopped. There was one last, drawn-out sigh, and then the steps moved away, the door shut from down below. He was safe.

Stepping toward the window, making sure he was hidden from inquiring eyes, Laurence had his guess confirmed. He watched as the senator settled into the backseat of his limo.

# Chapter Sixteen

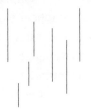

Emma wore her work uniform, black man-tailored suit will travel. Liam, on the other hand, was resplendent in his iridescent tux. To the River Café, making haste but arriving quite late in her '89 square-back Volvo Wagon. Of course, there was valet parking. And of course, as she stepped out and handed over the keys, the valet did a double take. "Careful with the chrome," Emma admonished as her reconditioned chariot followed the train of limos and Benzes.

Chavitz had chosen to hold his celebration here, at this spot on the Brooklyn waterfront, to make a statement about his allegiance to the borough. Not that he actually had his home here, the three he owned were in much tonier places. His primary residence was a waterfront estate in Greenwich, and there were two others: for skiing, a chateau in Aspen; for West Coast casual, a bungalow in Santa Monica. Still, you had to give him credit, he put his money where his mouth was. Chavitz was a major contributor to all the local cultural institutions; he'd sponsored exhibits at the Brooklyn Museum and was a platinum donor to the library, while the Academy of Music listed both Chavitz and his wife as members of their advisory board. All this, Emma thought, was good business sense, because in the last year, he'd spearheaded a group of investors who had done the impossible, getting governmental and community approval for a multimillion-dollar project on the Brooklyn waterfront that would include soundstages, a triple-tier mall, and a marina.

A velvet rope kept the walkway to the barge off limits. Emma showed ID after their names were confirmed, and the burly security guard let them through. Photographers were lounging nearby; the few who glanced up as she passed didn't bother with a second look. But as she ascended, Emma felt the sea change. Turning, she saw the men and women moving as a pack. A Hummer limo had pulled up, the back door opened, and a man who was obviously a bodyguard emerged, followed by Pru Ramone.

"Pru!"

"Baby girl, this way."

"Pru, talk to us, give us a look."

As they surged forward, the bodyguard shoved back, clearing a space. The protective rope was unhooked and Pru sprinted up the walkway, impetuously hugging Liam, then giving him a kiss, right on the lips, making sure to hold it just long enough for flashbulbs to pop.

"There you go," she said, to no one in particular. Liam, meanwhile, looked understandably dazed, not to mention enraptured. Once inside the door, in relative safety, Pru turned to take in Emma. "You're the mom, right? Your boy Lee here, he's the greatest." She gave him a chuck under the chin, like he was her best pal. "I've heard you're pretty fucking fabulous yourself," she added, and before Emma could even think of a response Pru was submerged by a crowd of well-wishers.

Emma surveyed the scene. She felt completely out of place. The room was packed to the gills. The buzz of conversation was so loud, it was mind-numbing. Everywhere she looked, she recognized boldface names. Donald Trump, with that mop of hair up top that was either a dead animal or a very bad hairweave. The mayor, a senator, and even an ex-president. Movie stars like Pacino, De Niro, and Streep. Her last gasp of rubbing shoulders with the rich and most definitely famous had been years ago, when she was a teen who looked older, and used a fake ID to party late into the night at various downtown hot spots, she'd been friends with Johnny D, a dealer who entered the back rooms at will. Danceteria. The Palladium. It had been a truly hedonistic period. Once she rarely looked back on at all. But this reminded her that, for every famous face she noted, there were a bunch of others who were undoubtedly equally powerful, the money men, and arm-candy women. If only Laurence had come. Did she feel intimidated? Totally.

"There's Dad," Liam said, saving her. He pulled her forward through the crush.

Will was seated at a table in the far corner. He waved to her, then looked past, checking for Laurence. She shook her head. Chairs were pulled out, introductions made all around. "This is Emma, my ex." How quaint. How truly civilized. Why didn't I stay home, Emma wondered.

"So Laurence couldn't make it then," Will said, looking a little too pleased.

"He's working a case." She could tell he thought it was an excuse.

"You're the famous Emma." The woman saying this looked awfully familiar. When Emma realized why, she did a double take. It was Kirsten Rogers. Like most movie stars, she seemed much smaller in person. Actually, Emma realized, she was exquisitely tiny, her body perfectly proportioned. Kirsten's hair was red in this incarnation. It framed her shoulders. Her skin glowed and she'd had work done—it had been apparent on the screen, and it was even more obvious in person. Her eyes were too feline, her lips too puffy, she was beginning to look like someone who bore a striking resemblance to Kirsten Rogers, the movie star. The overall effect was, to say the least, disconcerting.

"Your son never stops talking about you," Kirsten said, reaching forward and impulsively grabbing her hand, then squeezing it. "It's all good, don't worry."

What was the appropriate response? Emma squeaked out a "Thanks." That didn't seem right, but nothing really did. She was at a loss, racking her brains in an effort to remember the title of the first movie she'd seen Kirsten in; it had to have been at least twenty years ago, which made her, Emma realized, an approximate contemporary. Back in that film Kirsten had had Botticelli Venus looks, blond hair coursing down her shoulders in ringlets and a perfect body. When she'd revealed it naked, there had been a gasp from the audience; her breasts were at least C cups and definitely not surgically enhanced.

They were currently more than filling out the sheath she was wearing, a Chinese print in jade green. Did you pretend you didn't know who Kirsten was? That seemed totally ridiculous.

"I love your work," Emma said, feeling totally like a rube.

"Why, thank you," Kirsten said smoothly. Then she looked at something behind Emma and her expression changed. Her lips tightened. The mask slid on.

"And who is this?" The voice boomed out, announcing Greg Chavitz. Even rail-thin, he would have been an imposing presence, but he wasn't. He was at least two hundred and fifty pounds, and it wasn't all muscle by any means. His right hand was in front of Emma's face; she saw he wore a ring—large, gold, with what looked to be a diamond in the middle. He set his hand on Kirsten's shoulder, and Emma couldn't help but note the contrast, his bulk, her diminutive size.

"Emma Price, Greg Chavitz," Will said.

"The ex-wife? I take it back, Will, you do have balls." Greg removed his hand from Kirsten's shoulder and offered it to Emma. Her own was dwarfed inside his palm. "Quite a clusterfuck, isn't it?" His gaze swept around the table, taking in Jolene, and immediately passing over her to the empty chair at her right. "I don't know about you," he said, returning his attention to Emma, "but I definitely could use a drink."

He raised his hand, and a member of the waitstaff literally seemed to materialize.

"What can I get for you?" he asked, sliding into his chair next to Kirsten, his arm snaking around her shoulders.

Emma wondered if it was wise to have a real drink. She'd eaten nothing yet; on the other hand, her level of discomfort was reaching nine on the Richter scale.

"A rum and Coke, please." Perhaps the twelve cups of coffee she'd downed would inhibit the effects of the alcohol.

"What kind of rum do you have?" Chavitz barked.

The woman looked momentarily nonplussed.

"You don't know?" he asked. "Then go and check."

She scurried off. And Greg leaned in. "When Will said he was inviting his ex, I thought he was kidding. But here you are, how fucking civilized. My current wife, she'd sooner die than sit down to dinner with my ex."

Emma couldn't help glancing at Jolene. She was staring at Will with an excruciatingly pained look on her face, as if she'd swallowed a slow-acting poison.

"Ronrico, Bacardi, and Cruzan," the waitress said, returning.

"I'd go with the Cruzan," Greg said to Emma.

"Anything is fine," Emma offered in an apologetic tone of voice.

"Then Cruzan it is. Sweetheart, do me a favor, would you? Ask what you've got by way of a double malt?"

Off she went again.

"So . . ." Expanding himself to fill up whatever breathing space was left at the table. His attention returned to Emma. "What are you, some sort of lawyer, right?"

"No. I'm an investigator."

"Do tell? Death penalty cases, right?"

"Yes."

"At least I remembered that much."

The waitress was back. "We have Glenlivet, Dewar's, and La . . ." She looked bemused. "Sorry, the last one's hard to pronounce."

"Laphroaig," he said. "Sweetheart, you forgot to find out how long they've been aged."

"Sorry."

"How about you just choose one of them," Emma said.

He gave her a curious look.

"Really, it's no trouble," the waitress was saying.

"The lady says I have to choose, then I will." Shutting his eyes, he added, "Eeeny, meeny, miney, moe." His eyes sprang open. "Laphroaig," he told her. "You come back and see if you can pronounce it for me." As she turned to go, he reached out and gave her a fulsome tap on the rear.

"Jesus," Emma said under her breath. She was saved by the appearance of a man with close-cut, oiled hair and a mercurial smile. He kissed Kirsten Rogers on both cheeks, European-style, then glad-handed Chavitz. Looking around at the rest of them, he gave Will a cursory nod.

"Craig Klose," Will said, then to Emma, he added, "Craig's an agent at William Morris. You want a deal done with anyone, he's the man to talk to. This is my wife, Jolene, and this—"

But Chavitz broke in, "That's his ex. Can you believe this guy? He's so nice, even his ex-wife comes by to toast him."

"Remarkable," Klose said. Raising the glass he had clutched in his hand, he made as if to toast, then returned to the task at hand, attempting to broker a deal, Emma guessed. She was willing to wait and watch, knowing that Laurence had been unable to meet with him today, and now, here was her opportunity. But not here, she decided. She would have to pursue him, and get him more or less alone. Jolene, meanwhile, was in conference with Will. And Liam had contorted his body to talk on his cell phone. Emma caught a snippet of what he was saying: "Yeah, I'm sitting right here with her. You know who she is, right? She like played Pru's mom."

"You heartless fucking bastard." Swinging around, Emma caught Kirsten Rogers in mid-epithet. Her expression was classically pissed off, and she had lifted her fork, had it raised in her hand, as if she was preparing to skewer Chavitz with it.

"Baby, please." Humoring her.

"Don't try that with me, you know better."

"Kirsty, sweetheart, you know I can't cast you as the lead. You and Clooney? No one's going to believe it."

"I'm perfect for this," Kirsten countered. "You know it too."

"You shouldn't be trying to tell me what I am and am not aware of," he ventured, though more gently than Emma would have expected. "Kirsty, this is a sexual movie. There's nudity, okay? You told me yourself, it demeaned you, taking your clothes off."

Her cheeks reddened.

"Depending on the part," she said. "I said it had to be earned. Clooney's three years older than I am."

Chavitz rolled his eyes.

"He is," she insisted.

"Okay, so he is. That's not the point. You know how things work. This isn't some feel-good Nancy Meyers project. Kirsty, I'd give it to you if I could."

At which point, Kirsten Rogers's eyes welled up with tears. Even Emma realized it was a ploy. Chavitz's face darkened. "Hey," he said. "Stop."

"Go to hell," she said, and she sounded like she meant it most sincerely. "You too," she added, turning to Klose. Then she got up to make a dramatic exit and came face to face with Pru Ramone. "Ugh," she added in an expression of complete frustration before shouldering past.

"What was that about?" Pru asked, taking the seat Kirsten had vacated and receiving the customary Craig Klose benediction.

"Kirsten throwing a hissy fit," Craig said in a viperish tone.

Mercifully, the waitress returned, bearing news of dinner.

"Salmon or roast beef?"

The table split along sexual lines: fish for the women, beef for the men. Craig moved off, and Emma, dropping her napkin on the table, followed behind into the thick of the crowd.

"Excuse me," she said, virtually grabbing him to get his attention. Turning her way, he gave her a hostile look.

"Yes?"

"I'm Will Price's ex-wife, Emma. We have a mutual friend. Had, actually. Morgan Blair, he raved about you."

She watched Craig digest this news. He was clearly torn, easier to pretend ignorance, but Will still mattered enough, she thought, for him to reconsider.

"He was an extremely talented actor," Craig said, delivering his version of a eulogy. "A tragedy, what happened to him." His eyes darted past, apparently looking for an escape route.

"He was so excited about getting that part," Emma pressed.

"Was he?"

"Insisted you were the only reason he had even been considered."

"Nice of him," Klose said noncommitally.

"Morgan Blair." The voice was Will's. "I knew the name was familiar." The quizzical look was perfect. Will, coming to her rescue, a tarnished white knight. Just when you think you can write someone off, Emma thought, they go and surprise you.

"Were you at that casting session?" Craig asked.

"Must have been. It was a few months ago, right?"

"January. But I swear, I told Morgan not to get his hopes up. You and I both know how Greg is, he says he wants new blood, but in the end—" Then catching himself, he added, "Not that I'm not with him, a hundred and ten percent." His hand raised, he called out, "Ben, sweetheart." And, quick as a flash, he was gone.

"Fastest escape in the history of the world," Emma said to Will.

"He's got a reputation to maintain."

"What movie is he talking about?"

*"Los Alamos."*

"As in, there's a feel-good project?"

"Bad name, everyone knows. It's a working title. A passionate love story set against the backdrop of the A-bomb tests. The scientist who's the love interest may or may not be selling secrets to the Communists. And the waitress may or may not be an undercover FBI agent. The screenplay may or may not read like a bodice ripper. And Greg may or may not be making a bomb. He's been pushing Pru to say yes to it."

"You hate it."

"No kidding."

He started back toward the table. She caught his arm. "Thanks," she said to him.

"For what?"

"For being a mensch."

"I'm not sure that's the right name for it," Will said, offering his best, self-deprecating smile.

Back at the table, her meal was cold. She scarfed it down, regardless. Kirsten Rogers had not reappeared, and Pru was comfortably ensconced, holding court.

"You should know better by now," she was saying to Chavitz. Then emphasized her point, giving him a dig in the ribs with her elbow. "But you can't help yourself, can you. What a big bully you are." She put it fondly. Chavitz didn't argue, he beamed like a proud parent would, instead, and took the last bite of his very rare slab of beef.

"Hey," Pru called out to the passing waitress, who shot a nervous glance at Chavitz. "Could you get me a beer?"

"Since when are you of legal drinking age?" Chavitz asked.

"Since forever."

"You're going to get me busted." Joking, but also chiding.

"How quaint."

"Pru!"

"Gregory." She rolled her eyes at him, then added, "Fine. Forget the beer. How about a Coke?" Turning to Emma, she added, "Don't you just love how he plays godfather?"

Emma didn't answer. She took a drink instead, her rum and Coke, bottoming it out. Then sipped the ice water. And tried to think of how she was going to bring up this casting session, how to slip it into the conversation in a way that would seem deft rather than clumsy.

Meanwhile, she was aware of the shift, everyone's attention turning from Chavitz to Pru. It was interesting how Pru played to it, pretending ignorance but obviously knowing—even more clearly, loving—that she was the focal point. Look at what she'd chosen to wear tonight, a bustiere in black, with a see-through top over it; a leather miniskirt that barely covered her thighs; eleven studs lining one earlobe, the other left bare, a mix of "fuck you" and "fuck me."

She was striking-looking, Emma decided, which was better than beautiful: tawny skin, high cheekbones, and eyes with the permanently sleepy, bedroom look to them. Her hair had changed color since the awards; tonight it was a raven black.

"What're you working on?" Pru asked her.

"Me?"

"You're the only one here who does something useful. Come on," Pru said. "Give us the gory details."

"Emma wasn't invited for entertainment value," Will said sternly.

Pru turned his way, and Emma waited for the inevitable sarcastic quip, but it didn't come. Instead, she said, in an oddly chastened tone of voice, "Sorry, is that what it sounded like?"

"You know it did," Will asserted.

The look that they exchanged was a beat too long for comfort. Shit, Emma thought, and turned to find Jolene, eyes shooting daggers.

"I've been working on the Nevins case," Emma said.

"Yeah? I know that one. He capped his ex-wife, right? Did the kid and in-laws too." Turning to Chavitz, she added, "I saw a *Dateline* show on it. One of those that likes to make you guess about the outcome. I mean, give me a break, you can tell the guy's wearing orange, or they've got a fucking zipper in the front. What are you supposed to think? They're working construction? So, did he like slit his kid's throat? Do something kinky with the body?"

"Pru!" From Will, sternly.

"Hey, no harm in asking," Pru said. Playing cat and mouse with him. Enjoying it too.

Emma felt the cell phone vibrating in her pocket. No better moment for a diversion, she thought, getting up to answer. It was Suzanne, apologizing, but Katherine Rose was throwing a fit to end all fits.

"I'll be there," Emma said, then lifted her purse. "Liam, we have to go."

"Oh Mom!"

"I'll bring him by," Will offered.

"When?"

"Mom, come on."

"You have school tomorrow."

"Twelve at the very latest."

Will was up, apparently ready to escort her to the door. She sprinted, but he managed to keep pace.

"Is she okay?" he asked.

"She's Katie," Emma replied. Then couldn't help herself, turning to confront him. "What's going on with you and that teenager?"

"What teenager?"

"Will. Don't even think you can get this by me."

"Get what? We're friends." The martyred tone already in evidence, he'd heard this accusation before.

"Fine. Since you're such good friends, then you can ask her about Morgan Blair. See if she knows what happened with him."

"Cross my heart and hope to die," he said, with such sincerity she wanted to laugh. What an odd guy he was, she decided, half the time a Boy Scout, half the time a rake. Outside, she handed the parking stub to the valet. Waiting, she thought of the way Will had sworn fealty. *And hope to die* echoed in her head.

# Chapter Seventeen

So he hadn't wanted to get dragged along to that party; still, this was one hell of an excuse, Laurence thought, crouching down to get a different view of the bullet's angle of entry. Mrs. Rhonda Hawkins sat on her couch, her TV dinner set out on a tray in front of her. She'd been gut-shot, like a deer, or in this case, a rhino, Hawkins weighing in at a good three hundred–plus pounds.

"First I just assumed it was a typical domestic," Fitzsimmons said. He was crowding Laurence on purpose, basically breathing down his neck, hoping to provoke. Laurence knew better than to give him that pleasure. "Now I'm not of that opinion."

"Why would that be?"

"I had a talk with the kid who called it in." Fitzsimmons nodded toward the bedroom. "He basically confessed," he said. "Mrs. Hawkins was having a peaceful dinner, when he gets all up in her face about something, she won't listen, he pops her. Then gets scared and calls nine-one-one. By the time we get here, she's bled out."

"That's it, just him and the vic?"

"Two others, girls, they're back in the bedroom with him. They wouldn't say a word to me. Neighbors told us she's a foster mom."

"Nice home she made for them." Both of them standing in the filth, empty food containers, stray newspapers and magazines, and the worst of it, dog shit from the two pit bulls animal rescue had been taking away as he arrived on the scene. The sad part was, Laurence thought, he'd seen worse.

"The boy's named Karim. After he copped to the shooting, I pushed maybe an inch and he told me how she deserved it. When I asked why, he shut down."

Getting to his feet, Laurence felt his knee give.

"Anything else?"

"Nothing that comes to mind."

Laurence thought, Wasn't that the way? He'd been working Brooklyn South Homicide for almost two years and managed to avoid the pleasure of working with Fitzsimmons. Now here they were, roped together.

Which was making one of them a little too happy.

He went past Fitzsimmons's partner into the bedroom. Here was where those two dogs slept. There were pillows on the floor with their names embroidered on them; nice, fluffy names she'd picked: Butch and Spike. Mrs. Hawkins's oversized bedroom suite was decorated in girlish pink—pink satin pillows, a pink coverlet, even pink Venetian blinds. On the floor, more stacks of newspapers, *TV Guide*s, and a huge pile of shopping bags.

The three kids weren't sitting on the bed, they were on the floor too, huddled in a group. The girls looked to be maybe second- or third-graders, while the boy was definitely younger than Liam. Eleven? Twelve at the very most, he decided.

Gaunt didn't tell the story for any of the three, most particularly the boy, his skull a few sizes too big for his frame, the skin stretched extra tight, the eyes way too large for their sockets, his hands hanging down, outsized for the arms, the skin basically bandaging the bone, wrists so tiny you could wrap them twice with one hand.

"Karim, my name's Laurence. Laurence Solomon." Kneeling down again, he felt his knee giving back a dull ache.

Karim answered for them. "This here's Cherelle, that's Tama."

"Nice names," Laurence said. "Cherelle and Tama. Sooner I get this talk over with, the sooner we can all get out of here. Okay?"

A shrug.

He considered his options, ask them to separate or no. The way they sat convinced him. Let it go, for now.

"Your name is Karim?"

"Yes sir."

"How old are you, boy?"

"Seventeen," Karim said.

That took more than a second to digest. Even though the kid was seated, Laurence could tell how small he was. "How about you, Cherelle?"

"She's eleven. Tama's twelve."

"You three related?"

"No sir."

"Mrs. Hawkins, she was your foster mom?"

"Mrs. Hawkins, yes sir."

"How long you been with her then?"

"Three years."

"And the girls?"

"They come later."

"You called to say Mrs. Hawkins needed an ambulance."

"Yeah, I thought maybe they could fix her." He made a little sigh, pulled up his shoulders like the man he almost was, and added, "But I guess she's all done."

"Pretty much, yeah, want to tell me what happened?"

His face hardened, but his voice was still respectful. "I told her not to, but she didn't listen."

"Not to do what?"

He gave Laurence a searching look, trying to evaluate what he was getting himself into. Then he sighed, a small, hushed thing that said, What did it matter now. "All I meant to say was how she can't do what she done, not no more. Mrs. Hawkins, she likes to watch her shows. Sits all up there and eats watching her damn show. We got to stay in here the whole time. Got to sit on the floor. We do that, or else."

"Or else what?"

"You know, or else." His eyes roamed the room.

"This Mrs. Hawkins, did she hit you?"

"Sure, she done hit us all, you want to see?" And Karim lifted his shirt. There were welts all over his upper body. Marks that Laurence recognized as burn marks from cigarettes. Plus, his ribs stuck out, and his stomach was distended, like one of those Biafran kids who had made the news years back. This boy looked to be a regular poster child for starvation.

"How about your social worker?" Laurence asked.

"Mr. Franklin?"

"Did he visit you here?"

"He been here, sure."

"Recently?" Like, say, at any time during the last three years.

"No sir, not too recent."

"But he's seen you recently?"

"Yes sir. Someone called in from the school about whether we were getting taken care of. Mrs. Hawkins went down to make sure we got the check, she made us come along."

"He asked you questions, this Mr. Franklin?"

"Mrs. Hawkins, she told us what to say."

"And that was it?"

"I guess."

"The gun, where'd you get it?"

"Her gun," Karim said. "She kept it there." He fingered the drawer on the bedside table.

He'd have to separate them, go back at them again with the social worker present. And, in Karim's case, a lawyer. No mystery attached to this that he wanted to plumb, Laurence decided, his concern automatically moving toward the boy.

"How about you take them over to the precinct, see if you can find them something to eat, get them settled," Laurence said to one of the uniforms. Left it at that, although he couldn't help feeling like it was wrong, like he was just fattening them up for the slaughter. Stepping out, he saw the M.E. had arrived. Taking another look at the dead woman, he felt a rush of hatred for her, told himself not to jump to conclusions, laughed at that silently; the fact of it was, the more you saw of how human beings operated, the more you felt ashamed to be a member of the race.

Of course, Fitzsimmons was waiting.

"Like I told you," Fitzsimmons said.

It wasn't. Not at all. Laurence didn't bother illuminating him. Just stood there, watching the M.E. do her work. She had her notepad out, her gloves on, her kit open. In due course, the kids were escorted through, Laurence taking internal notes as they passed by the body, round-eyed stares from the two girls, knowledge from the boy.

The door closed after them.

"That boy says he's seventeen," Laurence said.

"He sure doesn't look it."

"Looks like she starved the three of them."

"And?" Fitzsimmons said. As in, your point? When it was so damn obvious.

"I hear you've been spending time with Lowry."

"Your girlfriend tell you that?" Inclining his head, the way a half-brained bird might. "Hey, all I did was give the man a ride."

"You figure, either way this breaks, you have a head start?" Laurence threw out.

Fitzsimmons shrugged.

"It's what I'd do, I suppose," Laurence agreed. Had to give him something, had to put himself out in some way, even if it ate at him, doing it. He knew Fitzsimmons could tell what it cost him. Saw the pleasure in his eyes.

"Nice of you to say," Fitzsimmons said. "I guess we're just brothers under the skin, you and me."

# Chapter Eighteen

"You don't even have to take bets how it'll end," Laurence said. "The shock, the outrage, the shame on you, they'll do a face-saving shakeup at DYFUS, this Mr. Franklin will get rousted, after which everyone will happily go on about their business till the next time something goes wrong and it's splashed across the news. When I left, the D.A. and that kid's lawyer were trying to work out a deal. No one wants him in jail for too long. Kid that size will get eaten up at Rikers. Meanwhile, you have neighbors up and down the floor, turning a blind eye. Whatever happened to 'It takes a village'? Seems to me there are a whole lot of villagers, doing a whole lot of nothing."

"You'll watch out for him," Emma said.

"Oh sure, I'm a great big help to him. Getting his confession on tape, making sure every detail was correctly transcribed. Handing it to the D.A. I'm most definitely watching that kid's back for him."

"Don't do this to yourself," Emma said, putting a hand on his arm. At least, he didn't pull away immediately, she told herself.

"I suppose I ought to be looking on the bright side. Not often you get a case that's likely to clear itself this fast."

Emma was torn. She understood his frustration. Here he was, basically doing cleanup duty for a system that rode on diesel, rails made slick by *your tax dollars,* polluting the air as it went, knocking over whatever hapless soul stepped into its path. She felt for those three kids, and even had sympathy left for this Mrs. Hawkins, because she knew from experience that there was always a story, always a reason behind behavior, no matter how heinous. Yet she couldn't help wishing for his undivided attention. Owning up to the wish made her feel ashamed.

"Here's the kicker. It was Fitzsimmons who got the nine-one-one call. Ironic."

"How was dealing with him?"

"Perfect," he said. His tone of voice made it clear: she was forbidden from pushing for more. Laurence was undressing. Emma watched as he dedicated himself to the details, folding his clothes up into a tidy package, setting them on the chair. All part of the practical act of avoidance. He was in his briefs and nothing else, when he slapped his head with an open hand. "Damn, I almost forgot!" He reached over, digging through his pants pockets. "This mean anything to you?"

A slip of paper with the word "Rosalita" written in sloping script, complete with pitch-perfect loops and a meticulously dotted *i*. She knew the handwriting immediately. "Dawn wrote this."

"I was by her house. She never did change that lock," he noted. Sliding in next to her, he leaned on her shoulder, taking a second look.

*Rosalita, you're my strong desire.* A Springsteen song, jotted down by Dawn whose taste was all classical, all the time.

"God knows," Emma said. It made her feel odd, the idea of him digging through Dawn's possessions in search of clues.

He leaned back, staring blankly at the ceiling.

"Who's the boy's lawyer?" she asked.

"Mae Barton."

"Really? That just happened?" She put her hand on his chest, directly over his heart. "You arranged it, obviously. You're a good man, Mr. Solomon."

"I don't know about that."

Still, the piece of paper she'd put aside was further evidence of how much he concerned himself. And part of his charm was his inability to agree, to accept her praise. "I spoke with Craig Klose," she said.

"Sorry?" As if he didn't know the name, another sign of his distraction.

"Klose, that agent. He was at the party. There really was a movie part Blair was trying out for. Gregory Chavitz is apparently producing."

"Chavitz?"

"You do know who he is," Emma insisted.

Laurence finally centered his attention, considering the name. "Will's boss?"

"Bingo. I didn't get a chance to ask Chavitz about the try out."

Laurence nodded.

"I'd like to, though," she said.

He was staring at her, but it felt like he wasn't seeing her. Or else, Emma thought, seeing through to something hiding inside. What sprang to mind was what had transpired just the evening before, Will's awkward attempt at reconciliation. It was something she would never share with Laurence—what would be the point of telling him? Emma added in Will's behavior tonight, his apparent desire to help, his flirtation with Pru. He was everywhere at once, she decided. A sure sign of desperation.

"I'm thirsty," Emma said. "Want anything?"

In the kitchen, she unloaded six cubes of ice into a glass, ran cold water over them, and took her time drinking it.

*Rosalita.*

Crossing the living room, she eyed the stack of documents. Squatting on the sofa, she reached over and switched on the light. There was plenty more to share—the talk with Arthur, the chance meeting with Hector Calderon, all of it swirling around inside. He hadn't pressed her for any details yet, he was busy with his own troubles. Emma wondered if he even would.

Then wanted to laugh.

He was nothing if not diligent, this man she loved. She saw Laurence, opening the door to her old house, saw him inside Dawn's bedroom, inside Millicent's. Emma bent over the file, her finger jabbing at the words, the description of what had been taken from Arthur

Nevins's apartment, what had been recovered from the basement. She turned page after page, searching for something that would pull all these disparate strands together, something that she had apparently missed before.

"Trying to find Rosalita?" Laurence asked. He was standing behind her. How long had he been there? Emma wondered. She flushed.

"I guess," she admitted.

"You've memorized that file," he pointed out. He went past her, into the kitchen. She heard ice clink, and knew it wasn't water he was after. Returning, he set the glass down on the coffee table then sat down beside her. Emma inhaled the peaty odor.

"What is it?"

"Laphroaig."

"What is it with that brand?" she asked.

"Straight from the peat bogs of Scotland. Why?"

"Chavitz made a special request for it."

"Then the man has taste."

"He's a prick," Emma said, remembering how he'd bullied that poor waitress.

"You don't get to be a success any other way," Laurence asserted.

Still, the man was complex, Emma decided. He'd seemed truly concerned about Kirsten, that is, before he eviscerated her. And he'd given Pru plenty of latitude. Was that because he didn't take her seriously, or because he was enthralled? Will certainly seemed to be, Emma decided. Pru, as in jailbait.

She set aside book one and picked up book two, news clippings that had photographs of the victims and of Arthur being led away in handcuffs, his head obscured. Here was his wife, Julie, again, the *Daily News* story, showing a little flair. Julie wore a bikini, sunglasses rested on top of her head, her dark hair was sculpted and shoulder-length. Around her neck hung a necklace rendering her name in gold, not exactly to Emma's taste, but Julie wasn't dressing up for her, Emma guessed. She was the sort of woman who kept the opposite sex in mind. Julie's gaze was seductive, her mouth pressed into an eternal pout. She was standing on a dock, in front of a boat, close enough so that you could see the lettering. "R," Emma read. "O . . . S."

"Would you look at that," Laurence said, then he let out an appreciative whistle.

The *Rosalita,* home port Sheepshead Bay, Brooklyn. Only one boat had ever been registered in that name. The license had expired a good three years ago, but for the previous seventeen it had been owned and operated by a Captain Jack Gallagher.

From the DMV where boat licenses were duly recorded, Emma took a cab directly to the Brooklyn Bay Marina. A mottled banner above her head announced FISHING CRUISES DAILY, although anyone taking a cruise this early in the season would probably need an icebreaker to get out to the open water.

A six-foot-high metal fence was undoubtedly supposed to discourage uninvited guests. But it was bound to be largely ineffectual, since the gate hung wide open. Stepping through, Emma saw a makeshift guard shack on her left, plastered with an array of bumper stickers. To her mind there was quite a gulf between "Jesus Was a Fisherman" and "Honk If You're Horny," not to mention "Rabid Dog on Premises," especially when said rabid dog was a tiny mongrel with wisps of white on its muzzle. It certainly didn't lunge at her, or offer a series of barks to announce her presence. In fact, it didn't even bother to open its eyes. Perhaps it was stuffed.

"Anyone home?" Emma called out, rapping on the wooden shutter. No response.

She tried again. "Hello?"

"Keep your shirt on," a man said, popping up. Emma thought if you were charitable, you'd call him a terminal burnout: stringy gray hair, red-rimmed eyes, and pockmarked cheeks. A cigarette, burned down to the nub, dangled from tobacco-stained fingers.

"Fucking socket don't work," he added. Looking inside, Emma saw a tiny TV, dark and quite silent.

"I'm looking for Jack Gallagher?"

"Looking for the captain. Why would that be?"

Taking a chance, Emma said, "I was interested in his boat."

"You missed the boat on that one," he said, laughing hard at his own joke. "The captain's retired. Permanently. Over in the Holy Rest Cemetery. Bum ticker," the man added, gesturing to his own heart. "As for his boats, they're long gone."

"You knew him pretty well, I'm gathering."

"Well enough." He gave her a harder look. "So what's this really about? He forget to pay his taxes again?"

Emma took out her card, offering it as collateral. Squinting, he read "Criminal investigator" out loud. Looking up, he said, "Too late to pin anything on Cappy."

"It's nothing like that." Emma set the copy of Julie Nevins's photograph on the counter; next to it, the blown-up version that showed the boat's name in blurred letters.

He glanced down, then threw out, "Yeah?"

"Do you know her?"

"Sure. I read the papers, same as anyone. Julie Nevins."

"I'm thinking she was on the *Rosalita,* at least once."

He didn't argue, but he also didn't feel it was necessary to agree. "Julie Nevins was pretty young in that photo. I'm guessing not even twenty. And she grew up, what, three blocks away from here?"

"Ain't that something." He took a last pull on his cigarette, then flicked it past her head. His gaze moved down to her wallet, which was still waiting in her hand. She pulled out a twenty, dropped it on the counter. As he reached for it, she withdrew it.

"Julie's been dead a good long time," he pointed out.

"So how can it hurt her, to talk?"

He grinned his acknowledgment. "String bean of a kid when she first started hanging 'round by Cappy's boat. From there to what she grew up into? Who would have figured that to happen? Cappy pretty much adopted her, even gave her a badge that said 'Junior Crewman.' If she had parents, they never seemed to mind. Tell you one thing, she could give you an earful. She was a real little know-it-all. When she was a kid, you got to telling her off, but once she grew up . . . No one could tell her nothing anymore." Still he let his gaze slide over the photo admiringly.

He took another tug on the bill. Emma released it, and it disappeared into his pants pocket. She set out another.

"What about Arthur Nevins?"

"The piece of shit that killed her? I hardly saw the guy. He came here maybe twice to pick her up." His mouth pursed at the taste of something so nasty. "As for opinions, he ought to be dead instead of wasting our hard-earned money." He spat, leveling the spray in the same direction as the discarded cigarette. Taking his payment, he coiled back onto his stool, his hands smoothing his knees.

Forty dollars didn't go as far as it used to, Emma thought ruefully. She took in the dock that stretched out past her, a motley variety of speedboats and cabin cruisers were berthed here, along with two large day fishing charter boats. Taking another twenty out of the wallet, she didn't set it on the counter, kept it in the palm of her hand and said, "Jason Samuels."

"Who?"

Emma didn't repeat the name. He was clearly testing her.

"I don't know him," the man tried next. Didn't bother reaching for the money either.

"I think you do," she said.

"Nope." And he leaned over, shutting the wooden door that closed up the window in her face.

The boats bobbed in the water. Not another sign of a living, breathing human being. She turned and tripped over the dog. It had managed to insinuate itself into her path. The animal lay on its back, its paws stiffly extended, not even bothering to open its eyes.

A healthy dose of paranoia kept her checking behind to make sure no one was following her. Emma crossed the Shore Parkway via a footbridge. During the walk, she noted a jogger, and an elderly man taking his miniature poodle out for its constitutional. Neither of them seemed particularly threatening.

Turning onto 29th Street, she paused in front of Julie's childhood home, a squat bungalow that looked in desperate need of some tender, loving care. The aqua tint on the exterior walls was flaking off, and the postage-stamp lawn was a patch of mud.

Julie had lived at this address till she was fourteen. Then her parents had divorced. Her mom had moved with her to Bay Ridge; her dad had left the state. Perhaps it had been their rancor Julie fled, venturing a mere quarter mile to the marina, using it as her own safe harbor. Really, Emma decided, she could imagine almost anything about who Julie had been as a child, they'd never pressed for details. The focus had been on Arthur; they'd spent their time attempting to develop his humanity, even, Emma knew, at the expense of his victim's. She reached into her purse and extracted the photo. To her eyes, Julie Nevins seemed both at ease and completely in her element.

Only a few blocks more and she would reach the subway platform. As she walked, Emma imagined Julie cruising these same streets. Who was Julie Nevins? she wondered, and blamed herself for not asking the question sooner. Yes, she'd arrived on the scene after the verdict was in, but that wasn't nearly a good enough reason. She'd taken her lead from Dawn. And Dawn had been concerned with appealing the ruling. They'd had lengthy discussions about the Nevins case. All she really knew about Julie was her history with Arthur, the testimony they had about the marriage, the fights where police had been called in to adjudicate, witnesses who'd heard him screaming threats and obscenities, and of course, the order of protection. At the time, Emma had assumed that was why Dawn had neglected to look into Julie's history, why go down that road, when you figure it will simply lead to more evidence of your client's bad behavior? It made much more sense to look somewhere else.

Or did it?

Now she was much less sure. That so-called guard had been happy enough to talk, until she'd mentioned Jason Samuels's name.

Circles within circles, Emma thought. The clipping was from a story in the *Daily News*. It was time, Emma decided, to call in a favor.

"Lisa Meyerowitz," Emma told the security guard. "Tell her it's Emma Price." Lisa M. had once been the bane of her existence. At the Bronx

High School of Science, Lisa had been voted prom queen. The heading under her photograph in the yearbook was "Future Mistress of the Universe." She'd risen like cream to the top, while Emma had spent four years smoking pot and cutting class every chance she got. Lisa had graduated second in the class, while Emma ended up near the bottom of the nine-hundred-and-eighty-student pack of graduates, managing ironically to ace her SATs. One of her mother's closest friends was dean of admissions at Barnard. Emma was admitted, which surprised her more than anyone.

During those formative years, Lisa, who lived down the block, had been spoken of in glowing terms at their dinner table. She was the stellar light in an ever-darkening sky of teenage trouble and angst. So when Lisa chose Barnard over Yale, it was a surprise to virtually everyone.

Emma had good reason to hate her, and did, right up until the moment Lisa approached her in the quad where Emma was sunning herself, cutting her Great Books class for about the umpteenth time. Lisa plunked down next to her, saying, "I hear you sell the best pot on campus. I wonder if I could buy a lid off you."

Perfect Lisa tarnished. It developed that Lisa had her own troubles, the main one being extreme travel phobias. She couldn't drive. Couldn't get on a plane. And couldn't ride the subway. Buses were the only mode of transportation she could face. And she never slept, or as Lisa liked to put it, "Sleep does not become me." Her life was circumscribed by anxiety, and until the dawn of Prozac, she was pretty much a basket case. Weed calmed her down. She told Emma all this within the first twenty minutes, as they ambled back to Emma's cubbyhole of a room, and the rest, as they say, was history.

Lisa now edited the Metro section of the *News*. Once she'd been touted as a possible managing editor, but then she'd had her first child; then, hot on the girl's heels, a baby boy. When she'd come back after both maternity leaves, Lisa had noticed a distinct sea change: she'd been put on the mommy track, and the only way to get off was to work twice as hard as her male contemporaries. She'd thought about doing it, but then her husband hit her with a bombshell: he was tired of living in the closet, he was gay, and damn it, he was proud.

And that was Lisa Meyerowitz, who was waving at Emma, calling her name, and looking, as always, slightly frazzled.

"You were in luck," Lisa said. "Not just the photo, but the original we cropped it off of." Handing it to Emma, she added: "And would you look who the lady's standing next to."

No surprise at all to see it was Jason Samuels, though what was hanging between them did take her aback. A shark that was so huge it literally dwarfed them.

On the back, the date: June 17, 1991; and the place, Brooklyn Bay Marina, Sheepshead Bay, Brooklyn.

"Where did the photo come from?" Emma asked, "It looks like a shot the family could have given you."

"Sorry, I've got absolutely no idea. I wasn't even working Metro back then." Lisa added a slip of paper. "Danny Lutz filed it; this is his number at the *L.A. Times*. Lucky bastard. Wish it was me."

Emma knew better than to respond truthfully. "It'll be your turn one day," she said. Los Angeles? Lisa?

"Right, when pigs fly," Lisa retorted.

Exactly, Emma thought. Lisa would never get on that plane, she'd barely managed to live at Barnard for four years. After which she'd moved back to Riverdale, commuted to graduate school at Columbia Journalism. She and her husband had bought an apartment ten blocks from her parents' house. Prozac could only help you so much.

"Samuels and a murdered hottie. That's got to be newsworthy. Looks like they at least fished together. And the couple that fishes together . . ."

Emma started to slip the photo away.

"Hey," Lisa told her. "Friend or no, you don't get the original. I'll make a copy." Holding it by the edges, Lisa paused, and Emma saw her mind working away. "Samuels took on the Nevins case, right?"

"When did you find that out?"

"About five minutes after you called. Word travels fast in the corridors of power. Now it turns out he knew the victim. Odd, representing the murderous husband when you were friendly with the ex-wife."

"Lisa, go easy with this. Give me a little time."

"It's a story, and a good one."

"Right now, you're the only journalist who knows anything about this."

"Really?" Lisa asked.

"I swear."

"And if I keep hands off for a little while, what's my special present going to be?"

"An exclusive interview."

"With who? You?" She laughed. "Try again."

"Look, I've had a pretty rough couple of days."

"Sorry." Lisa managed to sound sincere, for at least a heartbeat.

"How about I tell you a different version of what happened to Dawn." And before she could agree, Emma launched into an abridged version of the events that had filled up the last few days. Lisa's expression darkened, her forehead knotted.

"This is totally on the level?"

"Totally."

Lisa took a long look at the photograph. "Okay, I'll give you time. But you have to swear you'll keep me informed."

"I swear," Emma agreed. "Thanks."

"Don't thank me yet," Lisa told her.

Gazing at the photo one last time, she added, "Fishing. Man against nature, how do those idiots manage to believe that? On the one hand, you've got this guy with his two-thousand-dollar titanium rod-and-reel. On the other, the poor shark, who's basically got one thought and one thought only, where's my next meal coming from? What kind of a fair fight is that? Men! They're such idiots."

Lisa's disgust was fervent. There was no point in clarifying her vision of the event in question, though Emma guessed that Julie was as likely to have landed that fish as Samuels was.

# Chapter Nineteen

"We have to stop meeting like this," Fitzsimmons said. The lot was packed with vehicles; in the middle of them, the aging Subaru with a crack in the windshield. The span of the Verrazano Bridge glowed copper-red in front of the setting sun, and there was a wind, blowing ragged off the water. People dumped things out here, rusted engines and tires, this car with the man's dead body inside.

A car that had apparently been the deceased's palace; half-empty Burger King bags, soda cans, and copies of several-days-old newspapers. On the dashboard, a Hawaiian hula dancer in a grass skirt. Fitzsimmons stuck a gloved finger on it, to provoke the wiggle. "Ever visited our fiftieth state?" he asked.

"No."

"You should go, like a little piece of heaven." Jiggling the dancer again, he added, "Man, did I get wasted the whole time I was out there. And the local girls. Hot as they come."

*As if I want to know,* Laurence thought.

"According to the wallet, his name's Victor Bannion. The reason I got called? The cop who caught it found this in his wallet. Put the name through the system and came up with me as the primary."

He showed the evidence bag with the scrap of paper inside, Emma's name on it, her address.

"Sure looks like the description she turned in. Too bad we can't get him to speak a few words."

Lots of things were too bad, Laurence thought, like not being able to get this guy alone somewhere when he was alive. Not having the pleasure of trying to at least make him suffer. He looked too peaceful by half.

"Here's what the M.E. thought did it," Fitzsimmons added, lifting the sleeve to show the old track marks and the newest. "No needle, though. Either he dropped it somewhere else, then drove out here to die, or else someone was with him. What are your thoughts, detective?"

"I'm not betting on natural causes."

"See," Fitzsimmons said sarcastically. "That's why they pay you the big bucks."

# Chapter Twenty

Emma clicked her cell phone off before slipping into the back of the courtroom. Samuels was in the middle of a cross-examination. A narcotics detective wearing a badly fitting sports jacket and a pair of dark blue pants. Samuels, in contrast, wore a suit that had a certain timeless elegance; Emma guessed it was tailor-made.

"So you were in the car, across the street, and you saw my client, standing in front of this building." Samuels had the chalkboard up, and he was using the pointer to make it easy for the jury to follow. "The time again, Officer Lytton?"

"It was five-forty."

"On November seventeenth of last year, correct?"

"Yes."

"And you saw my client, you saw Mr. Richards, correct? You were in your car, just over here." Tapping again with the pointer. "It was getting dark, but you are certain you recognized my client?"

"Yes, positive."

"Positive?"

"That's what I said."

Samuels nodded, as if agreeing, albeit after the fact. "How was the weather that evening, detective?"

"Fine," Lytton said quietly.

"Cool?"

He paused, apparently sensing the trap.

Samuels had lifted a sheet of paper off the defense table. He dropped it in front of Lytton. "Detective, I'd like you to read that?"

"What is it?"

"The weather report for November seventeenth."

"Objection," came from the prosecutor's side. Samuels managed to barrel over it, then add, for the jury's edification, "That afternoon it was raining. Two inches of rain recorded in Central Park in under two hours. But you could make out my client? You saw him clear as day?"

A few minutes later, Judge Levy called for a lunch break, and Emma knew where he was off to; at the Five Brothers coffee shop, there was a small back room. The judge was a regular at the noontime poker game. He always took an extremely generous lunch break.

Samuels conferred with his client. The audience, such as it was, filed out: two metro reporters hoping for a story on a slow news day. Emma slid toward the aisle when the coast was clear, and only Samuels, his client, and the court officer were left. His back was to her; then the client was led out and Samuels packed up his briefcase, snapped it shut, and turned to leave.

She was up to him by then.

"A minute of your time," Emma said.

"You're stalking me now?"

He tried to shove past her. "Mr. Samuels, please."

"What story have you cooked up now?"

"Julie Nevins."

"What about her?"

"You didn't mention knowing her." Emma held out the photo. He glanced at it, then took another look, his jaw clenching. Finally, he managed a barking laugh. "Who doctored that?"

"No one."

"Bullshit. Is this your way of making yourself indispensable?"

"Does Arthur know?"

"Know what?"

"That you and Julie were acquainted?"

"What do you want from me?" he demanded.

"The truth," Emma said.

"You're asking for something, that's clear, but I don't think it's the truth."

He smiled thinly. "You ought to let this go," he said. "I believe it may be affecting your mental health. As a mother of two, it would behoove you to be concerned. Shall I continue?"

Emma didn't know what to say. Was this a threat?

"Liam. Fourteen. Goes to LaGuardia High School. Katherine. Two plus. Right now she's at day care. I believe it's called Tiny Tots in Flatbush. Now, I have a luncheon engagement."

He was gone.

Emma felt the anxiety coursing through her body.

"Bastard," she said through clenched teeth.

It had been a calculated risk, showing him the photograph. She'd expected anger on his part, certainly, but this? She felt physically sick. Emma had hoped that by using it, she could jar something loose, use the element of surprise against him. She's been foolish, he'd proved himself more than a match for her.

Emma's phone vibrated insistently. Lifting it, she saw a voice-mail message. It was from Laurence.

"You're certain it's the same guy?"

"Yes. Absolutely positive." As if she could ever forget that face.

Fitzsimmons sat opposite her in the interview room at the 61st; between them lay portraits of a dead man, looking way too serene for her taste.

"What did Detective Solomon tell you about him?"

"That his name is Victor Bannion, and he's got a P.I. license."

"Yeah, there's that." Fitzsimmons's face colored. "He has an office over in Bensonhurst, lived right above it. Sent some guys over to check, but apparently we weren't the first ones looking in. The place was trashed."

"How long do you think he's been dead?"

"The M.E.'s trying to pin it down. Last known sighting was over by your place, Tuesday. We need to speak to that guy who had the run-in with him."

Emma wrote down her contractor's number.

"Great."

It was now or never. Emma tried to decide how to spin it or whether he could even be trusted. And she felt Laurence watching through the glass. He'd come to get her, driven her out here, not even bothering to chide her as he'd walked her to the door. He'd touched her on the shoulder once, trying to give her whatever strength was needed.

"You know who Jason Samuels is?"

"Sure. Who doesn't."

Emma took out the photograph and laid it on the table. Fitzsimmons bent over, taking a careful look.

"I recognize two of the three," he admitted, albeit grudgingly. "Your point?"

"We were representing Arthur Nevins."

"Were?"

"Either he's decided to hire Mr. Samuels. Or Mr. Samuels has volunteered to work for him."

"Really." Fitzsimmons let out a low whistle.

"I recently brought this photograph to Mr. Samuels's attention and asked him why he hadn't disclosed his relationship with the victim. He told me to back off. Made threats against me, leveled them against my children. Mr. Samuels knew their names, as well as which schools they attended."

"Creepy," Fitzsimmons agreed.

Laurence was standing out front, working his cell phone. Holding up his hand for another second, he said, "I'll be there when I can. Yes, I understand what you mean by situation." Clicking it off, he thrust the phone back into his pocket. "Damn things make you always available."

Didn't she know. "What's going on?"

"Upstanding, churchgoing folk want to put in their two cents on the Hawkins case," he said. "The lieutenant needs me to give them some face time."

"He wouldn't rather take care of this himself?"

Laurence gave her a look that said she should know better.

"The man just got finished saying how he was sure they'd respond better to someone from their own community." He pulled the car out of the spot with a squeal of tires, a physical assertion of his obvious frustration. "I called up the day care, they're going to have Katie ready for you."

"Thanks," she said.

He made an extremely hard right at the corner. Emma had to work to keep herself upright. Between his anger, and her anxiety, she thought, they were a pretty pair. "Maybe I'm overreacting," she ventured, as much to calm him, as anything. "He's not going after my kids. He'd have to be crazy to do that."

"Emma, if you don't watch over them, who will?" Laurence pointed out.

You, she wanted to counter. Instead, she punched in Liam's cell phone number again. And got his message. "Hi, this is Liam, I'm not here right now. If you want to leave a message go ahead. I'll get back to you whenever."

She'd done as requested. Left message after increasingly irate message from the precinct, telling him to please get himself back to Laurence's apartment as soon as school let out.

"How'd Fitzsimmons respond when you brought up Samuels?"

Emma smiled.

"What?" Laurence asked.

"Creepy, that's what he termed it."

"And what's he going to do about it?"

"Take it under advisement."

"I could have predicted that. He's cautious, Fitz is."

While Laurence Solomon was anything but, he'd seemingly undergone a transformation.

They drove, flashing lights giving them permission to weave through traffic. In a few more minutes they'd arrive at the door of Tiny Tots.

"While you were in there, I did a little research on Bannion," Laurence said. "He's got a file, all right. Only it's from Nassau County, seems that he was one of their boys in blue, before he took early retirement. The exact same division as Lowry. Same time as the Nevins case broke." He shot a glance her way, their eyes met. "Gets you to thinking, doesn't it?"

He was right. It most certainly did.

# Chapter Twenty-one

Emma wished she had an answer for that. For any of it. Wished it fervently as she maneuvered the stroller through the door. Liam's jacket was thrown on the couch, his backpack lying next to it. Emma heaved a sigh of relief.

"He's home," she said to Laurence. "Lee?"

"Lee-um." From Katherine Rose, who clambered up the stairs to find him. "Let me in!" she demanded, pounding on the door.

"Katie, stop!" Emma said firmly.

"Hold on," Liam called out from inside.

Emma smelled the distinct odor of incense. A telltale retro giveaway. She took up where Katie had left off, knocking insistently. All she needed was this, her fourteen-year-old coming home early to smoke pot. She'd have to toss the room.

Emma definitely didn't have the energy.

Could he have planned a worse moment, she asked herself? The answer was a resounding no.

"Open up now," she insisted. Laurence was behind her, looking alternately nervous and harried. "Go on," she told him as the lock turned. "I can handle this."

Could she really? No sweet smell lacing the air, only the incense, and candles, and the bed that had clearly been made in the last minute, sheets still half off, with Liam's girlfriend sitting on the desk chair, pretending to be studious, her hair in tangles, her shirt buttoned wrong.

"Cleo," Emma said.

Turning, she blushed. "Hi, Mrs. Price."

"Does Cleo's mom know?" Emma demanded after Cleo had fled for the relative safety of her own dysfunctional home.

"Know what?" Sullen yet sheepish, the very same expression his father wore much too much of the time.

"Liam, come on. That she's sexually active? You're both fourteen. You know I'm going to have to talk to her mom about this."

"No you don't! It's none of her business. Or yours."

"How do you figure that?"

"Look, she's not getting pregnant or anything."

"How reassuring."

"Mom, you're so naive." Put in that incredibly supercilious tone that only a teenager could imagine was appropriate. She counted down internally, to avoid slapping him silly.

"Liam, having sex with someone, it makes the relationship much more complicated."

"Like it's ever not complicated," he threw back.

Touché. She supposed he'd been preparing for this moment for a while. Fourteen. She'd been fifteen; did a year really make any difference?

"I know you love each other," she said, trying to go the alternate route. "But this makes it so much harder. If you break up—"

"We're not going to break up," he said resolutely.

"You're planning your wedding already?" Hearing her own flippant tone, Emma grimaced internally. "Sorry," she offered, but it was too late. He scowled at her.

"You just don't get it," he said.

But she did. Only a few hours ago, Samuels had threatened to take him from her permanently. Ironic. Because, in one sense, he was already long gone. Emma didn't bother telling him that his attempt to escape was futile. He had already internalized her. You could run from a parent, run far and fast, but you could never really loose the hold they had on you.

It was both a curse and a blessing, Emma thought.

"You're grounded," she said. "You're coming home right after school. And staying in every weekend. Plus, from now on you're going to be dropped off every morning and picked up every single afternoon."

"Jesus, it's not like I killed someone or anything."

"This isn't about Cleo," Emma said. "I haven't been entirely honest with you. I wanted to protect you. But I see now I shouldn't have done that. You have a right to know exactly what's been going on. Starting with how I ended up in the hospital."

*Dora the Explorer* was blaring in the background. It was the only show that kept Katherine fully occupied. Glancing at her watch, Emma saw they had another ten minutes. She'd have to give him the abridged version.

That night, they ordered in, Chinese: cold noodles with sesame sauce, chicken fried rice, dumplings, and Peking duck. Eating seemed to lift everyone's spirits. After the meal was over, Katherine Rose forced them into a game of Candyland.

"Mom, your turn," Liam said, nudging her.

A roll of the die. A great leap forward. Into the Molasses Swamp. Emma was trying her best not to think, which meant that a million thoughts were colliding inside. Her confrontation with Samuels had left a residue of anxiety and anger. And there was the dubious relief of finding out Bannion was dead. A threat had been tendered; if the devil she knew was no longer around, what about his replacement?

Katherine Rose started rifling through the deck, giving herself the best cards.

"I win," she insisted. Liam rolled his eyes, then gave up and nodded, laughing.

"Lee-um," Katherine chanted.

He stood, attempting to beat a retreat.

"Do you have homework?" Emma asked.

"I guess."

"You guess?"

"I'll go do it."

Damn straight you will, Emma told herself. When he had escaped to the relative safety of the bedroom, Emma paced. Katherine Rose was busy, rifling through a pile of picture books. It gave Emma time to ponder what the currently deceased Mr. Bannion had hoped to gain by breaking into her house. He meant to kill me, she told herself, but wondered if that was all he'd been after. His office and apartment had been ransacked as well. Secrets, Emma thought, they tumbled out at the oddest times. And in the oddest places. That earring she'd discovered in Dawn's desk, for one thing. That was a mystery she felt she would never be able to solve.

"To bed," she said to Katherine Rose, and began the endless ritual. While she did, she pondered what was hiding behind Liam's closed door. And how she'd stumbled onto something he'd tried to keep private, though if he'd really wanted to, wouldn't he have found another place? Teenagers did, the world over.

You went one of two ways when you decided to become sexually active, Emma told herself. You were either obsessively vigilant, or you wanted to be found out.

She'd opted for the latter. She could admit it now, though at the time . . .

"I see you've decided on the Pill."

Her mother had cornered her in the kitchen, the plastic case in her hand. Emma could remember the entire confrontation as if it had taken place yesterday, the smoke from her mother's ever-present cigarette curling toward the ceiling. The air that day had been oppressive and leaden, late August with a thunderstorm threatening.

"Aren't you just a little young?" Louise had demanded.

"I know how to take care of myself, don't worry," Emma had retorted.

An absurd statement considering. She had been skating along the edge of danger, the boy she'd chosen clearly the least reliable; eight years later he would be dead of a heroin overdose.

"Don't do what I did," Louise had warned her.

And Emma had given back the appropriately hostile teenage response: "Mom, I'm just sleeping with him, I'm not going to marry him and ruin my life."

Her mother had stood there for a very long moment, then her face closed up, and it sat there, the hurt Emma had freely dished out.

*Like you.*

There were so many things one got to regret saying and doing, Emma thought. That was the bitterness in life. She shook her head as if to dislodge the image of her own petulant, prideful self. Because, she knew, she'd been lying to her mother, and lying to herself.

Still, what was even more remarkable was that her mother had forgiven her for it, had loved her, despite her own best efforts.

Emma lifted the phone and dialed Will's number. Of course, Jolene answered.

"It's Emma," she said. "Is he there?"

"No." Her voice sounded funny.

"It's important," Emma said. "Is he still at work?"

"I don't know where he's gone," Jolene said. It came to Emma that she'd been crying.

"What's wrong?"

"As if you give a good goddamn."

"Jolene, tell me."

"He left me, okay? We had a fight, and he told me he was going and he wasn't coming back. I'll bet you're thrilled."

And with that, she slammed the phone down.

# Chapter Twenty-two

The Right Reverend Ernest Garber of the Seventh Day Adventist Church was diligently popping his cuffs. Laurence had read about people doing this, but he'd never personally witnessed it before. Lots of things you didn't think you'd ever see, Laurence told himself. Garber was just the tip of the iceberg. Outside, on the steps of the police station, the choir section of the Reverend's church sang a hymn in praise of dead Sister Hawkins. Meanwhile, the Right Reverend had moved on to checking the buttons up and down the front of his white shirt, then adjusting his tie, and finally jerking his chin. It was a tic, Laurence had figured out, something like Tourette's, only the Right Reverend wasn't bleating out a stream of curse words, which might, in the end, have been easier to stomach.

"Sister was a righteous woman," Garber said yet again. Like that meant something. From where they were sitting, Laurence could hear the steady chanting.

*What do we want?*

*Justice.*

*When do we want it?*

*Now.*

*Amen, Jesus.*

He'd left Emma and the kids behind for this? He was worrying over what had happened after he turned tail, what sort of lecture she'd had to give, why she hadn't called to tell him the upshot. Maybe she resented that he'd had to leave, he thought, then told himself that was crazy, Emma wasn't the type, and she knew all about the job. How an order was an order. You ignored your lieutenant at your own peril.

Anyway, he'd already put in a call. There would be someone checking up on them while he was gone. But he kept going back over it; could he really protect them? Was having a car outside enough? Laurence knew the answer.

Meanwhile, his duty, according to the good lieutenant, was to get these people to talk sense. So here he was, riding in, Mr. Black Knight on his lily-white horse. It was making him feel physically ill, because what he wanted to do with Garber and the rest of his bunch of missionaries was to throw their sorry asses into a holding cell, then starve them for a while, see how much they liked it.

The Right Reverend daintily sipped on a complimentary soft drink. "Now, Rhonda, she was a good, God-fearing woman, don't come any better than her," Garber was telling him.

Good and dead, Laurence thought.

"Took in those strays, year after year. Never had no trouble with any of them. Raised them up, made sure they was neat and tidy, took them over to school and made sure they minded their lessons. Never had no trouble with any of them, till this batch came. Now what we got, we got you calling her unfit, got the news screaming about it, this woman, how she had no heart in her body, how she was practicing devil worship, starving them for sacrifice, all the rest, we got this story this boy has made up, and I don't know who's been whispering in his ear, or if it's all of his own accord, but I'm telling you, this boy? He's lying, plain and simple, blaming her when she's not here to say what's right. Trying to hold her accountable for his going and picking up that weapon, no one telling him how to do that but his own self. You hear me?"

"I hear you, Reverend. I understand your concern."

"Concern? What's that word s'posed to mean, son?"

Son? He was in no way young enough for that slap, Garber was likely his contemporary. Of course, the way it had been aimed was intentional, used in all its dismissive, small-minded retrograde thrust by this man with his head of black hair oiled tight to the scalp. Garber shot his cuffs again, playing with the streamlining buttons on his shirt all up to the top one, tugging the damn tie. Like to hang the man with it, Solomon thought, his patience just about run through.

"What we got here is a decent woman, doing more than most. What we need to know is how you're going to make this right for her." Garber moved closer, as if talking in confidence. "Now, I know you didn't have a thing to do with how the television gets ahold of this, spreads it right across the page and makes it fly. There are things they might want to know. That boy Karim was mixing with the wrong crowd. Sister told me about it."

"This was when?"

"Not long ago."

"So, Reverend, why do you think those three kids look like scarecrows?"

"High metabolism. The girls probably starving themselves, it's the fashion."

People saw exactly what they wanted to see, Laurence thought. It never ceased to amaze him.

"Mrs. Hawkins tell you that too?" Laurence asked. "Bruises up their backs. You think maybe they threw themselves against the walls?"

"All I know is what I know," Garber said stiffly. "Those children were trying her, the Bible says spare the rod."

"The Bible say something about flaying a child? Starving them to death? How about burning their fingers, holding them over the flame on the stove, how about locking them up in a closet, making them sleep on the floor by your bed so you can keep an eye on them. Dogs get their own nice pillows, not these kids, but then I'm sure you know 'cause you've visited Mrs. Hawkins in her home setting."

The man's mouth opened, then shut like a trap. He shook his head. "You ought to know better, children telling stories and you're going to listen."

"In my experience, children tell a lot less stories than adults."

"You're not calling my word into question?" Tapping his chest as if the idea was morally offensive.

"Why not? You're saying because you call yourself Right

Reverend that makes you different from the rest? Experience teaches me otherwise."

"What experience is it you're referring to, pray tell?"

"I work Homicide, Reverend."

"What's that supposed to be a reference to? You know, you ought to be ashamed of yourself," Garber said. "This is your people we're speaking of."

Now, that was tired! "My people?" Laurence stood and Garber did too, but that didn't help him much, there was at least a six-inch gap in Laurence's favor. "You know, Mr. Garber, what you ought to be asking yourself is how you can live with the way you let those kids get mistreated on your watch. If you want to go blaming someone for what happened to God-fearing Mrs. Hawkins, you might as well go look in the mirror. My final words."

Off he stormed. Laurence had pretty much fucked that up but good.

He couldn't help the smile breaking out. It stayed with him right up until the lieutenant poked his head in.

"How'd it go?"

"Perfect," Laurence said.

Just then from outside, the call.

"What do God's children want?" Garber asked over the bullhorn.

"Justice!"

"And praise the Lord, when do we expect it? Brothers and sisters, your answer?"

"Now! Right now!"

Justice.

Standing, Laurence gathered his things, thinking, *Hell, he was with them on that.*

Only a fool went round threatening a man's family and expecting him to idly sit by. Jason Samuels might not look like a fool, but he was damn sure acting like one.

# Chapter Twenty-three

Finding Will wasn't easy. He was not at the office, and messages left on his cell phone fell on purposely deaf ears. Emma had an idea why. She knew Will. Knew he'd undoubtedly made plans in advance, he wasn't nearly as casual as his persona made him seem. After all, he'd been having an affair with Jolene for a good six months before he had told her he was calling it quits. He was a man who definitely did not like being on his own.

Pru Ramone. It made Emma queasy to think of him with that girl, and that was all she was, a girl, barely older than their own son. Still, where else was he bunking? And why wouldn't he return her calls? There were only two viable possibilities: one, that he was otherwise engaged, and two, that he was ashamed.

"Stop!" Liam called out. "Mom, you'd better come here."

She did, out to the living room where Katherine Rose was playing difficult to catch. She had spilled the contents of Emma's purse all over the floor. "Mine," she insisted, waving Emma's bank card in midair.

Emma screamed, "Put that down now!"

For the first time ever, Katherine Rose stopped in her tracks. She looked up at her mother and dropped the card, there on the rug. Then she backed up, her bottom lip quivering. "Sorry," she said. And put her hand up to shield herself from the expected blow.

One that Emma had never, ever let fly. She'd wanted to, more than a few times, but the worst she'd ever done was shake the child a little too hard once. Katherine hadn't noticed, but Emma had, and it had scared her.

"I'm not going to hit you," she said.

Her daughter's hand went down slowly. "Sorry," she said again, cautiously.

"Oh sweet pea." Looking around at the mess on the floor, then back at her difficult child, Emma opened her arms to embrace her. Knowing she shouldn't, because it was sending the wrong message, but this was her child, actually cringing in front of her. "Who's been hitting you?" she asked gently.

"It was Jolene," Liam said. "I didn't know what to do." He looked so miserable. And there they were, suddenly, huddled in a group, Katherine breaking into somewhat elaborate sobs.

"You won't ever have to go there again," Emma promised.

At her feet, the contents of her purse, including the switchblade. She'd forgotten she had it along, having stuck it into the side pocket of her purse. Emma was grateful that Katherine Rose had chosen to play with the plastic cards instead. The purse had been ostensibly out of reach, hanging off the coatrack, and it was certainly off limits. Katherine knew that, but her daughter, Emma noted, loved living dangerously. Emma stuck the knife out of reach, high up on the topmost shelf of the bookcase.

Liam was helping, and Katherine Rose too, which was a mixed blessing, since the pills from the ibuprofen vial were spread liberally around the rug, being stepped on and crushed. Emma picked them up, one at a time, and dropped them back into their container.

"That's got to be the biggest tiger shark ever," Liam said, lifting the photo of Julie Nevins and Jason Samuels.

"How do you know it's a tiger shark?"

"From the markings. See the stripes? We just finished a cycle on creatures from the deep," Liam added. "Mr. Nesbitt says I'm a regular fount of information."

Emma laughed. And then the cell phone rang. Reading the number, she saw it was Will. She couldn't help hesitating a second more before springing it open.

"What's going on?" he asked. "Are the kids okay?"

She gave him credit, he sounded authentically worried.

"Watch your sister like a hawk," she said to Liam, then went to the next room and shut the door. "It's been an eventful day," she said. "For both of us apparently."

"You talked to Jolene, I guess." Will sounded slightly shamefaced.

"We had a very abbreviated chat."

"I know what you're thinking," he said.

No, you really don't, Emma thought, but had the good sense to keep it to herself.

"Em, you can't imagine what a shrew she turned into," he added. "I was always the problem. She was always on my back. About the work. About the hours I had to put in. Of all people to start with it too, she was a producer, for Christ's sake. She knew what she was getting into."

"Unlike, say, me?"

"That was different," he insisted. "You had reasons to be pissed off."

Nice of him to say eons after the fact. "You mean it was all about your job?"

"Yes."

Bullshit, she thought.

"So where are you?"

"Chav said I could bunk at his guest house for a while."

"You're that close with Chavitz? I didn't realize."

"What's going on there?" Will asked, swiftly changing the subject. "It sounded like an emergency."

"They found the man who assaulted me," Emma said.

"They did? Terrific!"

"Found him dead. And it looks like he had help getting that way."

"Is that good or bad?" he asked.

Emma hesitated. She felt wrung out, and to bring up Samuels, to explain, would undoubtedly provoke a laundry list of new questions. She just couldn't deal with it right now. "Suffice it to say, the kids need watching. Can you help with that?"

"Of course." And of course he didn't offer specifics. Chavitz's guest house was, she assumed, in Greenwich. He wasn't exactly around the corner. And Emma knew better than to ask whether he was alone.

"One more thing," she said, knowing she couldn't, in all good conscience, leave this for later. "It's about Liam. I came home early, and it seems I interrupted something. He and Cleo were in the bedroom."

"Oops. That must have been embarrassing."

He sounded so blithe about it, so completely unfazed. What had she expected, Emma wondered? He was probably proud of his son, Will's great moment had been detailed for her, blow by blow. Men. They really were from Mars.

"It wasn't just embarrassing. It was upsetting. We have to talk with Cleo's mother about this."

"Why?"

"I can't keep my suspicions from her."

"You're not understanding me," Will said, quietly. And then she did. She really was dense. He'd known!

"Liam told you? He said he was having sex with his girlfriend, and you didn't think to mention it to me?"

"Look, Lee asked me not to."

"So this was just buddy buddy? I don't care what he asked you! Will, you're his father, not his friend."

"Now, don't get nuts about this."

"I'd hardly call this getting nuts," she countered.

"No? Look, I thought it over carefully. I decided to keep this confidential. I believe I have a right to make that decision. What makes you think you know how to deal with this better than I do?"

"We parent together," Emma said. "It's essential that to do that, you keep me informed."

"Not when he needed this kept secret."

"Will, you shouldn't have made the promise then."

"And? He wouldn't have talked to me if I didn't."

"That was the chance you'd take."

"Emma, be reasonable."

She was being reasonable, Emma told herself, eminently so. For instance, she hadn't raised her voice to a harridan pitch. She hadn't threatened him with physical harm, and she hadn't accused him of trying to win their son over by pretending to be his best pal.

"You'd rather he talked to me than not, wouldn't you? I don't understand what *you* expect."

"Honesty," Emma told him. "But then, that's never been your forte."

There was a long, hostile silence. Then he drew breath and said, "It's been a really shitty day for me. I need to get some sleep. How about we figure out what you need me to do tomorrow."

Would tomorrow be any different? Only in the mind of the eternal child Will.

To bed then, first Katherine Rose, then Liam. She managed the first with subtle bribery and diligence, the second by simply ignoring the fact that his light was still on till half past eleven, then knocking on the door and saying, "It's time."

Amazingly, he complied, but then he was chastened, she supposed, and worried to boot. Laurence had still not called or showed. Not like him, and she finally broke down, leaving a message on his cell, asking what he was up to. She tried for a light tone of voice, not that either one of them was going to be taken in, in any way.

Emma wandered from the bedroom out to the living room. Pressing back the curtains, she saw the black-and-white cruiser settled in for the night. Laurence had apparently sent them in his place.

It was hardly an adequate substitute. Emma tried watching TV but found it impossible to focus on the selection of mind-numbing fare—several grade-D action movies starring Jean-Claude Van Damme, multiple reruns of *Law & Order,* and, on Bravo, no surprise, a documentary that they seemed to show in perpetuity, *The Origins of Cirque de Soleil.*

Giving up, she picked up the crumpled photo of the outsized tiger shark and its human companions and stuck it inside the Nevins file. Danny Lutz, that reporter from L.A., had never called her back. She could leave another message for him; after all, it was three hours earlier on the other coast.

Emma did. And felt no better for it. No closer to the truth. No more secure.

A tiger shark, Liam had said. Funny, the odd things kids knew. Emma herself had been the repository of all sorts of useless information, able to list every known breed of horse and dog. By eleven, she'd managed to memorize the winners of all three major East Coast stakes races, the Belmont, Kentucky Derby, and Preakness. You gave her the year, she'd tell you who. Citation. Gallant Fox. Man o' War.

When you were a child, your mind was a blank slate, ready to be scribbled on.

As an adult, she had trouble remembering her friends' names, particularly if she ran into them unexpectedly. Embarrassing moments. Pregnant pauses. Emma was becoming a specialist in both.

Stepping into Laurence's office, she saw the computer was still on, only sleeping, a dull pulse. Opening it, she realized Liam had been using it. She guessed it wasn't for research but for declarations of love.

Emma knew how to find out what he'd been up to. Her finger was wrapped around the mouse, but she found herself resisting. This was Liam's private business. Even discovering him in such a compromising position didn't exactly give her the right to intrude. Not with this.

Instead, she went to the search engine, typed in "tiger shark," and pulled up the first site. There it was, the same fish but a notably smaller version. The second site showed several different kinds of sharks and gave the average weights. The one hanging on that line looked to be definitely at the high end. And it had been brought back to port in one place, and one place only. Why not, Emma thought. She typed in "Brooklyn Bay Marina Tiger Shark."

The first site that came up was New York State Marine Fish Records. Clicking on that, she scanned the list of record holders' names. Nothing on the first page; opening the second, she felt a shudder: Shark (tiger), weight 1,090 lbs., June 17, 1991, caught by angler Gregory Chavitz.

\* \* \*

When she peeled herself off the couch at four-fifty and went to check, she found Laurence fast asleep in bed. He had obviously tiptoed past sometime in the night. As quietly as possible, she gathered up her clothes and turned to go.

"Where are you off to?" he asked.

"Just getting warm."

"Then come over here." He patted the bed, and she did as requested, sliding in against him, putting her head next to the small of his back. The cold was all-pervasive; outside, the temperature had obviously fallen precipitously. There was frost etching the windows.

"When did you come in?"

"A little after two."

"I didn't think it would take that long. What happened?"

"The situation got a little complicated." And that was all he was apparently going to tell her. What happened with Liam?"

"The good news is, he's drug free, the bad . . . those were incense candles we smelled," Emma said. "They appeared to have been setting the mood."

Laurence gave her a knowing look. "So that's what he was about." At least he had the wisdom not to add "Good for him." Still, it was there, in the crinkled corners of his eyes.

"They're both fourteen, you don't think that's a little young?"

"It depends," Laurence said. "Those two, they really seem to like each other."

"And?"

"Look, I was thirteen," Laurence told her. "It didn't do any lasting damage to either one of us, as far as I can tell. Liam and this girl have been serious now a good six months. It was only a matter of time."

So reasonable, so measured. She knew he would never be able to see it the way she did. Laurence was proud of Liam, he'd joined the club, he deserved a pat on the back, a raising of the glass. For Emma, the decision to give up her virginity had been awkward, painful, and she'd decided to do it for such complicated reasons. Yes, she had loved that boy, Emma supposed, but she had also brandished her new-found sexuality, using it as a weapon.

She'd needed one to separate from her family, the discovery of the birth control pills was, for her, a way of declaring independence.

Laurence saw Liam's burgeoning sexuality as a simple, logical step. He'd taken it. Liam would too. Emma knew better. Falling in love was never simple.

There it is, she thought, the fundamental difference between us. He believes in an emotional map that's linear, and one note. How male of him. Men want everything to be so uncomplicated, so fault-free, they act accordingly. While us women, we're the ones who try to ferret out the gray areas. We're the ones who are always arguing for a subtext.

"Will knew they were sleeping together," she said. "He promised not to tell me. Liam apparently made him swear an oath of fealty."

"Oops."

Not the reaction she'd hoped for. "Oops?"

He raised an eyebrow. "What?"

"You don't think it's a big deal, obviously. But I do."

He nodded, knowing enough to stay silent.

"And Will's apparently left Jolene."

"No!"

At least, that had gotten a rise out of him. As he chewed this over, Emma thought of what she was keeping back. Chavitz, showing up in the oddest places. Where and how he fit in was unclear. But Will, unknowingly, had given her a perfect entrée.

She knew better than to blurt out the plan, half-baked as it was. Besides, Emma had watched the eleven o'clock news. There had been coverage of an angry demonstration in front of Brooklyn South headquarters. Switching channels she found one station that had even managed to get a shot of Laurence, shaking the Right Reverend's hand. The crowd had not stayed late into the night, the reporter stood in front of the empty steps, opening with "Several hours ago, a noisy group of protesters . . ."

Whatever Laurence had been doing in the interim, was apparently confidential. Two can play at that game, Emma told herself.

\* \* \*

It was sixty minutes door-to-door in a rental car. Finding Chavitz's address was the easy part. Figuring out what she was going to say was much harder. Emma had reasoned she'd have time to come up with a brilliant strategy. Wrong. All she had, on arrival, was the same weak premise. She was coming there to speak with Will, there was a crisis with their children, and she needed to take some essential face-time.

That would have to do, she decided, buzzing at the gate.

"For Will Price," she said into the intercom. "He's staying in the guest house."

A second later, her husband's voice said, "Yes?"

"It's Emma."

"Emma?"

"One and the very same."

"Here?"

"Here."

There was a very pregnant pause, followed by the crackle of the intercom. Finally, he said, "I'll come out to get you."

He'd need a little time. Time to hide any evidence of Pru Ramone, if he felt that was necessary. Of course, he could just as easily decide to boldly thrust her forward. After all, he could reason, there was no shame in this.

Who knows, Emma thought, maybe he was there alone. She should at least try to give him some credit.

The gate opened, and she drove through. Will was waiting in the driveway, in the driver's seat of an Audi TT. It was the kind of car that basically screamed out midlife crisis. He waved, pointed, and she followed behind him down the winding road framed with cedars.

The architecture was Mediterranean, and the guest house looked big enough for a family of four to live in comfortably. Behind it, the hill sloped down to Long Island Sound. A beach. Perhaps even a boat slip.

If my luck holds, Emma told herself.

"You sure surprised me," Will said.

As intended.

"Where are the kids?" he asked. As if he really thought she'd bring them.

"Laurence is watching them. I thought we should talk this over by ourselves."

A worthy beginning. He stood there, hesitating, even though he'd ferried her this far. She'd given him the benefit of the doubt, but she thought much, much better of it. Some people got smarter as they aged, she thought, others got infinitely stupider.

Then the door opened. Emma took a deep breath, preparing, smiling grimly. And then blushed, her expectations met in an entirely unpredictable way. Kirsten Rogers stood there, dressed in a pair of worn jeans and an oversized man's shirt, quite possibly Will's. Her hair was swept back off her face by a headband, and she wore no makeup, looking exactly her age. So, he did have a few surprises left in him, after all.

That is, Emma told herself, if you looked at the smaller picture.

"Come in," Kirsten said.

Emma did. Inside, the cottage was extremely well appointed, albeit with a woman's touch. Almond was the color of the sofa, chairs, and ottomans. There was an Abyssinian cat purring in front of the crackling fire. Also, the smell of fresh-brewed coffee.

Emma didn't have to ask whose place it was. Blown-up art photos by Avedon, of Kirsten as a nymphet, fresh on the movie scene, nude but shot in soft focus in a bed of autumn leaves, framed either side of the mantel.

They sat in the kitchen. The coffee was good, rich, full-bodied. Kirsten's nails, perfectly manicured and tapered, in ruby red, gripped the handle of her terra-cotta cup.

It was impossible to think of what to say, but Kirsten managed to make it easy. She chattered on about all manner of things, including her facial appointment that was at ten, in town, and the winter weather advisory that was currently in effect.

"God, snow. It's so overrated," she said. "I hate the winter more and more. Not to sound selfish, but I really had hopes for global warming."

"It doesn't work like that," Will said companionably. "Some places may actually get colder."

"Really?" She reached out, ruffling Will's hair. "I'd better go, or I'll be late. And Frances, she can be so difficult if you don't come absolutely on time."

Off she went. The car rumbled away. Emma guessed it was the Audi. Not Will's at all.

"I was going to say something to you about Kirstie last night," Will told her. "But then things got a little sticky."

Sticky, he'd always had an odd way of putting things.

"How long have you been seeing each other?"

Will shrugged. "We've known each other for a while now," he said evasively. "This wasn't planned."

Which meant in Will's peculiar argot, Emma decided, less than a month, more than an hour.

"At that dinner she and Chavitz seemed to have a definite history."

"They did, at one time."

"So they're just friends," Emma said and couldn't help casting the first stone: "Like you and Pru."

"Exactly," Will agreed. He really was shameless, she decided.

"Is Chavitz around this weekend?"

Will shrugged.

"Kirsten invited you here without telling him?"

"She doesn't have to clear things with him. They have totally separate lives."

"Living on the same piece of property? Do you really believe that, or are you just trying it on with me?"

"Emma, you're wrong about this. Completely." But he sounded tentative, then added, almost petulantly, "Besides, we're all adults."

"You're the adult who just a few days ago was trying to do a little rekindling with me."

"You misunderstood that too," Will protested.

"How so?"

"I love you in a completely different way. If you don't know that . . ."

Oddly, she did. And told herself, What was the point of dragging this out? They were both falling into their time-tested pattern of doling out blame and ladling on guilt in equal measure. It wasn't about how much you loved someone, Emma told herself; love, by itself, couldn't make a relationship work. And to discuss it was to waste time, because if she had had a Spidey-sense, it would have been tingling. She was deeply suspicious of the whole convenient setup; Kirsten falling for Will and inviting him here for the night, if not for the duration, seemed not just unlikely to her but also criminally convenient.

She almost felt sorry for her ex.

"I'd like to get out of here," she said. No need to explain that further, because doing it would take time and he likely wouldn't believe her. "How about the two of us go into town, find a nice coffee shop, and hash things out."

"Neutral ground," he said, remembering lesson number one in couples therapy. "Okay, how can it hurt?"

He went to get his down jacket. Scarf. Gloves. Out to her car, and only when they were up to it did Emma realize that something was odd. It had sunk low to the ground. She saw why. The tires had been slashed. All four of them had gashes along the seams. The vehicle was basically resting on its rims.

"Who would do that?" Will asked.

"Kirsten?"

"Oh come on. She's got nothing against you."

"You're telling me vandals happen to be hiding out in the woods around here?"

"No." He stood there shaking his head, but then how could he really comprehend the potential gravity of the situation?

"How far away are we from the main road?"

"About a mile."

"Is there a path through those woods?"

"Yes. But why?"

Because taking the main road was pretty much like committing suicide, Emma thought, but didn't waste time trying to explain it to him. Instead, she grabbed him by the arm, urging him along.

"Show me," she said.

"Emma, you're being ridiculous. All we have to do is go up to the main house."

"That's exactly what they'd like us to do."

"They?"

"I can only tell you what I know," she said. As she headed into the woods, Emma pressed in 911 on her cell phone. When the operator came on, she agreed that it was most definitely an emergency. "Someone's been in my house. Yes, they still could be here, I'm at 1781 Ravenwood. This is Kirsten Rogers. Yes, the Kirsten Rogers. Thank you. Absolutely. No, I don't mind hearing it. One never gets tired of compliments."

Shoving the phone away inside her jacket pocket, she felt for the switchblade she'd taken with her that morning, retrieving it from the shelf where she'd stashed it. Frankly, it had been the only weapon she had available, other than Laurence's sidearm. She had not felt equipped to wield a gun, especially since her training consisted of a trip with Peggy out to a firing range in Jersey. She'd been thrust back by the whiplash, landing hard on her butt. And her aim was about as good—she'd gone wide of the target. The experience had not made her feel either competent or proud.

Will was resisting, posed by the car, smiling at her apparent lunacy.

"If you show me how to get out of here, I'll forgive you for being an asshole," Emma said.

"Do you think I need forgiveness? From you?"

At least he'd ignored the asshole part. That was progress of a sort. "I'd take what I could get," Emma noted. "Humor me, why don't you."

He shrugged, then led the way through a close-knit pine grove. They emerged onto the edge of a vast stretch of lawn. To their right, the hill sloped down to Long Island Sound. The sky was gray, snow definitely on its way; below them, the water had been whipped up, there were harsh whitecaps. Two boats were moored at the dock that jutted into the water, one, a large sailboat, covered in white canvas, the other a cabin cruiser.

"You can cut across the beach," Will said. And stood there, waiting.

"Come on," she insisted.

"Not until you tell me what this is supposedly about."

They were standing in what, Emma realized, was plain sight. Not the spot she would have picked for a conference. The main house was a good two acres away, but they were standing at the edge of what, in summer, was likely a beautifully manicured lawn. All anyone would have to do to find them was look out the windows that framed the back, stretching a full two stories.

"Chavitz is involved in Dawn's murder."

"You really are nuts."

"Do you think it's a coincidence that the man Dawn died with, the man who ostensibly killed her, was an actor whom Chavitz just happened to know?"

"Yes, absolutely."

"Then why are my tires slashed? They want to make sure I don't leave here. They're afraid of what I might know."

"Oh please!" Will said.

"Will, explain the tires."

He couldn't apparently. "So why did you come out here, if it's so dangerous," he ventured. "Was it to save me?

"They?" he continued, mocking her. "Who is they? And what connection could there ever be between Greg and Dawn?"

"If I knew the answer to that I could just go and have him arrested. Him, Jason Samuels, even your new friend, Kirsten."

"Jason Samuels, the lawyer?" he asked.

"What about him? You know him?"

"Not personally. But he does handle Pru's contracts."

"You know that because?" Emma asked.

"Jesus, Emma, she told me. We're friends, remember?"

The siren. Local law enforcement was making an appearance, at the very least they would be a welcome distraction.

"So how do we get to the road?" Emma asked.

He pointed straight across the lawn, to the copse of trees on the other side, a good three hundred yards.

"What about down by the beach, is there access to the neighbor's property?"

"I suppose. There's a rock jetty between the two beaches."

She was familiar with clambering over seaweed and stone. She made for the wooden stairway.

"Emma, this has gone far enough," Will insisted.

Behind him, she saw someone emerging from the back of the house.

"Shit!" Grabbing him, she pulled him back into the trees and knelt down.

"Emma!"

"Get down. Jesus, would it kill you to trust me on this?"

The man was heading toward them at a rapid clip. He had a cap on, and from this distance it was impossible to tell who he was. Then there was someone else stepping out, and a woman's voice lifted on the wind, making a request. "Could you . . ." was all Emma could distinguish, but the rest was apparently a demand for his presence. He stopped and turned, and the woman ran up to him, words were exchanged, and then both of them headed back toward the main house.

Safe. At least for the moment.

She made for the stairs.

"Samuels is involved in this how?" Will demanded, closing in behind her.

"He took over the Nevins case from us, lied about how that came to pass. It made me suspicious, so I did a little digging." She didn't add the help she'd had, from Dawn, indirectly, that name, *Rosalita,* had been the key. "He knew Julie Nevins, there's a photograph of the two of them together. When I confronted him, he turned on me, threatened the kids. He's had us followed, clearly. He knew their names, where they went to school. It was frankly, chilling."

Will's expression had changed. He was starting to believe her. "I've never liked that guy," he said. "But Greg, I can't see how he'd have anything to do with this."

She was halfway down. He was behind her. Looking out, she realized how precipitous a drop this was. Adrenalin had gotten her this far, but heights were most definitely not her forte.

No choice, she told herself stubbornly.

"You okay?" he asked. She heard the concern in his voice. He knew her so well.

"Fine!"

"Just checking, don't bite my head off," he told her. "You remember that ski trip?"

He was trying to make her laugh, and succeeded. "I should have warned you about my little problem," Emma admitted.

"I still wish I'd had a camera, you, hugging the snow."

The memory had carried her down, almost to the bottom. "Your boss Chavitz was there, the day the photo of the two of them was taken," Emma said. "I think they were all friends. Or something more."

"This took place when?"

"Twelve years ago."

"Okay," Will said reasonably, "So, even if Greg knew the woman, does that make him guilty of something else? In this business, you can't be too careful. People can get the wrong idea."

"Really?" Emma said, turning to him as she reached the sand. "I thought notoriety helped in the movie business."

"Only sometimes," Will offered weakly.

"Listen, if I could tell you exactly what was going on between those people back when, then I could explain why they're apparently willing to go to such lengths to protect themselves. From down below, she saw the Prescott's home, perched on a nearby bluff. "Dawn was up here visiting her parents, only three days before she was murdered," Emma said. "Her mother was running a charity event. It was a last-minute decision on her part. At the time, I was more than a little surprised. But now I have to think she decided to go because Chavitz was attending. It was an opportunity for her."

They had gotten to the sand, their shoes sinking down. The jetty was past the dock; to their right, a boathouse, locked up tight. And there was the cabin cruiser, small and definitely old-fashioned, not the sort of ostentatious boat she would have predicted someone like Chavitz acquiring. Looking up, she saw no one coming down the stairs in hot pursuit. It would take only a minute to confirm her hunch.

But, reaching the berth, she saw she'd been wrong. The boat was the *Beautiful Dreamer,* homeport, Greenwich, Connecticut. Emma turned to go, digging her hands into her pockets to warm them, and found the switchblade. Pulling it out, she flicked it open.

"Now what are you doing?" Will exclaimed.

"Defacing private property," she said as she used the knife to scrape away the paint and reveal what was hidden beneath—an *R* and then an *O*. So she had been right, this was Captain Jack's old fishing boat.

Just then, she heard voices. Looking up, over the bow of the boat, she saw Samuels at the top of the stairs, his back turned.

Jerking on Will, she pulled him down out of sight.

"I told you, I saw them heading toward the road," another voice insisted. Lighter, younger, and distinctly more feminine. Pru. "They're probably in town by now. And I don't see what the big deal is," Pru continued coyly. "Will wouldn't ever do anything to hurt me."

"I'm sure you think you've got him wrapped around your little finger," Samuels retorted.

"That's not very nice."

"Since when do I have to be nice to you?"

"Hey, unfair," Pru said coyly.

Emma couldn't help throwing a meaningful look Will's way.

"You pay me to be a bastard, so let me do my job," Samuels insisted. "Now go back to the house and let me deal with this."

"No."

"This isn't negotiable. Get back up to the house. Now. Or I'll have to tell Gregory what you've been up to. Imagine his disappointment."

"That's not fucking fair," Pru said.

"Oh dear, not fair," he mocked. "Don't even try saying that to me."

Emma took a chance and inched up; they were still standing at the top of the stairs. It was pure insanity to try and break and run now, only open space between the boathouse and the jetty, which was at least four feet high and several more wide.

Jason Samuels wasn't looking for them to tender an invitation for a friendly drink. Emma had no idea how much Pru knew or how deeply involved she was. And she certainly didn't want an answer to that question now, at least not if it involved bodily harm. Nudging Will, she grabbed onto the ladder and pressed her body flat against it. Then climbed, keeping her head low, and did a face-first fall forward onto the deck. Will followed behind as she crawled inside the cabin. From there, they were definitely hidden from view.

"This is fucking ridiculous," Will whispered.

Emma shook her head emphatically and pressed her finger to her lips.

He sighed. But didn't say anything else. She listened, as hard as she could. The small flags running up the line directly above their heads flapped in the wind. And then she heard the stairs creak. After that it was quiet. Waiting was excruciating. The minutes ticked past. And then . . .

"Hold up."

The voice was too close, it sounded as if it came from the end of the dock. If Samuels walked out, there was a very good chance he'd spot the damaged letters. But would he think they'd hide in here? No, she decided. Much more likely that he'd assume they'd have gotten away. Still, the only possible exit, other than the way they'd come, led down to what she assumed were sleeping berths. Better to be further out of sight than not. Samuels might duck his head in, just to make sure. She pointed to the hold and wriggled toward it.

"I thought you were taking care of this." It was Chavitz. The voice was even closer. He had to be standing only a few feet away. Emma had her foot on the stairs; she turned back and saw that Will hadn't budged.

*Come on!*

She wanted to scream it out. But he wasn't even looking her way. He was listening intently.

"I'm taking care of it," Samuels insisted.

"And doing a beautiful job too."

"There's no need to be snide with me."

"What should I be then? Elated by the way you've fucked things up so royally?"

"Me?"

"Who else?"

"Jesus, Gregory. Is that fair?"

"I can only call it like I see it," Chavitz said.

"Is that what you can do?" Samuels sounded completely exasperated. "Would it kill you to take responsibility for one fucking thing?"

"I see," Chavitz replied smoothly. "You want me to take responsibility. Okay, I'll say it. Mea culpa. Does that make you feel better?"

"You never stop, do you?" Samuels said. "Mea culpa. Say it like you mean it, for once." There was a moment of silence, then he let out a "Fuck! Look at this!"

One of them grunted.

"What about it?" Chavitz countered. "All she can say is I bought an old boat. It was someone else's and now it's mine. Where's the big deal in any of this? I keep telling you, there's no real proof. We took care of that."

"We? Make that me. I'm the one who's always got to take care of everything. And you're the one who worries himself sick. Remember how you told me we had to figure this out, just last week? We had to make sure nothing came up that could hurt either one of us. That was generous, including me. And now you want to pretend you didn't know what you were asking."

"It was a fucking accident," Chavitz said.

"An accident. After all this time, that's the best you can come up with?" Samuels's tone was harsh.

"I don't like the way you're putting that!"

"You think I give a shit what you like? I've always done exactly what you needed me to do. Most people would be grateful."

The boat tipped. They were coming aboard. Or at least one of them was.

Emma didn't wait to find out who. She took the stairs. And this time Will was right behind her. There were two small bedrooms, one with a bunk, the other a single bed, and a toilet in between. If, for some reason, one of them decided to search the hold, they were trapped. How did I get us into this mess, Emma wondered. She backed into one of the rooms and looked around for something, anything inside to use to her advantage. A small desk, with nothing on it, one drawer that looked way too thin to have anything inside that could double as a weapon. She didn't dare move. She stood, breathing as inaudibly as she could manage. There were footsteps right above her head.

"They're gone," Chavitz insisted. "You blew this totally. Getting Kirsten to invite that guy up here. And I fucking promised her that part."

Accident. Emma tried to reason it out, even as she listened for sounds that they were heading down to complete their investigation. Why buy this boat? Because it was a link in some way; Dawn had written the name down. And Emma had followed the trail back, perhaps Dawn had too. But what accident was Samuels referring to? There seemed nothing accidental in the wholesale slaughter at Julie Nevins's home. It all had the feel of something premeditated, although hardly brilliant. You didn't show up with gas cans and a match, did you, unless you wanted to burn something down to the ground.

Not to mention the .44-millimeter gun that had lodged bullets inside the bodies of the victims.

But then, there was Julie, Emma thought. She hadn't just been shot. A blow to the head had caved in part of her skull. And she'd been strangled, someone's fingers cutting into her windpipe. There had been a long gash in the skin. The coroner had theorized a piece of wire, or a metal chain, something soft that would break rather than cut too deeply. A necklace, Emma decided, like the one Julie had worn in the photograph, with her name written in what looked to be fourteen-carat gold.

Had Chavitz done it? A lovers' quarrel, Emma thought, then Samuels attempting to point the blame somewhere else. The plan had worked perfectly. Perhaps Lowry was even complicit, either beholden to Samuels or simply on the take. And, of course, there was the dead ex-cop Bannion.

"No one here that I can see." Chavitz, stating the obvious for him.

"She's probably back in town by now." He added a laugh, for effect. "The best-laid plans," he said.

"Fine, then we ditch the boat," Samuels told him.

"What's the point of that?"

"You never registered it. No one knows you have it. Who's going to be any the wiser?" Samuels's tone was tinged with anxiety.

"How would you suggest we go about doing that?" Chavitz said evenly. "I've got a meeting at noon."

"Jesus, you can cancel it," Samuels said. "This is more important."

"Is it? Why?"

"You know why. They have a record of this boat being docked in Glen Cove. You chartered it that night."

"I wonder who's going to make that connection?"

"Prescott did."

"That woman came up to me and asked me what I knew about my goddaughter's background. I referred her to you. And you took it from there. I find it hard to believe you couldn't stonewall her."

"I told you, it was obvious she knew about you and Julie."

"I know you told me that, but I can't help wondering what Prescott actually said to you. You've been awfully vague about the details."

"You don't believe me?"

"It's not just that," Chavitz said. "It's everything. Jason, look, if I'd known what a mess you'd make with this, I would never have sent that woman to see you."

"What would you have done, deal with it yourself?" Samuels sounded amused. "You wouldn't know how."

"I'm done," Chavitz said.

The boards creaked overhead.

"Where do you think you're going?" Samuels demanded.

"Back to the house," Chavitz said. "I have a business to run, or had you forgotten?"

"Who could fucking forget that? You're not leaving until we resolve this."

"Resolve this how, the two of them are gone."

"I'm warning you, don't walk away from me."

"Jesus, Jason, don't be so dramatic!"

There was the sound of movement, and then a derisive snort. "What are you going to do with that? Shoot me?"

There was only one inevitable answer to that. A shot rang out.

"Shit!" Chavitz said, aloud.

Will was up the stairs before her. That they both had had the same irrational response showed, Emma thought, that they were both insanely brave—or just remarkably stupid. Will came barreling out the door and threw himself on top of Samuels. He and Will crashed onto the floor, and the gun spun free. Emma went after it, but it was Chavitz who grabbed hold.

"Back up," he said to her. And got to his feet, exceedingly slowly. He put all the weight on his good leg, half lurching as he did, blood dripping down, drenching the pants. "I should do the same to you," he told Samuels.

He looked behind her when he said it, and Emma dug down into her pocket and grabbed the switchblade. She pulled it out, clicked it open, and sliced desperately at the hand that held the gun. Amazingly, she made contact. Chavitz dropped the weapon, and screamed out in pain. Emma dove and came up holding the gun.

Chavitz had frozen, he was staring at her, and it was clear that her acrobatics had given him the wrong impression. He actually seemed to believe that she knew what she was doing.

"Get down on the floor," she said, sounding much more confidant than she felt.

He did, sitting hard, his legs splaying out. Will shoved Samuels forward.

Opportunity, Emma thought, that was all it took sometimes.

"Make him kneel," she said to Will.

"What?"

"You heard me, make him kneel." Saying it, she almost saw herself as one of those tough guys.

"Why?" Will was staring at her. "Emma, what are you going to do?"

"What's the point of letting him go. He'll just worm his way out of it. He killed Dawn didn't he? Or paid someone else to do it."

"Emma, you're not serious."

She was. In a way. And for a moment, Emma let herself feel how the act of revenge could operate in her favor, purging her of every ambivalent feeling, washing her clean of guilt. She understood, so well, how people gave in. How easy it was to believe in this, as a cure.

Turning to Chavitz, she met his eyes, and there was fear in them, she noted. Good, she thought, he believes me. Then Samuels has to. "I'm not after you, not yet anyhow," she told Chavitz. Back to Will. "He was going after our kids," she said. "Remember?"

Will still looked uncertain.

"We have to do this," Emma insisted. Will looked hard at her, and she nodded, imperceptibly.

"Fine," he said. "Get down," he instructed Samuels.

Samuels shook his head, "This is . . ."

Before he could spit out whatever the judgment call was, Will kicked him, hard.

"Hey!"

"Do what she wants," Will insisted.

"All right," he agreed. "I'm going."

And then, he was kneeling, at her feet. He was smiling, still mocking her. Emma squatted down beside him, and pressed the gun against his temple. That managed to wipe the smirk off his face. "Why did you kill her?" she demanded. She said it the way she'd heard it, over and over again, in courtrooms where she'd been sitting at the defendant's table, while the next of kin demanded an answer.

There was never one that was good enough. Nothing could possibly assuage the grief. And yet, sometimes her clients tried, there were some who managed testimony that was almost elegant, certainly human, offering their apologies without excuse, their sincerest, most heartfelt regrets. Others simply read what had been penned for them, in one last effort to gain clemency, most often the accused refused to speak at all, they sat silently when the demand was made, their absence of regret or solicitousness taken as the ultimate slap in the face.

How many times had she watched bereaved parents and relatives crying hysterically, even being bodily removed from the courtroom.

"It wasn't me," Samuels insisted, shrinking away and blinking uncontrollably.

"Of course it was," Emma said reasonably. "Confess. Go on. It will do you a world of good."

He shook his head.

"All I have to do is press down a little," Emma said.

Samuels dropped his gaze to her fingers, wrapped round the trigger. "Okay, all right. I didn't tell Bannion to hurt her, only to get her away to someplace private for a while, so we could figure out what she actually knew. Then I get this call from him, things have gotten out of hand. I'll say they did."

"So, this was Bannion's fault? Bannion, who's conveniently unable to defend himself?"

"What can I tell you?" Jason Samuels offered.

"I'd settle for the truth," Emma said. "But you misunderstood. I wasn't asking about Dawn. I was asking about Julie."

"Julie Nevins?"

"Yes." She rolled back on her heels, getting a little more comfortable. The gun was unbelievably heavy. "Well?"

"Well what?"

"For Christ's sake, tell her," Chavitz said. "They've been on the boat the entire time. They've heard everything, Jason."

"Fine. If that's what you want." He smiled at Emma, and she felt her muscles contract, her fingers close around the trigger, the hammer bending under the weight. All she had to do was pull a little more and the bullet would roll in, then be expelled, drilling right through his brain, killing him or, at the very least, making him into a vegetable for life, it took so little . . .

And so much, Emma thought grimly.

"Chav went to talk to her. They got into a fight, and then he comes running back, says he killed her. I told him I'd take care of it. And I did."

"Talk to her about what?"

"About our daughter," Chavitz said. "Julie was making all these noises about wanting to see her, wanting her back. It just wasn't possible, okay? She made a deal with me, to keep away." Sternly, he added, "People ought to honor their agreements."

"I see, so she reneged. And you got mad."

"Look, I only did what I thought was best for the kid, Julie was fine with it for years. Then, suddenly, she decides she's ready to turn over a new leaf, which I didn't buy for a second. So I say what I have to say, which is, 'no fucking way.' And that's when Julie gets worked up, starts saying she's going to do things to get her, she's going to take her away. It's a mother's right. That kind of crap. To which I can't help but offer the counter argument, okay. Like that husband of hers, beating her up, landing her in the emergency room, the order of protection she had taken out against him, and how I didn't think any kid of mine deserved to be involved in that. How she'd agreed to give up her baby girl with no strings attached, how I'd paid her twenty-five grand for the honor and the privilege, how she'd signed papers. Julie didn't want to hear all that, she got hysterical, and when I tried to leave, well . . . she grabbed me, tried to pull me back. I guess I shoved her too hard, just to get her out of my face. She fell, hit her head. It was an accident." Chavitz sighed. "Look, I'm not proud of what I did. I panicked. Jason was waiting for me, I tried to tell him what happened, he went back to check, and he said, I was right, she was dead. He was the one who knew this guy who was a local cop, said he could be trusted, that he'd take care of everything for us."

"Bannion?"

Chavitz nodded. "I know how stupid it sounds. I should have stayed there. If I'd known what the guy was going to end up doing."

"You're saying it was Bannion who killed the rest of them? Why would he do that?"

"Jason said they walked in when he was dealing with the body. He didn't have a choice."

"And you believed him all these years? Come on, you didn't even buy it then," Emma insisted. She felt disgusted with his weakness, his obvious cowardice. "Samuels told him to do it. That was what he meant by fixing things. You knew as much."

"I swear, I didn't," Chavitz insisted.

"You know the irony," Emma said. "You could have saved Julie. She didn't die from the blow to the head. She was strangled. The coroner's report was clear on that. And whoever killed her, took whatever they used away with them. There were lesions in her neck. A metal chain might cut that way."

Chavitz stared at her. "That's not true." Then he turned, to confront Jason Samuels. "You swore she wasn't breathing. You told me, it was all over. You said you'd tried to revive her."

"That's exactly what happened," Samuels insisted.

But Chavitz was finally seeing the light. "The necklace," he said. "She never took the damn thing off. Said it brought her good luck."

"Come on," Samuels countered, weakly.

"Come on where?" Gregory Chavitz asked. "Jason, why would you do that?" He seemed genuinely bemused.

For a moment, Samuels looked as if he was about to protest his innocence yet again, but then, some shadow crossed his face, some level of disgust and even, Emma decided, relief. Perhaps, pride, as well. "Jesus, Gregory," he said. "Why do you think? She was only going to cause us more trouble. This way, we'd never have to worry about her again."

"Yes, that worked brilliantly," Emma put in.

"She was a whore," Samuels threw out.

"Whore?" Emma countered. "How do you define that exactly? Oh, right, you did pay her. That necklace, it was your gift, I'm assuming. And you knew that Julie wanted her daughter back, and she'd use every weapon at her disposal. She'd eventually use you, if she had to. She'd tell Gregory who the father really was and you couldn't have that. All along, you'd been working that angle so beautifully. You'd been getting him to pay for the girl's entire upkeep, every single dollar that went toward it, vetted by you, and every time he felt puffed up and proud, you patted yourself on the back, how you'd managed to delude him. She was your daughter, not his. What a perfect piece of one-upmanship that was."

There was a muffled sob.

Wielding a weapon had given Emma the oddest sense of being in control. The three men looked surprised, but Emma wasn't. She'd noted the boat rocking, heard the sound of soft footfalls.

"Join the party," Emma said.

Pru did as requested. Her hair was wet from the snow and her face grim. She was, without a doubt, her mother's daughter.

"I hate you," she said.

It was Chavitz she was saying it to. Pru Ramone came closer. "All you have to do is give me that gun," she offered. Her eyes glittered.

"No, Pru," Emma said. "That won't help."

"Yes, it will. They both deserve it. I'll make it a two-for-one special. What would I get? A couple of years at Bedford Hills?"

"Pru, sweetheart, you don't mean that," Chavitz insisted.

"No?" Pru laughed grimly. "Gregory, I'd do it in a heartbeat."

# Chapter Twenty-four

"She wouldn't have shot them," Laurence insisted.

"I think she just might have," Emma countered. "Believe me, it was tempting."

They sat inside his car, away from the show going on inside the local station house. Small-town police worked in resolutely opaque ways, kowtowing to whoever seemed the most powerful. At first, Laurence and Fitzsimmons had gotten sway, by virtue of being members of the brotherhood. That was how Emma had managed to give her statement and get excused. Will, Pru, and Kirsten were still inside. Chavitz was at the local hospital. And Samuels was safe for the moment, inside a holding cell.

Meanwhile, Laurence had confessed how he'd gotten to her, his night spent in doing due diligence, stopping by Fitzsimmons's apartment to hash things out. It was Fitzsimmons who'd taken up his post outside Samuels's brownstone, frying himself on the usual diet of Coke and doughnuts, Fitzsimmons who'd watched Samuels walk up the block to the garage, pull out in a silver Mercedes, and spin away. Fitzsimmons who'd called, waking Laurence only a few minutes after Emma had left the house, so that, while she was getting herself a rental car, he was already aware of her absence, already cursing under his breath and figuring out where he was going to park the kids, calling Suzanne and getting her into a cab and over to his apartment in short order.

Fitzsimmons had been parked outside the Greenwich home of one Gregory Chavitz by that time. He'd watched as a rental car paused at the gate to the estate. He'd noted Emma in the driver's seat. Just when he was thinking about how he would get inside himself, the locals pulled up.

And left twenty minutes later.

By then, Laurence was with him.

"Certain things troubled me," Laurence told her, offering a typically dry understatement.

He had been troubled enough to go up to the gate and insist on being let inside. Troubled even more when Kirsten Rogers claimed to have no idea where Will or his ex-wife, Emma, were.

Laurence and Fitzsimmons had conducted a search of the grounds, but not before phoning the locals, who eventually agreed to send in two cars for backup. By then, the snow was already coming down hard.

"I'd like to know what your thoughts were," he said.

"It's so complicated," she told him, knowing that he was angry because she'd put herself in harm's way.

"You looked authentic, holding that gun."

"Making fun of me?"

"Maybe a little." He stroked her cheek. She put her own hand onto his.

"I'm sorry," she said.

"You've got no reason to be." He kissed her, hard. Pulling back, he added, "The thing is, I happen to love you."

She would have replied in kind, except that there was a tap on the window. Fitzsimmons. "Samuels's lawyer just showed. He's some former hotshot. They're all scraping and bowing in there." Looking a little more closely, he added, "Was I interrupting?"

"Yes," Laurence said.

"Thought I'd let you know I'm going to stay around, see if I can provide a little backbone."

"I'll stay too."

"No need for it," Fitzsimmons said.

"Don't worry."

"I'm not going to forget about you," Fitzsimmons promised.

"Better not."

"Hey, niggah, I keep my promises," Fitzsimmons said.

"You're something else," Laurence responded, sounding almost amused.

"That's what people tell me."

The Starbucks on Greenwich Avenue was filled with teens. Most were clean-cut, but a few had donned the gangsta look, wearing their caps backwards, their pants slung low. Emma ordered her cup to go.

When the butler opened the door and gave the two of them an imperious look, Emma felt her courage desert her. Funny, what throws you, she thought to herself. Laurence showed his ID, and they were led into the library.

Emma had been here only once before, Dawn insisting she come along for one of the de rigeur Saturday visits. "It'll be fun," Dawn had said. "You'll see where I come from. Who knows, maybe down the road you can use it to blackmail me with."

Emma had rolled her eyes. But, of course, she'd given in. They'd driven up here, been ushered inside the very same room, and offered a round of tepid tea. It had only been them and Ruth, for quite a while, Hamilton popping his head in to say hello, then disappearing. He had work to finish.

To Emma, it was a foreign country. The grounds had been enough to stun her, not to mention the house, complete with butler and several maids.

"Miss Dawn," this very same butler had said, then he'd gone off to announce their arrival.

*Miss Dawn?*

Inside the library the floor-to-ceiling windows were veined with lead; the bookcases packed with first editions. Two rolling ladders rested against opposite walls.

"Don't think either of them reads," Dawn had said. "It's all for show, isn't it mother dear?"

"That's not true," Ruth had retorted, clearly annoyed. "You shouldn't make those sort of jokes. Your friend won't understand."

"I think she understands everything. She's much smarter than I am. That's how Jews are, quick."

Emma had flinched. She had not enjoyed the reference.

"Mom likes to call them 'those people.' Don't you, Mom?"

"Stop it, Dawn!" Hamilton's voice was coming from the doorway. He could have been watching for a long while. In fact, Emma decided Dawn had known he was there, that she'd baited Ruth, knowing it would get a rise out of him.

Hamilton saw Laurence first. "How can I help you?" he asked, walking past her, then realizing someone was sitting in the wing chair and doing a double take. From afar, at the funeral, he'd looked his regal, intimidating self, but up close, she saw the change. His shoulders were hunched, his face was pale, and there were sharp lines etched under the eyes.

Emma put out a hand to Hamilton. He refused to take it.

"You're not welcome in this house."

"There's no reason for you to take that tone with Ms. Price," Laurence said coolly. "She's come with good will on her part. I would like to think you'd be good enough to extend the same."

"There's ample reason not to," Hamilton replied. "As for you, Officer Solomon, I suppose for the moment, I'll have to give you the benefit of the doubt."

"It's detective sergeant," Laurence corrected him. "And I'm grateful you're willing to give me that benefit. However, Ms. Price is here to tell you they've arrested the man responsible for your daughter's death."

"The man responsible? That's absurd."

"How about you hear her out?" Laurence suggested.

"I don't seem to have a choice in the matter."

"Lowry got it wrong," Emma said, hearing her voice shake a little as she did. "This was no murder-suicide."

Hamilton muttered something under his breath. Emma could only imagine the content.

"I have to agree with Ms. Price," Laurence said. "I've had access to all the crime scene reports, and the medical examiner's notes. Whoever shot the man with your daughter was standing directly above him, the ballistics reports will definitely confirm that finding."

"I don't follow you, standing above him? So what?"

But, Emma knew he was following, was integrating it, even as he resisted.

"There was another person in that room." Laurence didn't add the rest, how the third person had undoubtedly had the weapon in hand, how he had orchestrated whatever went on, who was killed when was harder to determine, Emma knew that fear for your own life was a terrific motivating factor. Had it been enough to force an out-of-work actor to wrap his hands around Dawn's throat and choke the life out of her? Or had Bannion done the honors for him?

"I knew your daughter," Laurence said. "I considered her a friend. I want justice done for her. As her father, I know you can only feel the same."

"You know nothing about it," Hamilton said bitterly. His eyes met Laurence's.

"Is Ruth here?" Emma asked.

"Yes." He didn't move a muscle.

"She should hear this as well," Laurence said. A long moment passed, then he relented.

"I'll get her."

And they were left alone.

Emma joined Laurence by the window. Outside, the grounds were buried under the six-inch snowfall. The flakes came down softly now, the worst part of the storm had blown past. "His own little kingdom," Laurence said. "So this is where Dawn grew up."

"I wonder if he's really going to find his wife."

"Well, if he's looking for backup, he better bring an entire seven-nation army with him."

"You don't like the senator much."

"He hasn't given me reason to," Laurence said. "Although I don't get the impression he gives a good goddamn what I think about him."

Turning back, she took in the threadbare quality of the furnishings; the wear on the chesterfield, the color bleached out the curtains. It said, the owners have so much money they don't have to prove it to you or anyone. She heard footsteps. Ruth entered ahead of Hamilton, thrusting a dismissively hostile look Emma's way before settling herself into the most uncomfortable-looking chair in the room, her husband stood guard beside her.

"The man we believe to be responsible for Dawn's death was taken into custody a few hours ago," Emma said. "His name is Jason Samuels."

There was knowledge on both their faces. "Samuels? You mean the lawyer?" Hamilton asked. "What could he possibly have to do with this?"

"It goes back to a case we've been working on for several years."

"You mean this is over some case of hers?"

"The client's name is Arthur Nevins. He was convicted of murdering his estranged wife, their child, and members of her immediate family."

"Horrible people," Ruth muttered.

Emma ignored that. "There was a confession involved. Mr. Nevins claimed it was extracted under duress. Specifically he told us the arresting officer threatened to kill him unless he signed the statement implicating him. The murders took place in Nassau County. The arresting officer was Detective Shane Lowry."

She paused, to let that sink in.

"At the time, there were other things pointing to our client. A fire had been set in the house, gas cans were found in his basement, wrapped in plastic. There had been threats against the victim, to the point where she took out a restraining order. In due course, Mr. Nevins was convicted and sentenced to death. We've been working on his behalf since then. Not that either one of us believed him to be innocent."

"With good reason," Hamilton said.

"Can I ask how you know of Mr. Samuels?"

Hamilton gave her a stony look.

"We only just met him," Ruth said, intervening. "He came as Gregory Chavitz's guest. It was for the charity auction. Gregory is on the board of Angels of Mercy. We were raising money for our Meals-on-Wheels program."

"That was last week, wasn't it?"

Ruth nodded.

"And Dawn decided to come as well. You didn't expect her to, did you?"

"I hoped she would," Ruth allowed.

"But you were surprised. I'm sure she called first. Did she happen to ask you who was going to be here? Did she mention Chavitz specifically?"

"Actually, it's true. She did," Ruth admitted. "I said he was coming. I thought nothing of it." Her face flushed. "They were speaking, in the hall. Gregory looked upset. I assumed Dawn was castigating him about his money or some political view he held. You know how she could be. Anyhow, I felt it was my duty to make things go smoothly. I was the hostess, after all, this was my home." Ruth lifted her eyes to meet Emma's. "Is this really true?" she asked.

"I won't believe it," Hamilton exclaimed. "It's a trick on your part. A way to get the child."

Ruth looked from him back to Emma. "I don't think she would do that," she said softly. Then she reached up, touching her husband's hand where it gripped the curved back of the chair. Pulling away sharply, as if stung, he glared at her, then at Emma.

"You're being ridiculous," he told them. And stalked out of the room.

Ruth stood herself. Turning to Laurence, she said, "I have to apologize for my husband. He isn't quite himself these days."

"I understand," Laurence said.

"Do you?" Ruth said. There was a delicately ironic tone to her voice. "I'd better go take care of him. I'm sure you can find your own way out."

\* \* \*

On that day, so many years ago, Dawn and Hamilton had argued, non-stop, the topics ranging from politics to religion to sexual identity. At first, Emma tried to join in, but it became apparent how little she was wanted. She got up to leave, and Ruth said, "The bathroom?" Then pointed the way. Inside, she'd waited longer than she had to, washing her face with cold water, gazing at it in the mirror. When she'd finally stepped out and headed back, it was Ruth who motioned to her from the living room.

"A drink?" she offered. As she stepped in, Ruth added, "If you don't mind, dear, I'd prefer you shut the door."

Shut out the conflict. Shut out their love, which had depended on it for nourishment. If you couldn't change it, do your best to ignore it. Or deny its existence.

In the end, it seemed that the way you expressed love for your children was much more complicated than it felt on the day of their birth. Then, they looked so helpless and malleable. But that was one of the many illusions they shattered for you.

Emma could see Julie Nevins at seventeen, scheming to come up with a plan for her unwanted child. Why not make it into a lucrative transaction, how could it hurt? Why not lie to these two supposed best friends, Gregory and Jason? "Played them for fools and laughed all the way to the bank," was how Laurence had put it.

She wondered if Julie had known whose baby it was. There had been at least three choices. All these years later, it was more obvious, there, Emma thought, in the slant of the eyes, the squareness of the chin. Still Julie had gotten lucky, betting on genetics not to give her away, not to make this child darker than Arthur, who, himself, would have had little trouble passing for white, back in the day.

Where Julie had been naive was in thinking she could control the other two men, Chavitz wanting to be the father figure, not just for her but for their baby; Samuels loving that he could dupe his best friend, because Chavitz was the type who always had to lord it over everyone.

\* \* \*

Emma found Hector at the back of Gleason's gym, coaching a slip of a boy in headgear and red trunks.

"Harder than that!" he exhorted. "What are you, a pussy? Come on, make her bleed. I want you working on your combinations, that's what you have to use with her, you got to swing for your advantage. I want it to be like she doesn't even get a breath, okay? There's no mercy rule going here."

Only when she took off her headgear and leaned her head back, to drizzle water from her water bottle into her mouth did Emma realize her mistake, his student was female.

"Emma Price. Coming by for pointers?"

She shook her head. "Not my thing, boxing," she said.

Turning to his charge, he said, "Hear that, Frieda?"

"Yeah, I heard," Frieda said. "Maybe she doesn't believe in blood sport. Maybe it's the principle of the thing for her."

"That's what it is," Emma agreed. "Could we talk in private?"

"I don't know," Hector said. "I hear you can be pretty dangerous. Should I chance it?"

The bar down at the corner was called O'Shannon's. It was the sort that had a steady clientele. Three of them sat on stools up front staring at the hockey game. In the back there were booths, with fake Tiffany lamps hanging above them. Emma could barely see, but that was obviously the point.

In the booth, Hector leaned back, pretending to take her in.

"What?" she asked, meaning it in the true Brooklyn "try me" sense.

"I hear you gave Samuels a hard time."

"I did my best."

"Hmm." He chugged a little, set it aside, wiped the sweat off the glass.

"Hmm? What's that mean? Does it upset you?"

"Should it?"

They could play at this for a long, long while, but Emma didn't have the energy, or the time. "How was Hollywood?" she asked.

"Nice weather."

"You worked for Greg Chavitz. That's how you met Pru."

"And?" His smile was meant to provoke.

"How did you get that job?"

"Wrong question," he said in a mocking tone of voice. "*Why* did I get the job? That's the more important part."

"You don't get to tell me what to ask," Emma said. "We can do it here, or I can have you subpoenaed."

"As what?"

"Witness for the defense. Arthur Nevins has asked us to return as his counsel. He's decided Jason Samuels may not be the right person for the job. Too much of a personal interest."

"You think I wouldn't want to help Nevins out? What else has this ever been about?"

"So that's how you see it," Emma said. "I suppose it helps you sleep at night."

"Why wouldn't I be able to sleep?"

"Because, without you, Dawn would still be alive."

"Hey!"

Hector had reared back defensively. "You think I intended for this to happen with Dawn?" he spluttered.

"Dawn and you disagreed about how to pursue the defense. It wasn't the first time she'd disagreed with a subordinate, so I had to ask myself, Why was it so fraught? Why did the two of you come to blows over it? What had you invested that made you so convinced that there was only one right way to proceed? I tried to be objective about it. And I realized that both of you had valid arguments. Yours was that we should be looking into the dead woman's past, seeing who she'd been involved with, seeing if there were other places to go. Dawn's was that she had the confession in hand, evidence obtained at the crime scene, a police department that had been in the center of scandal. She chose to direct her argument that way. She tried to take Lowry's investigation to task. She decided not to try the victim. With hindsight, it appears that both of you were right. But you couldn't compromise, neither one of you could listen."

Hector didn't acknowledge her point. But he didn't get up and leave, either.

"When she was brought in to run the Capital Crimes Division, I remember Dawn saying she'd been one of two candidates for the job, that it was down to the wire. But then she prevailed. She didn't say why exactly, but she did tell me there was one person in particular who fought for her. Was that you?"

Hector's fingers were busy ripping the label off the bottle, rolling it up, knotting it, again and again.

"If it was, I'm guessing you two had a personal connection. And that it blew up in your face. I'm guessing she ended it. You must know, that was her MO. Dawn always tried to break up in a timely manner. She used whatever means at her disposal to make sure she wasn't hurt."

"You knew her better than I did."

"I knew her better than almost anyone," Emma said. "And I still didn't know half of what she was up to. Or what she was thinking. She was an extremely private person."

"Next you'll say how underneath she was soft and tender. Like a little ball of mush."

"No, I would never insult her by saying something like that. And I'm guessing neither would you." Emma took a sip of her beer. Behind him, at the bar, a woman yelled at the TV, "Fucking idiot, get the fucking puck away, you fucking, fucking moron."

"Look, it isn't what you think," Hector insisted. "I didn't know what I was going to find with Pru."

Emma studied him.

"I swear, I had no idea who she was. The job, it basically fell into my lap. Look, she was the one who came to me, asked if I could find out who her real parents were."

"You're saying it was fate?" Emma countered incredulously.

"I kid you not."

Emma didn't believe him, but there was no point arguing. "Go on," she said.

"Okay, so I knew Julie hadn't exactly been faithful to Arthur. But

I didn't know the full extent. Once I looked into the adoption, how it went down . . . I mean those are Chavitz's second cousins raising her, bringing her up just far enough away from the city so no one looks too hard into it. I had to think that this guy Chavitz was thinking he was the father. Or at least that he could be. Why else does he take such an interest in Pru, monitoring her whole career? Plus, you watch them together, it's just like he's her dad, the way he talks to her, the way he's always standing back and admiring, humoring her. Then again, Samuels, he's the one who arranged the whole damn thing, so he knows a thing or two.

"Meanwhile, it's Arthur's name on the original birth certificate. Pru says she wants to meet him, which I thought was pretty brave, considering. I mean, as far as she knows he's the one who's killed her mom, right? But that gave me a chance to go up and talk to Arthur again. I asked him what he knew about having another kid—well, let me tell you, it was some surprise. After he got over the shock, though, he was pretty open. Said he knew Julie wasn't exactly faithful, especially when he was away in juvie. He said there were signs. She'd be wearing things, in particular this necklace with her name on it. He didn't believe her when she said her mom gave it to her. Hell, who would?"

"Samuels gave it to her."

"How'd you find that out?"

"Hiding in plain sight," Emma said. "You'd think Samuels of all people would be more careful. But he was a snob, first and foremost. He bought it for her at Tiffany's. And they keep records that go back to the turn of the century."

"Look, you've got to believe me, when I found out about Pru, I tried talking to Dawn, I told her everything I knew. And she refused to believe any of it. Thought I was out of my fucking gourd."

"But she did believe you," Emma insisted.

"How could I have known that, I mean, from the way she was acting." But he sounded as if he was trying to convince himself. "Look, the woman had ignored me before."

There was no point in arguing about it. Emma opened her wallet and threw down a ten. She stood to go.

"Wait," he said. He was digging into his pocket, coming up with a card. On it, a bank name and an account number. "I was going to e-mail you about this. Samuels has a safe-deposit box. Who knows, maybe you can get inside. No one ever found that necklace," he pointed out.

"Because it's gone, at the bottom of some trash dump somewhere."

"Tiffany's. Pretty pricey. That guy, he likes to collect things. He's got the trophy cases, the trophy wife."

"You're taking up profiling?"

"I might. Who knows," Hector said. "Maybe an old dog like me can learn some new tricks after all."

# Chapter Twenty-five

"Foster Child Shoots Mom, Abuse Claimed." That had been the *Post* headline. A week later, the story had been relegated to the fourth page, most of it taken up by the Reverend, ranting about police injustice. By tomorrow, when the court date was going down, Laurence hoped it would be buried farther back, in the little columns next to the advertisements. Let Karim become a footnote.

Best thing for the boy, Laurence thought. Things were going in his favor, helped along by the final M.E.'s report, death from heart failure, the bullet passing through clean, not even nicking Mrs. Hawkins's vitals. Turns out the woman's medical history read like an accident just waiting to happen: diabetes, high blood pressure. Plus, she'd weighed in at a hefty three hundred and seventeen pounds.

The three kids had been put on the pediatric floor at Long Island College Hospital. Two rooms right next door to each other, with a uniform making sure no one got in or out.

Laurence stepped in to find Karim sitting on the edge of the bed, *Speed Racer* on the TV.

"Used to have that when I was a kid," Laurence said, by way of starting up the conversation.

Didn't even get the pleasure of a nod back.

Try again, he thought. "So they're taking care of you in here?"

That called for an answer. He got a grudging one. "Sure." Karim's attention was flush on the tube, on Speed with that pet monkey of his, Chim Chim. Laurence took a seat in the one chair. When he did, there was maybe a foot between their two bodies.

Pressing him again, "You need anything?"

A shrug.

"Ever been in the hospital before?"

A commercial came on then, and Karim deigned to turn his head, to say, "I guess I must have once. I got born, didn't I?"

Laurence laughed. "Yeah, that's one time at least." He set down onto the side table the comic books he'd picked up, along with the bag that held the Discman and a couple of CDs, a little selection of hip-hop 101: Run-DMC, OutKast's newest, Lil' Kim. "A few things to help the time pass."

"Didn't have to do that."

"Like you're telling me something I don't know."

"What's wrong, you feel sorry for me?"

That wasn't the half of it. But he wasn't going to try to explain all that to this kid.

Karim gave the bag a look, then fingered it, letting it go about as fast, like it just might bite.

"Don't worry, there are no books in there," Laurence said.

That got an almost-smile. "I know it. Says it's music."

"Well? Don't you want to see how bad my taste is?"

Karim shrugged, but he reached inside, took out the Discman in its hard plastic cover. "I'll get it," Laurence said, pulling out his Swiss Army knife, cutting away the wrapping while Karim removed the batteries, then the CDs.

"You know any of these?"

"Yeah," Karim said, making it clear he wasn't born yesterday.

"Like them?"

"They're aw'right." His show had started up again. He set the gifts aside, heading back to the fugue state.

"I thought you might have some things you want to get straight."

"How's that?"

"Questions, you know. About what's going on with you."

"The lawyer done talked to me about all that."

"And you understood every word he said."

"You think I'm stupid?"

"I'm not saying anything like that."

Laurence thought about what parents liked to say when their kids had worries, smoothing over the inevitable, coating it with sugar. That dragon in the window was just a figment of their imagination; come morning, it would go up in a puff of smoke. Only the dragon was real, the threat it gave substantial and to be reckoned with. But parents kept on saying what they had most likely since time began, how there were only blue skies ahead and clear sailing.

This boy Karim knew better, and had pretty much from the minute of his birth on down.

"I'll stop by again," Laurence said, standing.

"Yeah, sure, whatever."

He got all the way to the door before Karim threw out the question.

"I guess they're gonna put the needle in me."

So here it was, what the kid had worked himself up into believing. Putting that brave face on top of it. Trying to pretend he had street smarts. When he said it, Laurence heard that shit the Reverend had tried to pump out, how this boy was trouble for her, running with the wrong crowd. Any punk knew what he was likely to draw. But this boy was figuring he was headed for the "row."

"No one's fixing to kill you. Chances are you won't get but a few years at the most. No one thinks you were anything but hurt by that woman."

It was as if he'd said not a word.

"Your lawyer said as much. I guess you didn't believe him. Or didn't understand."

"I'm the one shot her."

"No one doubts that."

Laurence moved back, clicking the TV off. "Karim, you got to figure out what this is going to mean to you. All the stuff you've lived through, no one can change that. No one can make that up. But there's a chance for you here, you got to make something out of taking that woman's life, you got to make it mean more than saying enough is enough."

Karim blinked, hard, like he wasn't quite sure what he was seeing. Then he said, "That what you came by to tell me?"

"I guess it was."

"Okay then, I heard you."

"Fine." Reaching down, he grabbed onto the boy's shoulder gently. Karim didn't move away. His expression was unreadable. "There anything else I can help you with?"

Like he'd really helped at all? You get that much disappointment meted out, you stop believing, Laurence thought, you try to float, hope you can breathe a little, but there's another wave coming, and you know it can only get worse, most of the time it does.

Karim cleared his throat, the words sticking on their way out. "They won't let me see Cherelle or Tama." Not put as a request, to do that would be to court disappointment.

"I'll see what I can do about that."

At the door, he turned back for one last look. Karim had pushed the on button. He was staring hard at the TV, praying he could get sucked inside.

Outside, winter had gone again. Warm enough to melt all that snow into puddles, and soon, Laurence thought, spring would show. This street here was lined with magnolias, pink blossoms breaking out, mulberries raining into the gutter, tulips and daffodils, the only two flowers he knew by name.

Stopping at Sahadi's, he picked up some things to bring over to Emma's: spinach pies with that flaky crust, olives, dried fruit for the kids, and an espresso. Paying the bill, he stepped back out onto the street, thinking about Karim having to fight just to live his life, no one there to fight for him.

Thinking about Shaun. He hadn't in days. He'd pushed his own son away, told himself some things just were. Now he took a minute to look back, how he'd gotten the court to order him as sole parent, proved how his ex wasn't fit. She'd showed up for the wedding, all clean and tidy, with her new husband, wouldn't talk to him still. But Shaun had gone out of his way to invite her, to make up.

It was fine, having her there, the woman who hadn't managed to get her act together to raise him, hadn't even gotten herself straight and tidy till after he was all grown up.

Shaun could forgive her, find it in his heart for that.

In the wedding chapel, Laurence had felt his throat catch, looking over at his own boy, too handsome to put it into words, too filled up with pride for him, he'd wanted to hold him there, hold him back for one more minute.

"Why her?" Shaun had demanded, up for a visit north, Laurence getting him together with Emma for dinner, Shaun stalking off to the men's room to vent.

"What do you mean?"

"I can't stand the woman."

"You're not even giving her a chance."

No answer for that. The rest of the evening, Shaun had turned everything into a contest; by the end it was just him, one on one with his dad, Emma effectively cut out.

*This is who I hope to spend the rest of my life with.* Laurence didn't have to wonder how that would go over. Still, it was time he told Shaun that. Time he told the both of them.

# Chapter Twenty-six

"What you think is keeping them?" Mary Nevins asked the question to no one in particular.

Emma stood with Mary and Rafael under a bloody sun. Sweat dripped down her back, making her shirt stick. Across the street, standing outside the café, two guards were watching them, iced coffees in hand. Three people, waiting right outside the gate, next to their rental car. It had been a good hour now since Mary had gotten out of the car, standing off to the side where he would have to step out, the flowers she'd brought wrapped in tissue, wrung dry by worry in her hands.

How was it for Arthur, about to walk free, eight years of his life squandered? First came elation, then bitterness. Still, he'd done good things for himself inside. Perhaps he'd be one of those who could carry it out into the world with him.

One of the few.

"Something's wrong," Mary insisted.

"They're just taking their time," Rafael told her. He put his hand on her shoulder, gave it a squeeze. Patience. She'd had nothing but that for so long.

"I'm going to get something cold," Emma said. "Want anything?"

They both shook their heads. She'd buy them drinks anyhow.

Emma passed the guards and went inside. She placed the order, then leaned on the counter, looking out the window at her companions. They looked so fragile, dwarfed by the backdrop, the prison walls were immense, with that friendly topping of razor wire.

"That's Nevins's mom, right?"

It was one of the guards, he'd come in to ask. He was young, Emma noted, sweet-faced, with a bundle of freckles. The sort of boy you'd have a crush on, handsome in a purely nonthreatening way, which he made up for with the uniform and the holstered gun.

Emma nodded.

"Got to be tough on her, all this."

His tone was noncommittal. Emma wondered what he really thought, whether justice had been served or was being sidelined by this. Guards saw more than their share of what went wrong with the system. She took her coffee over to an empty booth by the window. He stepped out again; they were waiting too, Emma figured, waiting on history, this being the first time someone had been freed off of death row in New York State.

As for the man who Emma knew should have been sitting there instead, Jason Samuels? He'd gotten himself some excellent legal advice, and if it hadn't been for the necklace, he might have been able to cleanse himself of any connection to Julie.

Arthur was being released because the court of appeals had agreed that the evidence leading to his conviction was obtained illegally. A day later, Lowry announced his retirement.

She checked her watch. It was one-twenty-eight. She was hoping they would make the four-thirty flight back to LaGuardia. Her married friends who had opted to have three kids had told her, "You're outnumbered. That says it all."

But then, she'd been outnumbered with two.

Brian had worked up the agreement for shared guardianship, and the Prescotts had, surprisingly, consented to it. Emma got Millicent during the week, her grandparents on weekends. And the inheritance had been put in trust, till Millicent turned twenty-one. Emma got a stipend for all essential needs, food, clothing, and, the most critical of all, child care.

The three iced coffees arrived. But Emma stayed inside, and it wasn't just the air-conditioning, although that was definitely a factor. She hadn't wanted to come, had felt that it was not her place. Pru had begged off, pointing to the media circus. Emma wished she could have used that sort of excuse, or any excuse.

The gate was opening. Arthur walked out. For a moment, none of them seemed to know what to do, then there was a flurry of movement, the three of them holding on so tight, afraid to let go, and who could blame them.

Emma was smiling so hard she felt tears starting in her eyes. She'd never actually believed she would ever see this.

*In all the years we've worked together.*

*We.* It was hard to break the habit.

Opening the door, she walked outside. For a moment, a cloud went in front of the sun, casting the street into shadow. Emma knew better than to think it was a sign. No message sent from beyond the grave. There was even a prosaic explanation for the earring she'd discovered in Dawn's desk drawer. She'd come upon the mate in Millicent's diaper bag, hidden in the lining. "Would you look at this," Emma had said aloud.

Katherine Rose's face had turned scarlet. She'd scampered away as fast as her feet could carry her.

It looked as if her daughter had been the culprit all along, giving her friend Millicent a present, one she'd stolen out of her mother's top dresser drawer. Dawn had undoubtedly found it and set it aside, meaning to return it to her.

Then death had intervened.

Emma raised her eyes, for a moment, to the heavens. She didn't believe there was anyone up there watching, but still . . .

"What are you imagining?" It was Dawn's voice asking.

Emma couldn't say exactly. A better world? What a naive ambition that was, considering. People were too complicated by half.

The cloud drifted away; in its wake, the sun beat down even more relentlessly. Emma slipped on her sunglasses to protect her eyes against the glare. And when she did, Arthur raised his hand.

"Get yourself over here!" he yelled out.

Emma nodded. And crossed the street to join him.